FORT RENO

Other novels by Alfred Dennis

Chiricahua
Lone Eagle
Elkhorn Divide
Brant's Fort
Catamount
The Mustangers
Yuma
Rover
Yellowstone Divide
Sandigras Canyon
Shawnee Trail

FORT RENO

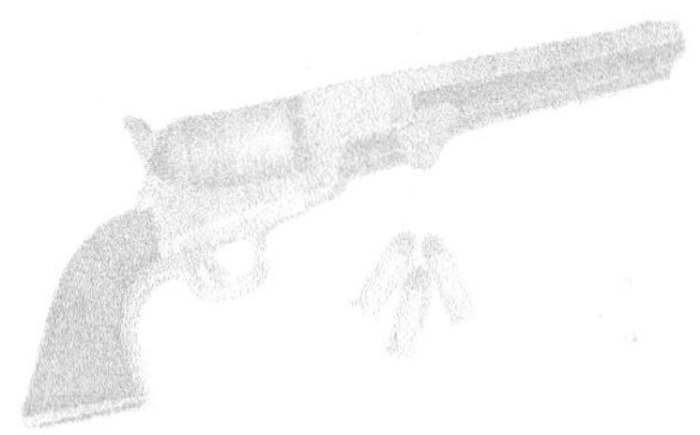

Alfred Dennis

WCP

Walnut Creek Publishing
Tuskahoma, Oklahoma

FORT RENO

Copyright © 2014 by Alfred Dennis. All rights reserved.
No part of this publication may be reproduced, transmitted, or resold in whole or in part in any form, without the express written permission of the author or publisher, except for the use of brief quotations in a book review.

This novel is a work of fiction. Names, characters, places, and incidents are either the product of the author's imagination or are used fictitiously. Any resemblance to actual events , locales, organizations, or persons, living or dead, is entirely coincidental and beyond the intent of either the author or the publisher.

ISBN: 978-0-9893241-6-8
Second Edition, Paperback
Published 2014 by Walnut Creek Publishing
Cover image, Certain stock imagery © Thinkstock.
Design and editing by KD Galbraith
10 9 8 7 6 5 4 3 2
1. Western 2. Historical Fiction 3. Western Romance

Books may be purchased in quantity and/or special sales by contacting the publisher;
Walnut Creek Publishing
PO Box 820
Talihina, OK 74571
www.wc-books.com

This book is dedicated to my mother,
Reba Faye Dennis.

Introduction

Early summer, eighteen seventy-four on the banks of the Canadian River in Oklahoma Territory, the U.S. Army builds a new army fort near the Darlington Agency to contain and guard the Arapaho and Cheyenne Tribes. Thousands of acres of grassland lay wasting and unused by the tribes. The great cattle herds only briefly use the grasslands as they pass north heading for the major cattle towns of Kansas.

Fort Reno is located across the Canadian River from the Agency. The Sixth Cavalry run the fort and they are within shouting distance of the newly relocated northern tribes. The great Chiefs of the Arapaho and Cheyenne Tribes, Charging Bull, Lone Wolf, and Little Bear know their nomad way of life roaming the northern plains is finished. Determined to make the best of a bad situation, the Chiefs decide to lease their grazing lands to two ranching families that are willing to pay with money, cattle, and horses.

Frank Kincaid is the owner of the great Running K Ranch that lays along the Trinity River on the Trinity Flats just a few miles from Jacksboro, Texas. He hears there will be a great demand for his horses when General Custer arrives at Camp Supply. Several cowpunchers from the Jingle Bob Outfit pushing cattle up from deep in south Texas to Kansas tell Kincaid of the market for his horses at the new fort. The cavalry units of the Fourth Cavalry move out of Fort Richardson causing the demand for remounts to go almost completely dry. Hearing the words of the cowpunchers and their promises of horse sales in Oklahoma, the rancher decides to move his great horse herd north across the Red River, deep into the Nations. Despite the unheeded warnings of his friends and hired hands, Frank Kincaid gives the order for the herd to trail north.

For years, Will Guthrie runs a stable and raises and sells mules in and around Hays City. Hearing of the new fort in the Nations across the Canadian River and knowing his wild young son Munday needs a fresh place to spread his wings, Guthrie decides to move his herd into the vast grasslands along the banks of the Canadian. He knows the cavalry will need pack animals and mules to pull their supply wagons north against the warring tribes of the Sioux Nation. He also knows if Munday remains in Hays and near the wild cattle drovers that bring their cattle north, trouble could erupt at any time. Munday is a good respectable son but he also has his wild side, quick to use the forty-four around his waist.

Both families with their herds come together on the banks of the great Canadian River, one family leasing land east of the agency and Fort Reno, the other taking up land to the west. Miles of grass and flatland separates the two families and their herds but is it enough to keep Munday Guthrie and the youngest son of Frank Kincaid apart. Clay Kincaid is the same age as Munday Guthrie. Both young men were raised with a gun in their hand and a horse under them. Neither knew the word fear, each throws a wide shadow wherever they walk. Both are proud but Munday Guthrie is arrogant, mischievous, and always ready for a fight. Whereas Clay Kincaid is laid-back and quiet never looking for trouble but none that know him doubt, if pushed he is not one to walk around or away from it.

As both herds move towards the Canadian and the lush grasslands, Ewen Galt and his band of ex-confederate raiders turned outlaws watch their every move like a pack of marauding wolves. Galt the outlaw leader wants both herds, one last big haul before moving his operations farther west into a healthier climate.

CHAPTER 1

THE RUNNING K RANCH OUTSIDE
FORT RICHARDSON TEXAS 1874

The dented up old coffee cup looks pitiful and small in the huge hands of the big rancher. Frank Kincaid stands motionless, his grey eyes looking into the eastern sun, staring out across the flat Trinity River Bottoms of his huge Running K Ranch.

"They're beauties aren't they?" The soft woman's voice comes from the porch behind the big man.

Shifting his eyes slowly, letting them drift across every horse in his sight, the man nods. "Yes Ma'am Miss Em, I do believe we've finally bred up the best remuda of broodmares in Texas."

Emily Kincaid whom everyone calls Em smiles knowingly, she knows his every thought, married thirty years now she can read his mind, almost before he speaks. "Imagine my husband, all these beauties came from a handful of handpicked mustangs and that thoroughbred bay stallion you brought back from the war. It seems like only yesterday."

"Yes Ma'am, it does." Frank smiles over at her. "We've had rough times but some real good ones too Mrs. Kincaid."

"They were all wonderful to me." She smiles softly. "Come in and get your breakfast while it's hot Mister."

Frank Kincaid nods absently then takes another swallow of coffee as he studies the band of mares and colts that drift in close to the ranch house. With the practiced eye of a born horseman, he automatically watches the movements of every animal for injury or lameness as they move about the pasture.

A herd of broodmares he bred for size and color, almost every horse imaged one other. All are blood bays, with black legs from their knees down; some have a blaze but most carry a white star in their foreheads. The big Kentucky bred stallion he brought back from the war definitely bred the finest of qualities into his colts. Every saddle horse branded with the Running K iron stood over fifteen hands and weighs around a thousand pounds or better. Harsh culling for over ten years finally paid off, producing some of the best horses in the state of Texas.

Small heads, slender necks, long backed with heavy thick hindquarters, straight strong limbs, and black hard feet are the trademark of every Running K horse. Any mare producing anything but a blood bay, dark bay or black was quickly removed from the brood band.

The original old stallion from Kentucky is still in use over a few quality mares. Several of his sons handpicked by Kincaid, are now the main foundation sires of the Running K. Kincaid smiles as he dumps the dregs from his cup. He accomplished his goal, two hundred blemish free mares with their colts, plus yearlings and two year olds ready to be broke graze freely on the lush grass of the Trinity River Bottoms. Nodding with satisfaction, he turns and walks towards the ranch house.

Entering the warm comfortable kitchen, he pulls a chair out from the wood table and sits down heavily taking his place at the table. "Buenos dias boss."

Frank nods at the tall beanpole of a man that was busy eating. "Good morning, Bandy."

"Miss Em has sure outdone herself this morning Frank." The tall man smacks his lips and grins, his dark twinkling eyes lighting up the deep suntanned face. "Yes sir, we've got us the best cook in Texas."

Emily shakes her head in frustration as she pours the two men coffee. "And just how would you know that Bandy Dedrow?"

"Why Miss Em, I should know, I've been eating your cooking for nigh onto ten years now."

"Ugh huh, if my cooking is so good tell me, why haven't you put on a pound of weight in all them years?"

The fork loaded with hotcakes and syrup stops in midair as the dark eyes wink. "Why that's easy Miss Em, it's your husband, he works me like a dog, and I just don't have the time to fatten up."

"Ugh huh."

Noticing Kincaid is quieter than usual Bandy hushes and looks down the table. "What's on the agenda for today boss?"

Frank let his grey eyes study the plate of eggs and pancakes for several minutes before picking up a bone handled fork. "Reckon me and the Missus will be headed into town right after breakfast."

The dark head of Bandy bobs up and down. "You're still planning on pulling up stakes ain't you?"

"Right now, I'm fixing to eat my breakfast." The words came out short and gruff as the rancher lifts his fork and looks down the table. "I suggest you do the same."

"Just asking, Boss." The tall man returns to his breakfast but not before grinning at Emily Kincaid. "Just thought those Jingle Bob Drovers might have put some bad ideas into your head is all?"

Frank lays his fork softly across his plate and then rests his square chin atop the big hands as he stares at his foreman. "Suppose Bandy, I do decide to head out. Are you and the boys sticking with me?"

"You know dang well most of the hands will stick but are you plumb sure you're gonna take the word of them lying cowmen and pull up stakes?"

Frank looks down the table at the man. "Bandy, do you and the boys like drawing wages?"

The question takes the tall man by surprise at first and then he grins. "I do, it's kinda hard to chase, umh I mean it's kinda hard to."

Frank clears his throat as both men look sheepishly at Emily. "I know what you mean Bandy."

"Sorry Miss Em." The tall man's face turns beet red.

Only a nod and a small smile comes from the woman as she turns back to the stove. "I'm an old woman Bandy Dedrow, wise to a cowhand's ways. I know boys will be boys."

"You're not old Misses Em, not by a long shot."

"All I know for sure is those Jingle Bob boys said the army is building a new remount station and fort near the Darlington Agency up in the Nations. They'll help try to police the Arapaho and Cheyenne Indians from raiding down into Texas or escaping back to their homelands in the north."

"And that means they'll be needing remounts." Bandy mumbles as he bit into his breakfast. "To help do their chasing is that it?"

"Exactly and we're gonna supply them remounts." Frank looks at the woman. "I'm ready to leave when you are Misses Kincaid."

Bandy grabs his hat from the floor and stands up. "Thankee kindly ma'am, reckon I'll get the boys to work on that new string of broomtails we just wrangled in."

Frank nods as he passes through the door. "We should be back around sundown."

"Okay Frank."

"Bandy."

"Yea Boss."

Frank looks towards the pole corrals where several men are standing looking over the milling horses. "Find out how many of the boys will be riding into Oklahoma with us, that is, if I decide we're going."

"Yes sir, I'll do it." Bandy looks towards the corrals. "Like I said, I reckon they'll all stick with you."

Frank exhales, "I appreciate that Bandy. You know the market is slow right now around Fort Worth and Dallas, except for maybe some replacements for the cattle drives passing through."

"Yep, most of them boys are already pretty well mounted." Bandy strikes a sulphur on his chaps and lights himself a quirley. "Want one Frank?"

Shaking his head the big rancher looks over towards the barn where a wagon is hitched to a team of bays. "I've got to go where the market is. I doubt it'll ever come back here again, at least not like it was when the Comanche's still ran wild."

"What do you mean, they're still out there?"

"The army's too strong now Bandy, too many soldiers." Frank pulls his Stetson down tight on his head. "Even old Quanah has to realize that by now."

"What about the ranch?"

"That's the main reason I'm driving into Richardson today." Frank looks towards the house. "I'll try to get Craig to ride out every few days and check on things. For now, I'll leave Ramon and his family here to run the place and feed the animals we leave behind at least until I sell, providing we decide to stay in Oklahoma."

Bandy shakes his head. "Don't know about Craig, he's pretty busy with his store and that new wife of his."

"I know but we both know Clay will be wanting to ride with us, he won't stay behind." Frank nods. "Craig will find time, he's a Kincaid."

"It just could be Frank; we may need Clay's fast gun up there in Indian Territory."

"Yea." Frank nods; his youngest son Clay followed Bandy Dedrow around like a puppy since he was twelve years old. The tall foreman taught him everything he knows about ranching, riding and how to handle the low-slung forty-five that hangs at his side. "Sometimes I wish you'd never taught him how to use that gun."

"You know he would have learned from someone, might as well have been me." Dedrow shrugs. "He's a good boy Boss; give him a little time to grow and mature just like those young colts out there. Don't rush him."

"I know he is." Frank nods. "He's never been in any trouble, at least not of his own choosing."

"His brother Craig is doing fine, and so will Clay."

"Clay is nothing like Craig and you very well know it Bandy Dedrow." Emily walked up unknowingly. "They're as different in temperament as a bulldog and a cur dog."

"Yes Ma'am." Bandy ducks his head. "Reckon I best get kicking."

Frank grins when her voice becomes sharp and the men know to find places to hide, real quick like. "We'll be back about dusk."

Jacksboro lay on the fringes of the Trinity Bottoms, ten miles east of the ranch, a small-town with a dark past and an uncertain future. Fort Richardson lies a mile or so south of the town. The great cattle drives turn farther south and east passing through Waxahachie, then on into Fort Worth or Dallas as they head north pointing the longhorns towards the Red River Crossing or Doan's Store. Kincaid's Running K Ranch lies ten miles east of the old fort. It is far out on the Salt Fork of the Trinity River and now with the cavalry slowly abandoning Fort Richardson, far from any serious horse market.

The great cattle drives drove thousands of cattle up from the south every year passing in a huge dust storm, the lusty young drovers working from daylight to dark, never dismounting except to change horses. The Running K sold a few replacement cow horses for the drives but mostly the drovers mount on the hardy mustangs that they catch off the wild rangeland of the southern plains. Two months back, word was sent to the ranch for twenty saddle mounts to be brought to the Northside cattle pens at Fort Worth for the Gordon Combine. Frank sold horses to this group of ranchers before. Frank dispatches his youngest son Clay and another rider named Bert Timms south with the horses. He finds himself gazing constantly down the dusty road leading to the ranch for the overdo men as he drives the buckboard towards Jacksboro.

"He should have been back two, three days ago."

"You know your son; he'll take his time seeing the sights." Emily smiles as the wagon bounces her against the big man. "He's a grown man now husband and he reminds me so much of you when you were his age."

"I've been too soft on him Missus." The grey eyes search the road for any sign of movement coming towards them. He knows exactly what she means by the sights. He knows his younger son is full-grown but he is still immature, yet he never gave his folks a minute's trouble and he always carries his fair load of ranch work and then some. Nevertheless, Frank knows his son, Clay is fast with the forty-five and he will not back down from anything. Bad horses, wild cattle, Indians, or bad men; the youngster will not back water for any of them and his father feared one day his toughness could just be his downfall.

The younger Kincaid is a throwback to his grandfather who fought with Sam Houston during the Texas Rebellion. Just an inch shorter than his father, Clay has eye-catching dark looks and handsome features that catch women's eyes and lure them to him. With the flashing smile, muscled up body and standing straight as an axe handle through the shoulders, Clay Kincaid in time will be a natural leader. Even now though still young, his charm and coolness when prodded draws loyalty from men, and adoration from women. Everyone who knows him likes Clay and all respect the young hellion. His brother Craig is well liked and respected as well but he does not possess the charm and natural leadership qualities Clay has. It is a well-known fact in Jacksboro, Richardson, and out on the range, to those who know him, the normally good-natured Clay could turn rough if he has to.

Frank pulls the team to a stop outside the mercantile store of his older son Craig Kincaid and helps Emily to the dusty ground. "Go have yourself a cold sarsaparilla with the kids Misses while I mosey over to the livery barn and check out the horse business."

"I can do that Mister." She smiles. "I'll be right here when you finish with your business."

Sloan's Livery is the last of the old time horse stables that still keeps its doors open in town. Horses bought and sold, horses rented, horses shod, the stable is indeed the last of its kind in Jacksboro. Old man Henry Sloan is one of the first of the settlers to put down stakes and open his livery when the town was first laid out. Arriving in North Texas, several years later Frank

Kincaid bailed Sloan out of a money problem by buying a partnership in the stable. Over the years, the Running K sold hundreds of horses through this barn.

The place is old; the barn smells of stale boards, horses and saddle leather. As Frank walks into the cool interior, he finds three old men sitting about a wooden barrel concentrating on the beat-up and scarred checkerboard before them. Frank looks at the McClellan Cavalry saddles that line one of the stalls, remnants of the Fourth Cavalry that stabled some of their horses in this livery barn. Once an intricate part of the Cavalry, the saddles are now like the old men playing checkers, just relics and reminders of bygone days. For years, the Cavalry from nearby Fort Richardson was a mainstay for the economy of Jacksboro. They protect the surrounding country and ranches including Jacksboro from the continual Indian raids of the Comanche and Kiowa Tribes.

"Frank Kincaid, you old hog thief." Henry Sloan stands slowly and shakes hands with the big rancher. "How are you Hoss?"

"Just fine Henry, how are you old friend?"

Sloan looks down at his two companions and grins. "Well Frank, to tell you the truth we sure ain't overburdened with work."

"I've heard word gets around."

"It's slow, slower than I've ever seen it since most of the Cavalry pulled up stakes and headed west to chase Victorio and Geronimo." Sloan looks into the troubled grey eyes. "Your youngest passed through here about two, three weeks or so back, left his horses here for the night and spent the evening with his brother."

"We were wondering he should be back by now."

Well, you know that boy." The old hostler shrugs. "He'll be along in his own good time."

"Yea, I've already heard that once this morning." Frank nods. "What do you think Henry, will the horse business return?"

"Well now, that's a good question, one I can't answer for sure Frank." Sloan scratches at his stubble of beard. "I doubt the market for those well-bred horses of yours will ever return. The cavalry will all be gone soon."

"What's wrong with the Running K stock?" Frank questions as he gazes into the old man's runny eyes. "There ain't any better cow horses in the state."

"Nothing, like you said they're the best cow horses in the country." The hostler looks down at the checkerboard. "I don't think you'd want to see them fine animals pulling a plow and that's what this country is fixing to come too, farming, nesters, and the like."

Frank nods slowly. "I know old friend; I've seen it coming for some time now."

"The day of the open range and big rancher is long gone, it's a darn shame." Sloan shakes his head sadly. "That's progress as they call it and you can't turn progress around."

The grey eyes of the big rancher look out through the weathered doors of the old livery. His eyes linger on the few horses that stand hipshot at the tie rails fronting the stores. "I can remember the time when there would be a hundred horses tied out there."

Sloan shrugs then smiles. "Yep and I can remember when I had more to do than sit around playing checkers all-day. Face it Hoss, the good old days are long gone, they've up and passed us by."

"I've heard rumors Henry."

Sloan cocks his head slightly then motions towards the big wide doors. "Let's step out front."

Curious why the old man does not want to talk in front of the others, Frank follows him outside. "Are we down to keeping secrets now Henry?"

"Nope but now we can talk plain." Sloan spit a stream of tobacco hitting a horsefly dead center. "What rumors you been hearing young'un?"

It always amazes Kincaid when the old hostler calls him boy or young'un. The hostler is nigh on twenty years older than he is and the old man practically raised him off and on for the last thirty years. He nods, "Word is the army is fixing to pull the few remaining men out of Fort Richardson completely when they get the Comanche's whipped back onto the reservation at Fort Sill."

"Uh huh, you figure that's gonna happen? Old Quanah might just have something to say about that."

Kincaid nods over at Sloan then looks towards the town square. He remembers well the day Quanah Parker rode into his small ranch yard with his warriors. He just sat on his horse unflinching and unafraid waiting for the white rancher to come from behind his wooden walls. Stepping from the house Frank remembers being amazed as he looked into the eyes of the great Comanche Chief for the first time. He always heard Quanah was a savage bloodthirsty killer but the tall Chief sitting his coal black stallion before his house was anything but. The dark highly intelligent face looked down on the rancher then extended his hand. No other words were spoken, only a handshake and Quanah was gone in a cloud of Texas dust just as he appeared.

"The Comanche, even with Quanah leading them can't whip the sixth Cavalry." Frank toed the stable dirt. "Not for the long haul they can't."

The hostler scratches his grey whiskered chin and grins a toothless smile. "I dunno about that, they've done a pretty good job of it so far."

"Hear tell, that crazy General Sherman is fixing to send Mackenzie and the Fourth Cavalry out into the Llano Estacado after Quanah."

"Ssh, I doubt Ranald Mackenzie could find his rear end with both hands." Sloan shakes his head again. "But, you know as well as I do that Sherman isn't crazy, he whipped the crap out of you boys all through Georgia a few years back."

"That's your opinion old man." Frank hates anything about a blue uniform and probably will until his dying day. However, he has horses to sell and to do that a man has to deal mostly with the army and that means Yankee Blue.

Frank me lad, you've got to let the war go." Sloan grins. "I've seen you whipped a few times over the years, you sure didn't hold a grudge against the boys that did that."

"Those boys are mostly Texans and they sure weren't dead set on burning my home down or stealing my stock." The rancher grins. "But they were like them Yankees in some ways; they had me outnumbered about five to one."

"If you want to sell horses, which you do, then you've got to be willing to deal with the devil himself, providing old Satan's a wanting to buy horses that is."

Frank glares at the old man then grins slowly. "I'd be willing to deal with Lucifer himself, it'd sure be better than dealing with Sherman."

"What you got on your mind boy?" The good-natured bantering from the old hostler is over as he comes to the point.

"I'm studying on pulling up stakes and moving into Oklahoma with my horses." Frank grows serious. "That's what's on my mind Henry."

"Just like that, you're pulling up stakes?"

"Just like that old man." Frank nods. "I've got animals to sell; I heard the army was building a brand-new post called Fort Reno up north."

"Blue army or grey?" The old eyes twinkle as they ribbed the rancher. "You've been listening to them Jingle Bob boys ain't you?"

"Maybe a little."

"And if'n the army ain't up there when you get there?"

"Well then, I reckon I'll head back this way." The big man kicks at the ground. "I'm leaving my son Craig and his Missus to watch over the Running K while I'm gone."

"Dang it Frank, you know darn well how those boys from down south of San Antoine can lie." Sloan shakes his head in disbelief. "They can take the truth and stretch it ten ways from Sunday, just like most Texans."

"Last season they sold some beef at the Darlington Agency on their way into Kansas." Frank nods as a saddle horse carrying a local farmer rides past the stable. "They told me that army surveyors were already laying out the new fort."

"Miss Em going with you?"

"She is."

"You know how dangerous that Indian Country and the Nations can be?" Sloan shakes his head. "You've heard the tales yourself."

"I have."

Sloan shakes his head. "Reckon you're just taking you're saddle broke stuff?"

Frank replies, "no sir, I'm taking the mares and colts, plus anything big enough to ride, that way I'll have horses to sell to the Yankee army."

"That's reasonable thinking." Sloan spit. "You taking Clay with you or is he staying here?"

"He's going." Frank explains, "that is if he ever gets himself back here."

"Dedrow going?"

"Him too."

"It was Bandy's idea wasn't it, that is to take the youngster?"

"Why?"

"Bandy Dedrow knows that Kansas border country and the new Oklahoma Territory. He figures you'll be needing the boy's gun before you reach this Fort Reno."

"You make Clay sound like a killer or worse, old man."

"Don't get your hackles up Sonny, I think as much of that boy as you do." The old eyes study Frank. "He may not be a killer now but one day soon men are going to find out just how fast he is and then he'll start to build a reputation. When that day comes and I'm afraid it ain't far off, then he'll have to kill or take off the gun which we both know he won't do."

"He won't, not if me or his Ma can help it."

"That's just it Frank old friend, you can't." Sloan smiles. "Clay has a good streak in him but he also has a wild streak in him and the boy can get downright ill-tempered if pushed."

"He's no meaner than most." Frank protests shaking his head. "He's just young and likes to sow his wild oats a little."

"Don't kid yourself Frank, if it comes to it you'll see what that boy can and will do." Henry waves his finger. "Just you wait."

"He'll be fine old friend."

"Okay, but I sure wish you'd reconsider and keep yourself here on the Running K graze where you're already got roots." Henry shakes his head. "It'll be safer for all concerned."

Frank nods slowly then looks at the old man. "Henry, I ain't sold enough horses this year to pay my wranglers. I've got to look for a new market, if the army closes up and leaves here, I'm in real trouble."

"The Comanche ain't whooped yet." Sloan spit. "You remember when Quanah came to your place to kill you for shooting up his warriors?"

"I remember." Frank nods, he well remembers the Comanche sitting in his front yard on their wild little mustangs especially Quanah. They are superb looking warriors, wild as a March hare and twice as dangerous as a bull buffalo.

The old man laughs, "That Comanche was sure surprised when you brung them three bucks out of the house a walking that morning. Course now they were a little shot up, had a few holes in them but they were alive."

"They started that little fracas."

"That they did, I remember old Quanah smiling as he leaned from his horse and shook your hand. Then he up and rode away leaving old Thunder Hawk to tell you that from then on you and yours could live in peace on the Trinity."

Frank nods. "That's what he said back then and he's kept his promise."

"That's just it Hoss, you head for this Fort Reno and you're fixing to run smack-dab into Arapaho, Cheyenne, probably Kiowa and who knows whatever other hostile tribe. And I'll guarantee they won't be as friendly to you as Quanah was."

"They're supposed to be friendly now and on their own lands."

The old hostler snorts then shakes his head. "Had me a pet rattlesnake one time, he was supposed to be friendly too."

The rancher knows better but he just had to ask. "Well, was he?"

"Was till he got mad one day and up and bit my fifth wife Nellie Bell."

Henry seems to grow sad. "And that's what an Injun will do, friendly one day and bang, he's got you."

"Henry, I ain't gonna sit here in Texas depending on a Comanche to hold my hand and keep me safe for the rest of my days."

"Well, so far he's kept you and yours safe."

"I'm pulling out before the cold gets on the land." Frank sullied up and stuck out his jaw. "I need a wagon driver and a cook for the trail, you want the job?"

"What about our stable here?"

"Craig can get us someone to see after it." Frank looks back at the half dozen horses that stood hipshot in the lots. "You can bring along your checker-board you old goat."

The old hostler smiles slightly then shakes his head. "Nooo son, these old bones are a mite old to be bouncing around on an oak wagon seat. No sir, I reckon not this time, I'll stay behind and play checkers with the boys, and tend to what little business me and you got left hereabouts."

"I've got to give it a try Henry." Frank reaches out and takes the old man's hand. "Adios old friend, I'll be seeing you in the spring maybe."

"Keep your powder dry partner."

"You do likewise Henry Sloan."

Both men turn as a lone rider reined in before the livery and looked down solemnly at them. A lawman's badge beat out from a Mexican Peso showed outside his denim shirt. Looking up Frank recognizes Abbot Rountree, a Texas Ranger from Dallas. "Howdy Henry, Frank."

Abbot Rountree, you old sidewinder." Sloan smiles up at the Ranger. "What in tarnation are you doing this far from Dallas?"

"I've been sent down here by Captain Winslow." The Ranger's dark eyes peer down at Frank and then the stocky Ranger slowly dismounts. "I've come here looking for a man Henry."

Frank nods, dreading the words he knows are coming. "Is it Clay, is he in trouble?"

"Afraid so Frank, I'm here to take him down to Fort Worth with me."

"What's my boy done Abbot?"

"I understand he kilt a man." Rountree shrugs. "It happened in Fort Worth after this gun slick killed a man named Timms."

"Bert Timms?"

"I believe so, you know him?"

"I know him, he rode for me, went with Clay to take horses to Fort Worth." Frank shakes his head because Bert Timms was always a friendly, likable rider. "What happened?"

"Way I heard it, Timms got himself shot dead, then your son came in the saloon and found him bleeding on the floor with this gun slick standing over him. Next thing him and this other feller were going at it, the other man went down before your son's gun."

"And now you've come for him?" The rancher looks at the littler man. "Sounds like a fair fight to me."

"The way they told it, it sounded like a fair fight to me to." The squat Ranger nods. "But orders came Frank, we're friends have been for quite a spell now but I'm still a Texas Ranger and the Captain sent orders for me to come down here and bring him back."

"How come they didn't send another Ranger?"

"They know we are friends I reckon, and want me to take him back friendly like."

"Who was it he supposedly killed?"

"Red Hooper." Abbot nods. "And it sure ain't supposedly; the man's deader than last week's chicken dinner."

"He was a fast gun slick out of Abilene, wasn't he?" Frank looks hard at the gun belt around Abbot's waist. "Killed several men I hear, and now Bert Timms."

"He was that, was your boy fast enough to take him in a fair fight?"

"Can't say, I never saw this Hooper pull a gun." The rancher shrugs. "Tell me Abbot, if it were straight up, why are you after Clay?"

Rountree never blinks as he watches the grey eyes of the rancher. Kincaid has a reputation as a fair and peaceful man but also as a dangerous and deadly one when riled up. After all this is his son, they are talking about. "Some say it was a fair fight, Red's friends say he didn't give Hooper a chance."

"And you're here to take him back to hang?"

"I don't think so but he's got to go back for a hearing all the same."

"Is Bascombe still the he hog down there?" Frank frowns. "Did he send you after my son?"

"If you're asking if Judge Bascombe is still the presiding Judge in Fort Worth, he is."

"Word is around here, he'd rather hang a man than eat his supper."

"He's a fair man Frank. The boy will get a fair shake."

"He ain't here Abbot, ain't returned from selling the horses I sent him to Fort Worth with."

"That a fact?" Rountree looks around the stable then turns to his horse. "Henry, can you put my horse and me up for the night? We've traveled many a mile today."

"Sure Ab, sure."

"You haven't ever lied to me old friend." Rountree looks over at Frank then passes his reins to Henry. "I doubt you are now but just so you know I will be taking him back, it's my job."

Without a word or backwards glance Frank turns and walks to where Emily stands watching the conversation, lifting her bodily into the wagon he takes up the lines. "We best be heading home Missus."

"What's wrong?" She knows him, she can feel the tension in his body and something is amiss.

"Nothing." Frank put his big hand on hers. "We'll speak about it when we get to the ranch."

Dedrow can tell the look on Frank's face is serious as the rancher pulls the tired team up in front of the barn. There was no joking as usual, as he helps Emily down from the buckboard. Uncharacteristic of her not a word of greeting comes from Emily as she touches the ground and hurries on towards the house.

"We've got problems Bandy!"

"Is it the horse's boss?"

"No, that would be simpler, its Clay, they say he killed a man in Fort Worth; Abbot Rountree is in Jacksboro looking for him."

"Ranger Abbot Rountree from Dallas." Bandy's usual smile fades slowly like a wisp of smoke. "He's a bad one to have on your trail. Who was the young'un supposed to have killed?"

"Red Hooper, after this Hooper killed Bert." Frank looks out across the flats hoping to see Clay riding up. "I want you to saddle-up right now and ride. Find the boy and catch up to us across the Red River, get him into the Nations as fast as you can."

"Bert Timms is dead?"

"He's dead alright, grab some supplies and ride."

"You sure that's what you want Boss?" Dedrow questions, "He'll be wanted if he runs. Rountree will just follow him into Oklahoma. Besides Hooper is a gun slick, a killer, everyone in Texas knows that."

"I know that." Frank nods. "But, if he goes in he could be hung, that crazy carpetbagger Neal Bascombe still presides in Fort Worth."

"Bascombe! You may be right about the hanging. I'll get him into Oklahoma; it's still just a territory." Bandy starts for the barn. "It's mostly lawless across the Red River in Indian land; I doubt they'll spend much time hunting him there. I ain't real sure the Rangers have authority to arrest a man in that country anyway."

"I know Rountree, he makes his own authority." Frank frowns. "Find him Bandy; we'll meet on the trail up north somewhere."

Emily stands on the porch clenching her fists as Bandy rides out of the ranch yard in a hard dust-raising run. Frank never speaks as he walks by her and into the house. Pulling up a chair, he places his hat on its peg then sits down and drops his head tiredly.

"Tell me husband, what's wrong?" Emily pulls up a chair next to him.

"It's your youngest son woman."

"I figured it was something like that, the way you were so quiet coming home." Her voice had a catch in it. "Has he been hurt, killed, what has happened?"

"He killed a man, I figure it was a fair fight but I ain't turning him over to find out." Frank takes his old battered cup she offers. "With Clay in trouble maybe you should stay behind and not go north with me just in case he comes here."

"When are you leaving husband?"

"Maybe day after tomorrow, the boys have the horses separated and ready to trail, so there's no use waiting."

"Okay Mister Frank Kincaid, I'll be ready to leave when you are." Emily turns her back to him. "And Sir, I wouldn't say another word about leaving me behind if I were you. I can use a rifle as good as any man and you know it. Clay can get himself out of this trouble alone; he got himself into it alone."

An understanding smile crosses his face as he lifts the cup. He knows she loves each of her sons but he is her husband and where he goes she will follow. It has always been this way between them, they were always inseparable and he knows they will always be together.

Chapter 2
Hays City, Kansas the year 1874

Will Guthrie's Livery Stable sits east of the town square, four city blocks along Dodge Street. It is easily the biggest building along the broad thoroughfare. A huge sign was painted in what was once bright red but now fading to a dullish red, proclaiming Horses and Mules Bought, Sold, Boarded and Shod, not particularly in that order.

Two head high tall corrals surround the stable on three sides leaving the huge front open for customers to enter. Inside the normal smell of horses, sweaty horse blankets, leather oil, and hay accost a man's nose as soon as he enters the barn. A pack of tall rangy Russian Wolfhounds the hostler uses for running down wolves lay scattered about the alleyways that separate the horse stalls. Several barn cats lounge about on top of the hay or corrals fearful to get within reach of the fierce dogs.

Heat emits from a coal forge that sits in front of the barn doors to heat the raw bar stock of iron for horseshoes. The heat also keeps the coffeepot hot for the paying customers and friends that are forever wandering into the stable. Several men stand in a group close to the front of the barn hollering and laughing as a square built sturdy man with a ruddy complexion waits before a huge anvil. Muscles flexing in the man's forearms and biceps as he adjusts a one-inch thick rope around the horn of the heavy anvil.

"How much does this thing weigh Will Guthrie?" A fat man wearing the apron of a shopkeeper or saloon man asks laughingly as he slaps the huge anvil.

"Two hundred pounds, Mister Lawrence, to the ounce." The sandy brown haired man of about fifty years answers proudly.

"You're betting all comers that you can curl it with one hand, your elbow cannot touch your body in anyway, the anvil has to swing clear of the stump, and you only get one chance at lifting it." The fat man speaks again doubtfully. "Is that the bet Will?"

"That's it and you can bet on me or against me." Sweat runs down the stocky man's face, as he studies each man's face waiting for them to decide which way they would wager. Guthrie is not too tall but he is powerfully built and strong as a bull.

Naked down to his waist, he has a thick leather belt looped around his rough denim pants. Thick muscles cord across the man's chest and shoulders making him look almost deformed. Average of height, it is his bulk of muscle that makes other men look at him in awe. Scars cover his face from his days as a prizefighter back east. His ring days are over, marriage and his brand-new bride demanded before she said yes to his proposal that his fighting days in the ring were over and finished forever. A legendary right hand with lethal knockout power put Will Guthrie next in line for a championship bout but that is all past and done with for several years now. Over the years, many boxing promoters offered him big money to return for one last fight but one look at Alder Guthrie's frowning face convinces most to leave well enough alone.

"It can't be done, no man is that strong." A short cowboy tosses money on the stump. "Ten dollars says you can't lift it, no sir."

A younger man stands next to the strong man and takes the bets marking down the wagers in a small black book. "Thank you Billy Locker."

"It can't be done Munday, no offense mind you but no man not even your Pa has that kind of strength." The cowboy takes a seat on a bale of hay and watches the younger man place his money on the growing pile.

A tall powerful built man takes the rope with both hands, tests the weight, and then gives up quickly as he cannot budge the anvil from its perch. "I'll take twenty of that."

"Pretty heavy, huh Sam?" The apron man speaks up.

"It's heavy enough boys." The man grins confidently. "I feel like Billy, it can't be done."

Close to four hundred dollars lay stacked around the anvil as the sandy haired lad of about twenty counts the money. A low-slung forty-four hung about the narrow waist, shifting slightly as the young man gathers the money and finishes recording the bets. Almost the spitting image of the bare-chested man except in muscle mass, he returns the money to the stump.

"There's four hundred and thirty dollars here Pa."

"Okay Munday." The green eyes of Will Guthrie study the men silently. "Anybody else want to make a wager against this Welshman?"

"I'll take a hundred of your money Mister Guthrie." The voice is a slow southern drawl filled with contempt. "I'm betting on the anvil."

All eyes turn towards the open doors where a broad shouldered man stands propped against the wall holding a fistful of bills. Munday Guthrie looks over at the man with a glare. "Your money's no good here Ewen Galt!"

"You letting this snip of a kid speak for you now, Mister Mule Man?" The man straightens ready as a striking viper as he sneers at the bare-chested man holding the rope. "Or do you speak for yourself?"

Only a blur comes as Munday whirls and crouches, ready to draw. Will Guthrie releases the heavy rope and steps between the two men. "One of these days Mister Galt you're gonna let your alligator mouth overload your tad pole tail."

"Am I talking too much today or is my money good here?" The well-dressed man grins wickedly at the younger man trying to goad Munday Guthrie into drawing. "You've got yourself a real bad man there."

"Your money's good Galt!" Will frowns, "I'll cover anything you want to wager but keep your smart words to yourself."

Galt steps forward and places his money on top of the rest. "I don't see any of your money yet."

Will Guthrie gives a slight nod then Munday pulls several bills from his pocket and counts them out before slamming them on top of the growing pile. "Five hundred and thirty dollars."

"You boys all know the rules." Will wipes his face as he studies the men and waits for an answer. "Angus, you and Charlie are the judges, here we go."

Leaning over to pick up a handful of dirt and straw that littered the stable floor, Guthrie steps up closer to the hickory stump that holds the anvil and he plants his feet. Rubbing his hands together once more, he looks around the stable before slipping his broad powerful hand under the loop of rope.

"Remember Mule Man, no part of your arm or elbow can touch your body and you have to curl your arm, no dead lift." Galt grins broadly. "Nothing touches or you lose the bet."

"I should remember Galt, they are my rules."

Not a whisper of sound, not even a shuffle or slight noise from the animals in the stalls sounded as Will puts tension on the rope. Veins stand out as muscles ripple up and down the great arm as the man begins to exert raw power against the rope. All eyes focus as the heavy hemp rope begins to tighten around the anvil. Every man in the barn holds his breath expecting the rope to snap, hoping something will give way as it stretches.

"It's moving!" The fat man wearing the apron whispers hoarsely to the one beside him. "It's actually moving."

"The rope stretches some but I believe you're right Angus, the anvil is moving." Billy Locker nods his head in disbelief.

"It ain't cleared wood yet by a long sight." Galt argues.

The huge bicep of Guthrie balls-up in a small mountain as he strains harder making sure no part of his arm touches his body. With a final effort, he clears the anvil from the stump by six inches or better.

"He done it." Munday Guthrie yips in triumph. "You done it Pa, you done it."

Will drops the heavy anvil letting it settle back to the stump then rubs his arm as his muscles relax. Both Angus Lomax and Charlie Wallace proclaim Will the winner in the contest and pat him on the back. Glaring, Galt whirls and stomps from the stable. All the men stand about laughing. They do not like losing their money but it is worth it to see the hated outlaw Ewen Galt get his comeuppance.

Will slips his shirt back on and raises his hands for quiet. "Boys, the beers are on me and my son Munday. Let's mosey over to the Rainbow and cool off."

Charlie Wallace looks about the stable and shakes his head. "Sure wish you folks weren't selling out and leaving us Will."

"Me too." The green eyes of the Welshman light up. "Those drovers said they'd be a big market for my mules down in Oklahoma at that new army post they're building along the Canadian River."

"This stable won't be the same again." Angus Lomax starts towards the door following the rest. "You know old Jim Kipps ain't gonna work hard enough to shoe a horse. We'll all be afoot in less than a month."

Will laughs, "Don't matter none now boys, come sunup tomorrow he owns the stable lock, stock, and barrel, except for my mules."

"What about them hounds?" Another man looks to where the wolfhounds lay in the alleyways.

Will grins. "They stay here to keep you boys in line."

"Here's the rest of our stake Pa, now we can head for Oklahoma and that new fort called Reno." The younger Guthrie hands the wad of bills over to Will.

Looking at the bills, Will stuffs them in his pocket. "Let's just hope we're making the right move boy."

"We are Pa, we are." The younger man smiles crookedly, Munday Guthrie wants to move on and he has for years. He outgrew Hays City; it no longer is wild enough to hold him.

The Rainbow Saloon is almost empty as the men pile into it and sidled up to the long scared up bar. The day is young yet, the cowboys and town men are still working. Only three men sit at a back table playing poker. Will Guthrie shoulders up to the bar and slaps a twenty-dollar gold piece down hard on it.

"Drinks for the house, Lon." The Welshman grins. "When that's gone yell out and I'll find another one just like it."

Jack Fritch, Paddy Murphy and another man all look up from their game and survey the room. All three men are drinking steadily and their red eyes show it. Leaning his chair back in curiosity Fritch looks at the door as Ewen Galt steps into the saloon.

"Lon, when did you start letting snot-nosed, wet behind the ears kids in here?" The tall man starts in on Munday Guthrie as soon as he settles at the end of the bar. "The place has kinda got itself a milk smell about it."

Silence blankets around the room as all eyes glance to where Will stands talking with Angus Lomax. However, their main attention is on Munday, they know the hair-trigger temper he possesses.

The barman shrugs his shoulders. "Anybody can drink in here Mister Galt, long as they got the money."

Galt steps slowly away from the bar with his hand hovering over his pistol. The men in the saloon quickly move away from the trouble. "This kid ain't drinking in here with grown men."

Before Munday can move, the iron grasp of Will Guthrie's huge hand locks around the butt of his pistol. "Turn it loose Pa."

"Boy, you loosen your gun belt and let it fall to the floor." Will looks over to where Galt stands ready, waiting to draw.

"You pull that gun Ewen Galt and we'll hang you." Angus points a finger at the tall man. "Marshal Vetter has gone down to the Nations for a spell but we'll get it done just the same."

Munday's gun belt hits the floor inside the saloon sounds like a cannon going off, the saloon is so quiet. "Now Galt, you drop yours."

"You boys take it outside." The saloon man laid a double-barrel sawed off shotgun across the bar. "You ain't tearing my place up, especially on a Wednesday."

A wide smile spread from ear to ear on Galt, as he looks bewildered at the slender youth. "You mean you want me to fight him, that scrawny beanpole?"

"If your man enough?" Will's voice is hard as iron. "But, it'll be a fair fight."

"It's his funeral."

Every man in the saloon troops outside to watch the fight. They all know Munday Guthrie is overmatched. Galt outweighs the boy by at least forty pounds and stands a couple inches taller. They know the boy is a scrapper, they saw him in some kind of trouble almost his entire life, Fighting with every boy and even some grown men in town at one time or other. They know the boy has sand, they saw him get whipped several times but they never saw him stay whipped. If a man or boy whips him one day he had it to do the next and the next until Munday finally wins. He is trouble by most standards but there is not a man in town that does not respect the youngster's courage and spirit.

Will turns on Fritch and Murphy. "You two try to interfere in anyway and I'll break you in half."

Galt grins and waves them back. "I ain't needing any help boys, not against this snot-nosed kid."

Both fighters peel out of their shirts and step further out into the dusty street. Will takes Munday's shirt and turns his back to walk away. "Box him boy, he's too big and strong for you to wrestle with or go free-for-all with, you box him."

"I ain't scared of him Pa."

"I know you ain't lad, didn't say you were." Will steps back. "I said box him, you got age, speed and more air on your side. Just box him until he tires."

"No funny stuff Pa, I aim to beat him good."

"Ugh huh, well son you do as you think best." Will shakes his head. "If I were you, I'd box him."

Will Guthrie is a fighter. He was taught to box since childhood back in his homeland of Scotland and the Welch Isles. Physically strong and well trained by his fighting kinsman he was in many a boxing match inside the ring during his boxing days and on several occasions in a free-for-all on the streets. A man with a level head and fair-minded, he never was a bully or went looking for trouble. Today he gives his only son, Munday, the best advice he could, always box to outlast a larger and stronger opponent. The old adage, that it is not the size of a dog in a fight but the size of the fight in the dog is just that, words. When Will hears someone say this, he only shakes his head. He knows given equal skills the larger man most always comes out on top in a free-for-all. It is just a fact of fighting; the heavier man has the advantage of weight on his side.

Since childhood, Munday was always cocky and arrogant and lately as he grows older, he begins to swagger even more. The older Guthrie knows if the lad does not slow down he will eventually come up against someone that does not mind killing him. Today could possibly be that day. Munday is tough as boot leather and he is not afraid of anything walking. However, he is young and did not learn enough humility to listen to his elders. Well today might be the day and Ewen Galt might just be the man to teach him that lesson.

"You ready for a lesson in boxing kid?" Galt flexes his arms as he moves forward.

Munday Guthrie does not answer only glides forward and lands two sharp jabs to the bigger man's chin then dances quickly back out of range of the longer armed man. Will Guthrie nods, maybe the boy did listen. The youth is quick, faster than a striking rattler as he slips punches and lands his lightning fast counterpunches. Galt continues to plod forward waiting for an opening as Munday dances around taunting the older man.

"You're slowing down old man." These were the first words from the younger Guthrie's mouth since the fight started. Will frowns; he taught the boy better, never taunt your opponent while a fight is in progress. It could give a beaten man renewed energy and the will to fight harder.

"I'm still here boy, you hit like a sissy." Galt grins, wiping away a little blood that trickles down from a split lip. "You're a girl."

Enraged at the words Munday springs forward, forgetting his father's words to box the man. Several heavy blows land against the rock hard heavier body of Galt. The larger man absorbs the punches. Then he grabs the smaller man coming inside, he pulls him close then let loose with a thunderous left hook followed by a straight right that knocks Munday backwards into the dirt.

"I've got you now you little whelp." Galt starts forward.

Grinning as he staggers to his feet and raises his hands, Munday spit blood. "Maybe you do Sir but you've got it to do yet."

A short man even shorter than Will slips up beside Guthrie and looks curiously first at the fighters, then at his boss. "The lad's kinda overmatched, isn't he Boss?"

"It's his fight Mister Killian." Will never looks sideways at his ranch foreman. "We will not interfere."

"That's not what I asked."

Galt is landing punches regularly as Munday tries his best to move away from the bigger man. The heavy punches take away most of his speed, now his legs are wobbly like rubber refusing to move as he asks them.

"I heard you." Will nods. "The boy needs to learn, just like we did."

Tom Killian starts forward as another heavy blow sends Munday to the ground again. "He's had enough."

The strong-arm of Guthrie grabs Killian by his arm. "We'll stay out of it for a while yet."

Killian rips loose from the powerful grip. "He's your son Boss but your wife is across the street watching her only son get the crap kicked out of him."

Will looks back to where the small figure of Alder Guthrie stands in the bed of their buckboard watching her son take a beating. Her light blue eyes look a hole through him as she frowns. Turning he watches as Munday takes two hooks to the stomach then a hard right to the chest knocking him down once more. Pulling himself to his knees the young Guthrie shakes his bloody face and staggers to regain his feet.

"You've had enough young man." Galt steps back as Munday throws one last feeble right. "I apologize Mister Guthrie, you aren't a kid anymore."

With a nod, Will steps forward proudly and takes his son by the waist. The youngster tries to break free but for today the fight is finished. "It's over son."

"You want to try someone more your size Galt?" Tom Killian steps forward with his fists balled up.

"We'll go home now Tom." Will helps Munday towards the buckboard.

"Perhaps another time, Mister Killian." Galt laughs then turns to where his friends wait with his shirt and gun. "I wouldn't want to whip two of you Guthrie riders in the same day."

Tom Killian is burning, his blood is up and he wants to fight. He never liked Ewen Galt and more than that, he loves a good fight. Fifteen years ago when Will Guthrie brought his first herd of mares and Missouri Jacks into Hays to breed and raise mules, he was a thirty a month bronc rider for the Slash Y outfit near Wichita. Killian was in Hays delivering a small bunch of cattle to the local butchers when he and Guthrie tangled in the same Rainbow saloon. It had been a real humdinger of a fight, the town people talked about it for years as the best they ever saw. Both men wound up in jail and charged for the damages, and then they lay behind bars until Alder Guthrie relented and paid her husband's fine.

Looking at the battered face of Killian and knowing the cowboy is broke; Will paid his fine and herded him to the nearest diner. Before the dinner was finished, the stocky man was working for Will Guthrie and at his side for the last fifteen years working his way up to foreman. They still argue over who won the fight for years but they grew close and neither would think about fighting each other again.

Munday Guthrie sits on a wooden bench as his mother gingerly washes his bloody face from the horse trough outside the stable. Grinning up at the frustrated woman, he can only shake his head. "Reckon I forgot to duck, didn't I?"

"Well, you ain't as pretty as you were son." The face of Alder Guthrie was still beautiful after forty-odd years. A small woman, she is said to have the softest heart in Kansas but it could turn stone-cold in a blink. "I hope you enjoyed it?"

"I did." Munday frowns painfully. "Every bit of it."

"You learn anything boy?" Killian hands Munday a clean handkerchief.

"One thing, I'll know how to fight him the next time."

Will shakes his head. "That's all you learned?"

"Well Sir, you told me to box him, next time I will." Munday grabs his pistol from Killian. "He ain't got me whipped yet."

"You didn't learn to keep your mouth shut?" Will looks down at the weapon and frowns. "That thing there won't get you out of trouble every time."

Munday looks at his father out of one-half closed eye. "Ain't a man alive Pa, that'll keep me whipped and if I have to use this thing as you call it, I will."

The resounding slap of Will's open fist coming up against Munday's face sounds across the darkened stable area. "You may talk smart to others boy but don't you ever dare back sass your Pa."

Will Guthrie clucks at the team and sends them trotting towards home. The light squeaking of the wagon's wheels as they turn, the crunching noise of the small gravel they cross, and the jingling of the trace chains keep beat with the horse's hooves, as they head east from Hays City.

Killian helps Munday to his feet and propels him towards his horse. "That wasn't to wise youngster."

"Man." Munday tries to grin. "He still hits like a mule kicking."

"You learn anything?"

Munday touches his swelling face. "Yes sir, I sure did."

"What was that?"

"To keep my mouth shut or duck quicker." Munday kicks his horse into a hard run and quickly catches the wagon. Looking down at his folks, he grins. "Sorry Pa, it won't happen again."

Nodding, Will clucks to the team as Alder Guthrie squeezes his arm and smiles.

Chapter 3

Trinity River Bottoms Texas 1874

Bandy Dedrow sits atop the high cliffs of the Trinity Crossing scanning the horizon with the battered field glasses that he carried since the war. He was sent south to intercept Clay Kincaid and keep him out of Fort Richardson and out of sight and the clutches of Abbot Rountree. Dedrow cannot understand why a Texas Ranger even bothers to come all the way to north Texas to arrest anyone for killing a lobo wolf like Red Hooper. The man was as deadly a killer as ever walked in Texas, except maybe for Bill Longley. Nevertheless, to come this far after a mere boy for killing a man like Hooper is a curiosity. Dedrow rode with Rountree in their younger years before the Rangers, he is a friend of the Ranger or he was at one time.

He knew Clay Kincaid since he was a child, he helped raise the boy, he knew the lad was a little wild but most young men from the Texas plains are. The younger son of Frank Kincaid was raised on the open range where every man must grow up fast and tough. At heart the boy is a good man; he is not mean or cruel to anything or anyone. The Running K foreman was responsible for teaching the boy the use of the forty-five pistol before he was strong enough to hold it steady or cock it with one hand. As the young Kincaid matured, he became cat quick with a pistol and better yet, he is accurate with any handgun or rifle. In time and with hours of practice and tutoring from the foreman, Clay Kincaid is now faster than his mentor and friend Bandy Dedrow.

In the wilds of post war Texas, every man and boy, old enough to pull a trigger, were always armed to the teeth. Comanche's, Comancheros, outlaws from the recent war, and fights over the open range made it suicide to go unarmed. Neither Frank nor Emily Kincaid are opposed to the boy learning the use of the pistol if only their youngest will settle down and cool his hair-trigger temper. They know it is natural to go armed, just a way of life out on the Texas Plains and here in the Trinity Bottoms.

Dedrow strikes a sulphur to his quirley and draws in a cloud of smoke as he thinks about Abbot Rountree. He knew the man when they were younger and full of vinegar. Some said Rountree rode the outlaw trail before signing on with Captain Winslow and his Rangers. Some people think the rumor is true but none dare voice the matter or question Rountree. He is a rough one, maybe the toughest lawman to wear a badge of all the Rangers. Bandy Dedrow studies on it, he rode with Rountree and knew the truth to the rumors, yet he never speaks of those long ago bygone days. Even Frank Kincaid does not know when he mentioned the Ranger and sent Dedrow after Clay that he knows the man. Still he just cannot understand the Rangers sending their best man on the trail of a youngster like Clay Kincaid.

"You lost or just killing time?" The soft Texas drawl comes from behind Dedrow. Recognizing the speaker Bandy stands up and walks to where the man sat his gelding. "Abbot Rountree, you old tom-cat. How the heck are you?"

"Can't complain Bandy, how about yourself?" The rough beat out badge reflects the sun as the Ranger sticks out his hand.

"Tolerable, just tolerable." Bandy grins and shakes the strong hand then pulls out his sack of Bull Durham. "Light down and have a smoke with me old friend."

"Alright compadre, it's been a year or two." Rountree dismounts on the off side of his sorrel, something Bandy notices.

"You've always been the careful one Abbot but don't tell me you don't trust me either?"

Rountree nods as he accepts the quirley. "Just habit but a man in my profession lives longer, if he's cautious."

"I understand."

"What you doing out here Bandy?" Rountree looks off to the east. "You work for the Running K west of here don't you?"

"I do." Bandy agrees. "Been with Frank Kincaid for several years almost since me and you parted company."

"Now you're waiting to warn the Kincaid kid that I'm here looking for him?" Rountree draws in on his smoke. "Kincaid sent you, is that it?"

"In a nutshell, I reckon."

"This is official business for the state of Texas and the Rangers."

"I understand, what I don't understand is why a Texas Ranger was sent here looking to arrest a youngster for killing a skunk like Red Hooper?"

Rountree pulls himself up a patch of sand overlooking the Trinity and sits down. "I was sent, that's all there is to it."

"Yea and I'm a two-legged billy goat." Dedrow sits back down. "This is me Bandy Dedrow you're talking with old friend."

"I know who you are." Rountree squints into the sun. "Told you, its official business, that's all I know."

"Un huh, now suppose you tell me what this crap is really all about."

Rountree grins. "The kid didn't kill Hooper; Bill Longley did the actual shooting. Your boy is fast all right but he hit Hooper in the shoulder, Longley's thirty-eight didn't miss. Judge Bascombe wants Longley bad, he figures this young Kincaid is a friend of Longley and maybe knows where he is. Anyway the lad left Fort Worth without the Judge's okay, that's breaking the law and his honor wants him back muy pronto."

"His honor, Judge, that's all bull Abbot. I knew Bascombe when he was still rustling cattle down south before he got himself educated and became a carpetbagger."

"Yep, and he wasn't even a good rustler." Rountree exhales. "But then like now, he's smart and tricky."

"So he trumps up this killing on a pretense to send a Texas Ranger after the boy?" Dedrow cusses. "The boy doesn't even know Longley."

"You sure of that?"

"Positive." Bandy nods. "I've known the lad since he began wearing short pants."

"He must be pretty fast with the hog leg he carries to beat Hooper to the draw?"

"He's fast Abbot, real fast."

"Faster than you Bandy?"

"I'm not in his class anymore and old buddy that's a pure fact." Bandy nods. "You sure you've got to take him back with you?"

"I reckon that's about it." Rountree smiles. "Way you talk that might just be a job in itself."

"You already know Frank Kincaid his old pappy; he's a mighty tough hombre." Bandy looks over at Rountree. "He ain't about to let you take the boy back."

"I know he's a real tornado when he gets riled alright." Rountree tosses his smoke. "Trouble is he's headed down the trail for Oklahoma with a herd of horses."

"Already heard that, have you?" Bandy nods. "No he ain't here Abbot, but I am."

"It's like that is it?"

"We've rode the long trail together for many a year old friend."

Rountree taps the homemade star on his vest and looks at Dedrow. "This badge goes beyond friendship Bandy, you know that."

"Reckon I do at that."

"You gonna try me?"

Dedrow nods slowly. "Are you going to force it? You know I was always faster than you in our younger days."

"Yes you were but those days are long gone now." Rountree stands up and squints down towards the river before backing away from Dedrow. "I'll be riding for now but don't get between me and the Kincaid kid."

The Running K foreman stands and watches as the Ranger rides away from the river in a slow lope. He got his answer, an answer he does not like but judges are powerful carpetbagging politicians that control Texas these days and they are as crooked as the day is long. Trouble is he does not know how honest Rountree became since swearing an oath to the Rangers. If this Judge Bascombe could bag Bill Longley, he would have bragging rights and walk his way right into any office in Texas he desires, even the Governor's Mansion in Austin.

Pulling his cinch tight, Dedrow mounts and turns towards the south. Clay could have cut across the range and headed straight home, then again, he could be riding straight into Rountree's arms. The youngster has no idea he is being followed or that he is a hunted man. If Rountree confronts him, Bandy knows Clay will fight. The young Kincaid is fast but Rountree is older and cagier when it comes to confronting a man in a gunfight. Bandy is an old hand at shooting, he would bet on the older man with experience every time. Bill Longley is a youngster who broke that rule but there is only one Longley. He knows Clay has not become as cold and hard as Longley; he is not a natural born killer.

Clay Kincaid stands holding his hand over the yellow horse's nose as he watches the two men high up on the bluff. The bright blue eyes are sharp as an eagle, he can tell even from a distance one of the men is Bandy Dedrow. The other man he does not recognize and never saw him before in the Trinity Bottoms or anywhere else in these parts. His eyes follow the lone rider as he rides away to the southeast; he knows the man saw him from the cliff just before he pulled back into the shady mesquite thicket. Clay watches as his old friend Bandy mounts up and starts south.

"Well Yeller, let's go catch old Bandy and see what he's doing way out here on the grass lands." The young man pats the yeller horse and steps lightly into the saddle.

Kincaid knows whoever was talking with the Running K Foreman could still be up on the ridge and from where he stands, they would have a bird's-eye view of the bottoms. There is no helping it; out on the flats there is nothing to hide behind unless you find a Texas size gopher mound. Angling to cut off Dedrow, he kicks the yeller horse into a slow ground-eating lope. The old-timers said when he brought the horse into Jacksboro the first time the yellow colt could lope all day in the shade of a Mesquite Tree and never stir up dust. He remembers his Pa throwing a walleyed fit the first time he laid eyes on the young colt traveling alongside his dam. What the older Kincaid did not notice was the ground-eating running walk the colt was already displaying as he moved.

After two days of arguing and threatening to tell everyone, the old Kentucky stud threw a yellow colt Clay manages to buy the little feller. However, he had to swear to everyone listening he bought the colt from a passing Comanche Buck. His Pa squirms every time he sees the colt but as he matured and was finally saddle broke, he had to admit the horse was a real looker and could walk a hole in the wind. Worse still, there are few horses, even the old stud that could run with the yellow horse, something Frank Kincaid is secretly proud of.

Dedrow catches a flash of yellow as Clay rides out of the mesquite with his lanky frame rising and falling in rhythm with the horse's lope. Smiling from ear to ear, as he reins in the yellow horse, Clay laughs as Dedrow looks over his shoulder at the near ridges.

"He's long gone Bandy. Who was he?"

"Did you see him?"

"Sure, me and him stared at each other just before he rode away."

Bandy nods. "So you're what he was looking at down there?"

"I reckon."

Dedrow looks around the flats. "He's a Texas Ranger sent here to take you back to Fort Worth."

"For what?"

"For killing Red Hooper, that's what."

"Someone's been spoofing you, old hoss." Clay laughs easily, his grin showing off his straight white teeth. "I didn't kill that fat man, I got one in him but someone else killed him."

"Who was it?"

"Bill Longley, I believe was the gentleman's name."

Dedrow strikes a sulphur and nods. "Some gentleman, now we've got to ride for the Red River, there's another gentleman looking for you.

"Who's that?"

"You're Pa."

"He finally decided to go north did he?"

"He's gone."

Abbot Rountree lies belly down on the high cliff over the Trinity and watches the two riders as they turn back north. Grinning he stands up and brushes the sand from his clothes.

"That's one you owe me old friend." Mounting his gelding he turns back towards Fort Worth thinking Bascombe, the Yankee carpetbagging judge, will just have to wait for the Governor's Mansion.

Dedrow turns and raises the glasses towards the far-off ridge, then hands them to Clay. "Thank you old friend."

"Was that the Ranger, Bandy?"

"His name is Rountree, you seen him a time or two when you were small." Dedrow smiles. "He's a good friend."

"Sure he wasn't scared?"

"Scared?" Dedrow looks at the youngster. "Number one, he's a southerner, number two he's Abbot Rountree and a Texas Ranger. Neither one knows what the word scared means."

"If you say so."

"Don't ever sell him short boy, he'd chase a longhorn bull with a switch."

Emily Kincaid drives the heavy chuck wagon north leading the way for the herd of horses being driven by Frank and six other wranglers. After the third day, the mares quit trying to turn back to their home range and start following the old bell mare that is tied behind the chuck wagon. The old Kentucky stud was left behind at the ranch, with the other stallions. All the mares have colts at their side and all were bred back so the studs would be an unneeded nuisance on the trail.

All day Kincaid holds the herd to a pretty good clip, tiring them out so they will graze at sundown and not try to stray. He is eager to reach the Red River Crossing where he told Dedrow to wait on them. He has no way of knowing if he found Clay or if Rountree was following the herd. Rountree was an old acquaintance of Kincaid but he is still a Texas Ranger. Frank is not sure about the boundary between Oklahoma and Texas but he knows the Red River will not stop Rountree. He has no idea where the Ranger's jurisdiction ends. Knowing the Ranger as he does, he doubts the man will honor boundaries. Oklahoma is just a territory, owned and settled mostly by the Cheyenne, Arapaho, Sac and Fox and the hostile Comanche, Kiowa and other tribes. If Abbot Rountree takes it in his mind to cross the Red, Frank knows he will.

Loping forward the rancher reins in beside the noisy cook wagon and smiles over at Emily, accepting the cookie she offered. "The boys will be jealous if they see me eating."

She laughs her throaty laugh. "I'll just tell them I'm trying the dough out on you so I wouldn't poison them."

"We'll camp at the next crossing ahead; Pecos said it was some kind of small tributary or creek with good water." Frank nods forward.

"I was hoping to see Clay and Bandy ride in today." Emily looks worried.

Frank nods. "They'll be along anytime now."

"You sure husband?" She clucks to the team. "I remember Abbot Rountree from the times he came through Jacksboro hunting a fugitive."

"He wouldn't hurt one of our boys or see any harm come to him."

"Are you sure he wouldn't?" She looks up at him. "Plumb sure, he was always pretty rough."

Frank swallows a sip of water to push the cookie down and then nods. "I'm sure wife."

The small creek is running shallow but clear as the wagon bounces across the old buffalo crossing and pulls in under some huge oaks that border it. After drinking their fill, the horse herd spreads out and starts grazing on the ample grass that grows belly deep on the colts. Old habits happen as Frank let his gelding pass through the herd checking every animal for signs of lameness. Counting the colts and two year olds his count when he left Jacksboro was over four hundred head.

That many animals stir up a lot of dust and Frank knows that a dust cloud that large will not go unnoticed for long after they cross the Red. The river lies two days ahead at most, if the herd has not already discovered it, it will not be long. Across the river lies what they call the Nations, miles and miles of wild hostile land inhabited by all sorts of unscrupulous men, red and white. Before the week is out, he knows many eyes will covet the large herd following on its flanks like wolves after a buffalo herd. Most men riding the vast untamed Indian lands were honest hunters and cowmen but they were not alone, there were also horse thieves, cattle rustlers and outlaws enough to go round. Not counting the young bucks of the Cheyenne, Arapaho, Kiowa, and Comanche tribes looking to steal horses and win their coup feathers.

Frank looks back down the trail they just came up on looking for Clay and Bandy. He is worrying about Clay running into Rountree but he also needs their guns if a large band of horse thieves rides in on them. Times are tough and out here in this almost unknown grass country many things can happen in a hurry, the land across the river is dangerous, bloody ground. Turning back towards the wagon, he reins in beside a rangy rider.

"You ride herd until after we eat Lebo, then me and Pecos will take over until midnight."

"Yes Sir Boss." The slender rider folds his long leg around the fork of his saddle and lights a quirley. "The Misses cooking sure smells good, even from here."

"I'll be back pretty quick." Frank nods. "Then you can ride in and eat your fill."

"Take your time."

Pan bread, beans, side meat, and coffee emits its smell around the small campfire as Emily spoons each of the rider's food out on tin plates. Thanks and more thanks are spoken as each man takes his plate then finds him a seat on the wagon tongue or ground. They were used to riding but these long hard days behind the herd is more than they experienced in many a year.

"You boys get a good night's sleep." Frank takes the plate Emily holds out to him. "Maybe we'll see some sign of Clay and Bandy tomorrow."

"Knowing them shirkers, they'll wait until we reach this new fort we're heading for before showing themselves." One of the younger wranglers gives a good-natured laugh.

"Si amigo, they would if they were smart, that's for sure." A Mexican vaquero speaks up.

Emily waves her large spoon at the two men. "I guess you boys are gonna want breakfast come morning?"

"Yessum, we were just fixing to shut up." Ben Doss laughs.

Frank finishes switching his saddle to another horse when a rider followed by Lebo Booker rides slowly into camp. "Found this feller checking out the herd Mister Kincaid."

"No Sir, I sure wasn't doing that." The rider looks slowly over at the chuck wagon. "Now, I ain't looking for trouble or calling your rider here a liar, I was just riding by and spotted your fire is all."

Booker spit a stream of tobacco. "Then what did you ride in for mister?"

"Told you hoss, I seen your fire and came in for a look-see." The slender rider shrugs. "Truth is, I ain't eaten in two days and I came in hoping to maybe get a feed."

"You got a name?" Frank studies the man.

"Yes Sir, names Tom Hatton."

Frank nods at Booker who turns his horse and rides back to the herd. "Lite down Mister Hatton and grab you some chuck."

"Yes Sir, thank you Sir."

"Jorge, give the man's horse a scoop of oats." Frank looks over at the Mexican rider.

"Si Senor."

Good manners demands that the owner wait until the man finishes eating before engaging him in conversation. It would not do any good to question Hatton anyway as his mouth is busy shoveling Emily's beans into it. It appears he is not lying about not eating in days, as he hungrily devours two large plates of her cooking.

"Thank you Ma'am." Hatton returns his plate to the washtub. "Can I wash them for my keep?"

"You go sit down and talk Mister Hatton but thank you anyway."

"Yes Ma'am."

Frank waits until the rider seats himself before he speaks. "Where bout's you from, Mister Hatton?"

Shrugging the man takes a quirley offered by Jorge. "Everywhere but most recently I been up towards Wichita."

"You happen to pass the new post they are building down around the Darlington Indian Agency on your way here?"

"No Sir, a man riding alone ain't got no business anywhere near them heathens." Hatton shakes his head. "No Sir."

"Well Mister Hatton, you can toss your blankets down anywhere." Frank stands up and heads back to the horse he was saddling. "You're welcome to have breakfast with us before you ride out."

"Well Sir, if it's all the same with you I reckon I'll be riding on." Hatton acts embarrassed.

Frank shrugs. "Suit yourself but peers to me your horse could use a rest."

"Yes sir, reckon he could but I've urgent business in Fort Worth." Hatton looks towards the herd and nods. "Speaking of horses, you boys sure have a good-looking bunch with you."

"Yea, we do." Frank mutters low, Hatton can sense the friendly just went out of the big man's voice.

"I'll be riding on then."

"You do that Mister Hatton, just that."

Frank watches as Hatton disappears into the darkening night and then rides out to meet Booker. Curiosity crosses his mind as he turns in the saddle, the man seemed likable enough but perhaps too likable. His last parting words about the horses sent the hairs on his thick neck to rising.

"I circled camp and watched him ride out." The slender night guard calls out as Frank rides up. "Personally, I don't trust that fellow."

Frank grins. "You don't trust anybody Lebo; go get your supper and some shuteye."

"Mister Lebo es right Senor Frank." Jorge rides in behind where they sat talking. "This one he lie, his name es no Hatton."

"Do you know him Jorge?"

"No, I don't know him but I see him once in Waco Town." Jorge kicks his gelding as it tries to graze. "His name was Jack Fritch back then, a very bad hombre."

Frank looks back towards the chuck wagon. "You sure you got the right man?"

"Si, I sure." The sombrero tips as the dark face nods. "Him kill another man in bar fight with knife, him same man."

"Sure wish Bandy was here, he might shed a little light on the man." Frank rubs his chin thoughtfully. "He knows every bad man in Texas."

"He'll be along anytime now."

"Sure wish I was as sure of that as you are Lebo."

The tall slender wrangler kicks his horse. "I'm hungry."
Frank watches the man ride away. "Send Pecos out here."
"I'll do it."
"Jorge, can you follow this bad man, see which way he went?"
"Si Senor but not until daylight."
"Be careful."

CHAPTER 4

Jack Fritch alias Tom Hatton waves cheerily at Emily Kincaid as he rides away from the Kincaid chuck wagon. He told the rancher the truth; he was heading for Fort Worth before he found himself in the midst of the big herd. Not anymore, as soon as he is out of sight and hearing of the fire he is fixing to head back north into the Nations as fast as his horse can carry him. He left Ewen Galt back in Hays City a week or so earlier, now he has to catch Galt before he attacks the Guthrie's mixed herd of mules, broodmares, and Missouri Jacks.

Fritch knows Guthrie; he rode for the Welshman at one time and he wants no part of Galt's plans to steal the mixed herd that Will Guthrie is pushing south into Oklahoma. Guthrie will have many riders with him so Fritch knows he must kill Will Guthrie in the raid or he will track the horse thieves clear to Mexico to get his animals back. No sir, he told Galt that very thing, the herd of mules are sure not worth the agony they were fixing to bring down on their necks. Guthrie is a bearcat when you steal from him or wrong him or his family in any way. No sir, it is not worth it but this herd of fine broodmares and colts he stumbled on is a gold mine on hooves. They are worth taking a chance on plus they have fewer wranglers guarding them.

On his way south, he rides around the mule herd without a farewell or howdy-do. He wants no part of Guthrie or Munday that crazy tempered wild son of his, and Tom Killian the foreman is as bad, maybe even worse than the rest of them. No sir, stealing horses or those cantankerous mules from the Guthrie Clan is the craziest job Galt ever planned and Fritch wants no part of it at all. He rode with Ewen Galt for several years now. They were involved in shady deals, rustling, stealing horses, and killing all across Texas and Oklahoma since the war. Nevertheless, Fritch does not like to take unnecessary chances and Will Guthrie is a holy terror when he gets riled. However, this herd of horses out here in the grasslands of the nations is different; it is made-to-order. Fritch just hopes he can reach Galt before he strikes the mule herd.

Fritch kicks the gelding and picks up his speed, the horse is tiring but he will try to make Longs Store down in the Nations by midweek. There he can change horses and pick up a meal. He cusses, why does he bother with Galt and this deal at all? If he is smart, he will turn back and find Blaine Pitts, owner of Pitts Fur Company in Fort Worth, who is holding money for him for a load of pelts he left with him last fall. The trader thought he trapped the wolf pelts but he stole them from an old trapper he met out on the range.

To Fritch stealing beat working every day of the week, the only drawback is the danger that goes with it. Fritch does not mind danger, for five years during the war years he rode with Bloody Bill Anderson on the border and those times were loaded with danger but also plenty of loot. With Lee's surrender and Anderson dead Fritch refused to turn in his weapons or be pardoned, instead he and Galt rode into the Nation's and lost themselves in the open grasslands. In time, they rode into the wild town of Muskogee with two saddlebags filled with paper money. To Fritch's disgust he found out the money was worthless with the end of the war as it was all in Confederate bills. Unknown and dead broke in a wild open town; the two became hard-bitten card sharks and outlaws practically overnight. After a few killings, people in the surrounding towns decided to walk a wide berth around the two killers.

Other men, outcasts and ex-soldiers from a losing cause soon begin to join with Galt and Fritch and form a gang that runs unchallenged, pillaging the vast grassland. Oklahoma is wild, mostly unpopulated, controlled mostly by the Indian Tribes with few law officers policing the no man's land. Only a few Indian Police that are mostly ineffective except against the Native Indians and a few U.S. Marshals sent down from Arkansas by Isaac Parker try to bring law to the open lands.

The situation is tailor-made for Galt and his bunch of cutthroats who run amuck, causing havoc wherever they ride. The fight Galt has with the younger Guthrie finally makes up Fritch's mind. Unhappy for the last year, he wants to break with Galt who is fast becoming crazier and more daring with his depredations. Watching Galt whip the younger Guthrie did not bother Fritch. However, afterwards Galt bragged long and hard over a bottle of rotgut whiskey how he whipped the youngster and how he was fixing to steal the whole herd of mules from Will Guthrie.

Fritch heard only days before the fight U.S. Marshal Hank Vetter stationed in Hays City was dispatched to the Darlington Indian agency across the Canadian from where the army is building a new fort. The Marshal probably will not stay longer than necessary, just long enough to make his presence in the vicinity known. The Galt gang already had two run-ins with the hard-bitten old Marshal and both times, they came out second best. He also knows his name and Galt's name. They head the eradication list Vetter carries in his pocket. Oklahoma Territory is fast becoming too hot with all the outlaw gangs using it for their hideouts. Jack Fritch is no coward but he is not a fool either, it is time for him to get out of the Nations and the sooner the better. However, the unprotected horse herd caught his interest. With one quick swipe, he could pocket enough money to see him to Arizona or even California. Just one more quick raid, the last in these parts, then he can retire from the outlaw trail into a life of ease. No Sir, this one job and there will be no more cold camps, cold food, or cold ground for him.

The Red River was two days behind him and his gelding is completely done in as Fritch dismounts in front of Long's Store. Emptying his vest pockets, he counts two hundred dollars in gold into his open palm. He counts the gold then replaces the money in his pocket and steps up onto the board porch. Knocking dust from his clothing and hat before stepping through the open doorway Fritch takes one last look around the yard where Kiowa lodges with a passel of Indian children cover the place. Knowing the old reprobate Shiloh Long was married to a Kiowa woman and probably another squaw or two Fritch grins as he approaches the plank bar.

"You're back pretty quick Jack." A grizzled old man sporting a long grey beard and even longer hair nods and places a bottle of rye on the makeshift bar. "Did you get turned around?"

Fritch wipes the filth from a whiskey glass and nods. "Nah Shiloh, I just became lonesome for your company."

"Do say, well now that's a first." Long tosses a roll of tobacco towards the newcomer and laughs. "You want whiskey, supper, or what?"

"I need a horse Shiloh, one with lots of bottom." Fritch downs a heavy jolt of the rotgut and smacks his lips. "Then I best be riding on."

He gives a long curious look through the open door. "Is someone on your trail Jack?"

"Shucks, there's always someone on my trail. Now, how about that horse?"

"It ain't Vetter, is it?" Long swallows hard, "That man scares the by-golly out of me."

"It ain't the Marshal; I just need to get back to Hays pretty quick."

"You know the Marshal passed through here maybe two days ago right after you were here." Long shrugs and downs some of his whiskey. "He was acting his normal closemouthed old self and then when you came back I figured he was after you."

"Now Shiloh, you know full well that I'm following the straight and narrow now."

"Following it where, to hell?" Long laughs at his own joke, "That's pretty funny ain't it Jack, to hell?"

Fritch frowns at the laughing old man. "Get me a horse old man."

"Right away son, I was just funning with you is all."

Fritch runs his hands over the well-muscled roan horse then hands Long two gold eagles. Nodding as the trader put the money in his pocket Fritch steps into the saddle and takes the flour sack of food that Long hands him.

"That'll keep you a few days Jack."

Fritch looks around at the playing children and nods their way. "Tell me Shiloh, how many of them are yours?"

The chest of the old trader rises slightly as he laughs. "All of them Jack, every one of them little rabbits."

Shaking his head Fritch kicks the roan into a lope away from the trading post. Normally he stays a day or two, rests his horse, and feeds up before moving on. Today he does not have the time to rest and enjoy himself. If Galt is going to raid Guthrie's herd, he will do it quick before the herd nears the Darlington Agency where the Cavalry could give chase if the alarm sounds. To steal a large herd of horses or cattle the thieves need some time to lose their tracks in the vast grassland. A well-mounted posse or a cavalry patrol could run down the slow moving animals quick. Fritch travels north in a good lope, causing the country to pass quickly underneath the powerful roan.

Fritch knows this land, he rode it, been chased through it, and was lost in it during the heavy snows of winter. Yep, he knows this land well. He also knows Galt is close; the mule herd is just a few miles ahead. He must ride cautiously, circling the herd without any one discovering him and then find Galt before he can act.

Will Guthrie rides the point following the chuck wagon that Pete Jumper his cook and swamper drive. Looking over to where Alder Guthrie rides flanking the left side of the herd, he smiles. The thirty-eight pistol seems huge on her slender hips. No bigger than a minute, Will knows she is a spitfire when she gets upset. He also knows the little gun is not for show, he saw her use it on too many occasions. Mainly Indian attacks in the early years, but he has no doubt she can and will use it on anyone who rides against them.

The herd settles down and are traveling south at a good clip. Will looks over at the wagon where Jumper is pointing off to the west. A lone rider appears across the swale of the tall grass as he comes towards them at a lope. Kicking his horse, Will lopes over to where Alder sits watching the approaching rider.

"Looks like Moon from here."

"It is Moon." Will agrees with her. "That Indian sets a horse better than any man I have ever seen."

"He's half Indian husband." Alder smiles her white teeth shining in the afternoon sun. "Riding comes natural to that young man."

"Might as well be a full-blood, his old pappy was raised by the Cherokee."

"Yes he was but Silam Moon was black."

"And a good friend of mine, thank you very much Miss Guthrie." Will grins, "Anyway it doesn't matter; you're right the boy can ride the hair off of anything that walks."

The rider comes in at a lope where finally the olive dark face is plain to see under the wide brim felt hat. He is slender but wide of shoulder and straight through the back. He sits the black gelding as if he is part of the horse, moving in perfect rhythm to the motion of the gelding. Good riders out on the range are abundant but seldom does one see anyone that can sit a horse like this rider. Even at a walk when he enters Hays City people watch the young rider as his horse prances proudly down the main thoroughfare.

Grey Moon was named after his father and his mother's father but as a rule, he only uses the name Moon. Life for a half black and half Indian was kind to Moon because he found a home with the Guthries. They were good to the youngster and he was completely dedicated to Will and Alder Guthrie. They took him in after the Fourth Cavalry attacked the village of his mother's people and killed both his parents. His father Silam Moon worked off and on for Will Guthrie over the years before his death in the cavalry attack. Once even bringing back and rescuing Munday and Grey Moon after the Comanche found the boys out hunting alone and took them along as prisoners. After escaping from the attack on his Grandfather's Village and the death of his parents he made his way to the Guthrie Ranch and was with them ever since.

Will smiles as Moon sits back in his saddle lightly causing the black gelding to slide to a stop and then he takes two steps backwards without touching the reins. Moon could train a horse or a mule to rein and handle better than any wrangler he knew. Many of the white riders are jealous of the Indian but it does not matter, Will Guthrie likes his animals trained quiet. With Moon there is no rough handling like sidelining, hobbling or bucking a horse out until he is thoroughly fatigued. No, there is no cheating a horse if Moon breaks him and that is the reason the young man is the lead horse wrangler on the Guthrie ranch. Several of the white wranglers learned the hard way out behind the stable not to square off against Moon. Most find out that Will Guthrie taught the youngster he looks upon as a son how to box like a prizefighter since he came to live with them. Will knows the boy is a natural in the ring, he knows the boy could be champ but one sharp word from Alder Guthrie dissuades that kind of thinking real quick.

"It's good to see you back Grey Moon," Alder smiles.

"It's good to be back Missus." Moon looks over at Will. "Ya'll are making good time."

"How far you reckon it is to the Canadian River?"

"Two days will do it." Moon dismounts and checks his cinch without looking up. "But, we've got other problems right now."

Will is instantly alert; Moon is steady in a bad situation, he never was one to jump to conclusions. "What problems we got?"

"There's several riders been shadowing the herd for some time now."

"Great!" Will slaps his leggings with his gloved hand. "How many?"

"Ten, maybe more." Moon shrugs.

"You see'em?"

"I seen some of them, they're part of Ewen Galt's gang." Moon looks off behind him as if he is expecting to see Galt and his men ride over the hill hell-bent for leather right behind him. "They're trouble, a real bad bunch."

Will nods, "I know your figuring they're sizing us up?"

"Only reason I can figure they're shadowing the herd like they are." Moon looks over at Alder. "Maybe the Missus should ride in the wagon beside Jumper."

"Go get Jumper to give you something to eat."

"Yes sir." Moon nods. "I am a bit hungry."

"Wife, circle the herd and have the boys close up and keep them tight." Will looks around the grassy range. "Tell Munday, Tom, and Little Bit to cover the point, flanks and drag. Tell them to stay alert and make dang sure we don't get surprised."

"I doubt they'll hit us until dark." Alder checks her thirty-eight.

"I hope you're right but I don't want to take chances, Galt's bunch are all seasoned gun hands and if there's ten of them, they'll have us outnumbered pretty good."

Alder nods and kicks her gelding into motion back to the rear of the herd. Will pulls his forty-five and checks the loads. He knows both Galt and Fritch, he cannot believe either man would dare raid a herd of his but they are outlaws, some of the worst killers that rode the range. Riding over to where Jumper stands beside the chuck wagon getting Moon some left over cornbread and side meat, he dismounts.

"Jumper, break out the long guns and plenty of ammunition."

"Okay Boss."

"Arm yourself and stay on your toes; we could get company any time now."

Jack Fritch sits in a grove of blackjack and oak trees and watches the mule herd pass slowly. It is plain; Guthrie somehow knows the herd is in danger. He can see the mules and horses are bunching in close, every rider carries a Winchester across his saddle, and not a rifle in their scabbards; they are ready for trouble. Watching the herd move out of sight, Fritch dismounts and rolls himself a smoke then drops his reins and kneels smiling as he strikes a sulphur. Guthrie is shrewd and he is fearless, Galt might just have run into a wildcat if he attacks the mule herd. Will Guthrie is as hardheaded as his mules, there is no doubt he will fight. Fritch knows Galt and his bunch will be following, how long he will have to wait, he does not know for sure but he knows they are not far behind the herd.

Galt is in shock as he hears his name coming from the cluster of oaks off to his right. Wheeling his gelding, he thumbs back the hammer of his pistol and studies the trees and scrub oaks. Surprised he holsters the gun as Jack Fritch rides slowly from the timber.

"Jack!" Galt in shock at seeing him. "What are you doing here, thought you were heading for Arizona or someplace where the climate is safer?"

Fritch studies the riders as he rides in. Most he knows but there are a few new faces in the crowd. "I was but thought I'd keep you from getting your heads blown off."

Galt studies the face he knows so well, rode with over many years. "Uh huh and who's gonna do this dirty deed?"

"Will Guthrie if you raid into his herd." Fritch looks around at the new faces. "He's armed and ready for bear."

"That dang half-breed Moon, we thought we seen him lurking around spying on us a couple days back."

"Moon doesn't matter, I've got us a better deal due south of here." Fritch pulls out the makings. "And a lot more profitable haul for all of us."

Galt reaches for the smoke Fritch rolled. "What kinda deal?"

"A big horse herd mainly mares and colts, is coming right at us."

"All horses?"

"Yep, all horses." Fritch blows smoke as he hands Galt the unfinished quirley. "That means we don't have to mess with them dang long eared mules."

"How many outriders are with them?"

"One woman, six men maybe seven at most."

"Why not take Guthrie's herd then move on to this other bunch." Another rider chimes in.

"I told you, Guthrie is ready to fight." Fritch looks disgustedly over at the new man. "Every man of them is carrying a rifle across his swells."

"You never wanted to tangle with Will Guthrie." Galt stares hard at his old partner. "Why?"

Fritch frowns and looks over at Galt. "I told you he's a bad man to mess with. Why take the chance of getting shot all to pieces?"

"Where is this herd now?"

"Last time I seen them they were two days south of the Red River Crossing."

"The Canadian is two days of hard riding and then at least another three or four days to the Red." Galt calculates quickly. "That'll take us at least five days hard riding, we'd have to change horses with Shiloh Long and that'll sure cost us."

"Why not just steal the horses from him?" The same new rider spouts off and laughs crazily.

"Who is this idiot?" Fritch glares at the new man.

"Moss Shadrack, from Kentucky."

"Tell him to keep his mouth shut when men are talking." Fritch rests his hand on the big pistol. "It's maybe less, that herd is headed at us at a pretty good clip."

Galt looks hard at Shadrack and shakes his head at the man, as he turns red in the face. Pointing off towards the woods where Fritch just appeared from he tosses his burned-out smoke. "Let's make camp and have us a talk, Guthrie can wait another day."

"If you're dead set on raiding that mule herd Ewen, count me out and I'll be riding on."

"Just like that, won't even have supper with us, old hoss?" Galt grins over at his friend. "Old Moss here cooks up a real tasty chuck."

"Maybe he doesn't like our smell Galt."

Shadrack's smile fades as Fritch pulls his pistol out and points it at the man. "I told you to shut up big mouth."

"It's shut Mister, just don't pull that trigger."

Fritch nods. "That's better, now let's eat."

"Where's Pine and Paddy?" Fritch looks at the mounted men surrounding him not seeing either of the older men.

"They'll be here soon."

"Good, we may need them."

Chapter 5

Horse Thieves on the Red 1874

Clay Kincaid and Bandy Dedrow finally pick up the wide beaten track of the herd. Hundreds of horses trample the ground making a path simple to follow. Smiling at the thought of some good cooking they study the tracks then kick their horses into a trot.

"I'll betcha we catch up before they reach the Red." Dedrow pulls his hat down snugger. "If we hurry along that is."

Clay agrees, "I'll be glad to see the folks and get some of Ma's good cooking in me."

"Sounds good, by the looks of these tracks I don't figure they could be over a day ahead."

Frank Kincaid watches as Pecos rides up to him from the flank of the herd. "We've got ourselves some company Boss."

"I see them." Frank looks up on a small ridge where several Indians sit looking down at the herd. "They've been watching us for some time."

"They don't have rifles, at least I don't see any." Pecos' dark brown eyes study the mounted Indians. "That's some help I reckon."

Holding up his hand the rancher halts the chuck wagon and the broodmare band that scatters to graze on the flat pastureland. His mind is set on leasing land near the new Fort Reno they are building, he sure does not want to start a small war here on the flats and ruin his chances.

"Get Lebo up here and we'll go have a talk with them." Frank looks over at Pecos. "Tell Missus Kincaid and the boys to stay ready but don't fire a gun unless they have to."

Frank along with Pecos and Lebo are heavily armed and ready to ride towards the watching Indians when a shrill whistle sounds out across the flats. Frank whirls his horse and grins as he recognizes Clay's lifelong claim to fame, the lad perfected the recognizable loud shrill whistle since childhood. The yellow horse stands out like new copper in the bright sunlight as he comes on in a hard run.

Frank yells loudly over to the chuck wagon as the two riders race their horses towards the waiting men. "Our missing boy is here Missus."

Dismounting Clay pulls his yellow gelding to a halt and vaults from the saddle, the two men bear hug then Frank shakes hands with Dedrow. Grinning from ear to ear, the older Kincaid shows relief. Now he has two extra guns for backup. Out here on the open range, anyone with anything of value needs all the guns he can get.

"Well Pa, we're finally here." Clay looks up at the hill. "Took us a spell but we finally made it."

Frank follows his gaze. "We were just fixing to ride up and talk with them boys up there."

"No need." Clay speaks up. "We had us a talk with them yesterday."

"What do they want?'

"They've got a few lodges about twenty miles from here." Clay hugs his mother as she dismounts the wagon. "They're starving, there's nothing left out here to hunt and the cattle herds haven't passed through yet."

Frank looks over at Bandy. "I was under the impression the government was supposed to issue the tribes rations and supplies."

The foreman shakes his head. "Apparently not, you know our Yankee Government, long on promises short on do, these people are starving."

Emily turns from Clay and smiles at Dedrow then looks over at Frank. "Why don't we cut them out a few horses?"

"A few horses?" Frank looks aghast. "Every horse I've got is prime horseflesh woman, do you want to let them Indians eat them?"

"Husband, they're hungry, it'll be better to give them a few head than have them slipping in here and raiding our herd during the night." Emily frowns at him. "And it just might make us a few friends where we're headed."

Frank shakes his head. "You said you talked to them?"

"We did for a fact." Clay nods. "We let them have what little food we had with us."

"They already know about the horses?"

Clay nods. "They do, they're Kiowa from old Satank's band and at one time they were the best horse thieves that ever lived."

"I've heard of that old devil." The rancher nods. "Why didn't they hit us already?"

"They may be afraid of the Cavalry at the new post the army's building but I figure they really are trying to survive in peace out here on practically nothing." Dedrow looks up at the waiting Indians. "Give them a few head and keep them off our backs Boss."

"You think they'll raid the herd?"

"I do, just as sure as you're standing there." The foreman adds. "The warriors have women and kids hungry and starving in their lodges."

Frank's teeth grit at the thought of killing his beloved horses for food. "Alright Lebo, you and Pecos cut out five of the older mares with older colts that are ready to be weaned and don't need their mothers."

"Okay Boss." Lebo turns his gelding and motions at Pecos and two other wranglers sitting nearby.

Frank turns his back and starts towards the wagon. "You boys grab some biscuits and side meat, and then drive the mares up to them."

Dedrow knows what the rancher is feeling as he takes the food from Emily. Many years of hard selection brought the Kincaid broodmares to the level they are and to watch them walking off to be eaten is a hard thing to take. Frank and Emily start the rest of the herd on down the trail as they drive the five mares up towards the waiting Indians. They drive the newly weaned colts to the inside the herd. The colts nicker for their mothers and run around crazily but the mares are already out of their sight. With the dust and movement, they can no longer smell them. The colts are beautiful; Bandy knows if he tries to get Frank to send the colts with their mothers, there would have definitely been a fight.

Smoke from the chuck wagon's fire, curls around the cooking pans, skillets, and coffeepot as the men gather around for their supper. The herd covers almost twenty-five miles since sunup and the men are tired. Frank finally finds time to sit down with Clay and Dedrow and they fill him in on their meeting with Abbot Rountree. A lone rider plods tiredly into the light of the camp and dismounts near the fire.

Frank stands up and empties the left over from his cup. "It's good to see you back Jorge."

"Si Senor Kincaid, it is good to be back." The Mexican wrangler smiles tiredly.

"Clay, take his horse and turn him loose in the herd please." Frank motions at the fire. "Sit, the missus will bring you a plate."

"Gracias Senor, but first I will tell you of the gringo Jack Fritch." The Mexican accepts a hot cup of coffee from Emily. "He is like I say an outlaw. He leaves here and rides hard back to the north where he met up with another bad man, I think is Ewen Galt."

"I've heard of him clear down in Texas, a guerilla that doesn't know the war is over." Frank cusses, "A real hard case."

"Si, I think so too." Jorge tastes the coffee. "I follow them for one day, I think this bad man Fritch will lead them here muy pronto."

"He's probably right Frank." Dedrow speaks up. "I knew both Galt and Fritch when they were younger before the big war, they're both bad medicine."

Will Guthrie looks over where Moon stands beside Alder eating the cold food she threw together from the chuck wagon. He is proud of the youngster, thinking of him like his own son. He is tall over six feet in his flat leather moccasins and dressed in the rough trousers of a cowboy. Moon always wears a slip over buckskin shirt with fringe and no buttons, the one thing with the exception of his dark countenance that set him apart from the other wranglers. Broad of shoulder, Moon seems graceful on the ground, not like other riders who are awkward walking in their high heeled, tight boots. A huge bowie knife sports the wide belt that buckles around the narrow waist. Expert with a rifle Moon was never a pistol shot, the knife is his main weapon and several scars across his chest and arms shows he was in many fights with it. In their early youth, Moon and Munday at one time or another fought with every boy or young man in Hays.

Across the grasslands, many black cowboys rode with the cattle herds, good horsemen all, but none handle the wild unbroken horses like Moon. Horse gentling and training is a characteristic of many horse cultured Indians of the Great Plains, none are better. In his youth before the destruction of his village, he witnessed to and learned from many of the great Comanche and Kiowa horse tamers who are able to calm a bad horse with just the touch of their hands and soft crooning of their voice. Will watched many a day in the dusty corrals as Moon would top out a horse or mule in the same way. With his gentle touch and soft voice very few put up much of a fight and most were ready for the less experienced riders after a couple of rides.

"You think you can slip back out there and see what they're doing?" Will looks over at Moon. "Without getting shot at?"

Replacing the battered water dipper Moon nods. "Let me cut out a fresh horse and I'll go have a look-see."

"You be careful boy." Will slaps Moon on the shoulder. "Real careful."

Alder smiles, "I'll have you a mule lip blackberry pie baked when you get back."

"I sure wouldn't miss out on that Miss Alder, no Ma'am." Moon laughs. "You just keep Munday out of it."

Fritch spoons the last of the hot stew from his plate then pulls out the makings as he sat about the small fire "That was mighty good Mister Shadrack."

"You want more Jack?" The lanky hill man grins toothlessly. "Plenty left."

"No reckon not." Fritch looks over to where Galt sits eating. "Let's hear it Ewen I ain't joking, you ride against Guthrie and I'm pulling stakes right now."

The dark eyes of Galt stare back at Fritch. "If I didn't know you better old friend, I'd think you were yellow."

"I call it being smart." Fritch looks about the camp. "Any of you boys want to call Jack Fritch yellow, just step right up here!"

Galt holds up his hands and shrugs. "We all know better than that."

"Then listen to me and pay heed." Fritch strikes a sulphur but does not use it to light his smoke; he lets it burn his fingers. "I ain't saying it again; messing with Will Guthrie is suicide. If we don't kill him; he'll hunt us until we're all dead."

Every eye is on the burning match, noses can smell the burning skin as the sulphur burns right into Fritch's finger. The man did not blink; he acted as if he did not notice the pain from the flame of the match. Galt watches the sulphur then smiles. "Alright, you've convinced us. We'll take the horse herd."

"Good." Fritch strikes another sulphur and casually lights his rolled quirley. "But, I sure wish Pine would show."

Moon's moccasins leave no impressions as he prowls around the vacant fire that was just abandoned. The ashes are still warm, he knows he only missed Galt's bunch by an hour or less. The tracks of the raiders lead off to the south skirting around the herd, something that puzzles him. He did not pass the riders or caught sight of them as he rode out scouting the plains where he saw the gang two days before. By the signs of their horses for some reason, they deliberately skirted the herd and rode off to the south towards the Red River and Texas.

Kicking his horse, he rides straight back to the herd and reports his findings to Will Guthrie. "They're gone Will, they rode wide around the herd then took off to the south in a straight line."

Will rubs his chin as he sat his bay gelding. "You sure boy, it ain't a trap of some kind?"

"Sure as I can be." The grayish black eyes appear to stare straight through a man. Night wranglers riding with Moon on dark nights swear he can see in the dark like a cat. They told more than once about how he points out a lone horned owl sitting on a limb in the pitch dark of night. Some doubt his word but riding closer to where Moon pointed they watch in surprise as sure enough a great horned owl would fly off into the night. "I followed them for a quite a ways, they seem to be in a hurry, I don't think they're planning on circling back for us."

Guthrie nods slowly. "That's good to hear, I sure didn't want to mix with that bunch."

Moon smiles, "I figure it was Fritch, he ain't forgot about that whipping you gave him a few years back when he worked for you."

"How'd you hear about that?" Will looks over at the young rider.

"Secrets like that get out sooner or later." Moon looks over to where Little Bit sat his horse. "Little Bit was watching it all when ya'll mixed it up."

"Little Bit has got a big mouth."

"Don't get riled, he meant no harm just bunkhouse talk."

Will nods then turns his horse. "Thank you Moon, now let's get this herd moving."

"Yes sir, we'll be at the Canadian in two days."

Fritch and Galt sit out in the dark and listen to the soft guitar music sounding across the flat grassland. Both men smile over at each other thinking they slipped in on the horse herd completely unseen. Little do they realize several sets of dark eyes are watching their every move since they rode in close to the horse camp.

"What do you think Ewen, we gonna hit them tonight?"

"Not tonight, I want that herd and I don't want any survivors left alive to accuse us later of stealing it." Galt studies the dark horse camp. "We sure don't want the cavalry on our heels."

"You gonna kill them all?" Fritch looks over at his partner in shock. "Even the woman?"

Galt snickers cruelly. "Well now, is she pretty?"

Fritch turns his head in disgust, he rode with Ewen Galt during the war and ever since, still at times he does not understand the man. Killing is one thing but complete slaughter of all the victims is a different matter, something Fritch does not like; since the war he lost all stomach for cold-blooded killing. Still he knows the volatile nature of Ewen Galt an ex-Confederate Raider who rode with Bloody Bill Anderson and learned killing during some of the most violent years of the Great War.

"Someone plays the guitar beautifully."

Galt grins. "Well then, we'll let him enjoy himself tonight."

"Yea." Fritch just shakes his head. He remembers the woman's face; she had been kind to him. He hates to think of her being slaughtered with the men but he needs his share of the horses for a new start in the west.

Two Kiowa warriors stand next to Frank Kincaid nodding out into the dusky dark. Jorge's guitar strumming across the camp gives a calm feeling that all is peaceful and quiet. However, Frank was forewarned already of the impending danger. Unseen but carefully camouflaged under the wagon; Clay, Bandy, Booker, Pecos, Doss and Emily lie hiding. Their Winchesters pointing out into the dark ready to pour a volley of death and destruction into the raiders if they attack.

"You have fed our people white man." The older of the warriors speaks broken English. "Now, we will help you."

"No." Frank shakes his head. "If the Kiowa kill a white man, the Cavalry will come to make war on them. I cannot allow you to put your people in danger."

"There are many more white men out there than you have."

"But, our friends the Kiowa have given us warning, now we can take them by surprise." Frank presents the two warriors with tobacco plugs. "Thank you but this is a fight between white men. When we get to the agency the Kiowa will always be welcome at our lodge as friends."

"We will watch from the hill." The older warrior nods. "If you need us, give us a sign."

"Thank you my friends." Frank watches the warriors melt silently away like ghosts in the night.

Slipping back to the wagon where Emily and the rest calmly wait behind boxes of supplies, saddles, and whatever else they could drag under the wagon for a barricade, Frank smiles at Emily. How many times after they settled in the Trinity Bottoms she stood by his side and helped defend their pitiful small horse herd, and their homestead. As steady and courageous as any man, Frank looks at her with respect, love, and deep admiration for her courage. Marrying young, no one thought the marriage would last because both have a strong will and deeply independent but it lasted. Clay and their older son Craig are the product of their marriage. There were several other children but they died in childbirth or as infants. Both know that is the reason they are so protective now of their wild younger son.

"Are they out there husband?"

"The Kiowa say they are." Frank lights a smoke and hands it to her. "Here, settle your nerves a little."

Laughing lightly she takes the quirley and puffs on it. "They might hit the herd while we're all laid up here waiting on them to come in."

"I doubt it, they don't want to leave any survivors they have to fight again, if they leave us alive they know we'll just follow and try to get them back."

Emily hands back the smoke. "Are you sure they aim to kill us all?"

"Yes Ma'am, that's Galts way." Dedrow pulls on his own smoke. "Way I see it, they have to."

Reaching over she takes the smoke back from Frank. "In that case I reckon I need another puff."

Laughing quietly he pats her shoulder then moves behind the wagon. "Those boys don't know what they're fixing to get themselves into, do they wife?"

"No husband, if they come against us we're fixing to smite them like the Good Book says."

Ewen Galt with Jack Fritch mounts beside him sits with the other raiders strung out in a single file a good horseback run from the chuck wagon. Dawn slowly spread over the land, lighting it up as the sun shows itself in the east. Galt's plan is to wipe out the wranglers sleeping at the wagon then move on and kill the riders with the herd. Ten riders heavily armed sit lined up silently staring across the shadowy grass at the peaceful camp. Every man is armed with at least four revolvers strapped to their saddles, an old habit of being heavily armed during the war. Racing across rough ground on a running horse, they found out early in the conflict it is next to impossible to reload an empty pistol on the back of a charging horse and while engaging with the enemy.

"You boys ready?" Galt motions them forward with the familiar Cavalry motion. "Let's get them all with the first pass, then move on to the herd."

Broodmares and colts drift out of their way as the men move slowly walking towards the camp. Suddenly the shrill cry of the confederate soldier burst from Galt's lips as the men charge in one long line. Fritch's good dun horse outdistances the others much to his regret as his eyes focuses in on the Winchesters protruding from under the wagon as he nears.

Reining in the dun, he tries to turn back as a burning sensation racks his chest. Trying to pull the wounded horse around he feels another hot piece of lead tear into his right leg then gunfire erupts in a heavy roll from under the wagon. It is too late; he knows they rode straight into a trap set for them. Slowly losing his grip on the saddle, he slips to the side of the dying horse and both animal and man roll to within touching distance of the wagon.

Seeing Fritch fall Galt throws up his arm trying to halt the charge but it is already too late. Whoever defends the camp are all expert marksmen as saddles are emptied with almost every shot. Whirling his lunging horse Galt spurs the excited gelding and hollers for what is left of his men to retreat. Racing away across the flatland the outlaw screams in rage as a slug takes him in the side. Only four men of his original ten are left, he saw Fritch fall crumpled like a doll; there was no doubt, Galt knows he is dead where he lay. Galt himself was wounded twice before during the war; he knows he took a hard hit in his lower left side and one in the shoulder, how bad he cannot stop to tell.

Frank crawls from the safety of the wagon and stands up as the raiders disappear from his sight. Five men lie on the ground about the camp their bodies contorted in death; one more lies closer to the wagons. Walking to where the nearest man lies staring up towards the morning sun Frank kneels down and recognizes the rider who ate supper at his chuck wagon only days before.

"Tom Hatton, who are you really?" Frank looks into the pain-racked eyes. "Tell me, you don't have much time. Don't go to your maker with a false name."

"The name is Jack Fritch, how did you know we were coming?" Fritch looks off into the sky blankly. "And I was scared of Will Guthrie."

"Will Guthrie, what did he have to do with this?"

The eyes glaze over as the man tries to talk. Emily walks to where Frank is kneeling beside the downed man. "He seemed like such a nice young man."

"Yep, but he probably won't be getting much older now." Frank looks down at Fritch and nudges him gently. "Who was this Will Guthrie, was he one of the ones that rode away?"

"No." A burst of bubbles left the dying man's mouth raggedly as the head slowly turns sideways.

"He's gone." Emily turns away. "I hope it wasn't my bullet that got him."

"He and the others were out to kill us and steal our horses Em."

"How many got away?"

"I don't know for sure, maybe four or five." Frank looks off into the distance. "I believe we got some lead into the big man racing away in the lead."

Frank and Dedrow take the weapons from the dead men then herd their horses up the hill towards the waiting Kiowa who quickly cut the saddles from the animals and dump them onto the ground.

Dedrow laughs. "Those bucks don't realize them saddles are worth more than the horses."

"Reckon not." Frank never broke a smile as he turns away. "Maybe they'll eat those horses and not kill my good mares."

Emily looks down at the dead body of Jack Fritch lying beside his good dun gelding who took a shot directly to the head. "Such a waste." She mutters.

"Of what Senora Em, a bad man or a good horse?" Jorge quips coldly.

Chapter 6

Canadian River 1874

Will Guthrie studies the flat lands that lie along the Canadian River and he likes what he sees, perfect grazing land for his animals. With his mind made up, he sends Moon on ahead to pick out a good range with plenty of grass downriver at least ten miles from the Darlington Indian Agency. Riding into the agency Moon meets with the agent John Miles, a pleasant short statured man who looks at the half-breed young man with curiosity.

"Young man, this land is Indian land for many miles up and down the Canadian; most of the Territory of Oklahoma belongs to the red man." The bespeckled agent looks across the desk at the dark skinned Moon. "It's open to be leased and used for grazing but you people will have to pay the tribes for its use."

"Yes sir." Moon agrees. "The owner already knows that."

"Any buildings you erect will become the property of the Indian when you leave."

"Yes sir."

"You are of split parentage are you not?"

"My father was black, my mother was Cheyenne." Moon looks quietly at the agent. "She was Northern Cheyenne."

"I see." The intelligent eyes almost close. "Well, tell me who do you work for?'

"Mister Will Guthrie from Hays City."

"The mule trading Welshman." Miles shakes his head. "I have heard of your Mister Guthrie, a man with a good reputation, in and out of the ring."

"You've seen him fight?" Moon was curious.

"That I have Sir, three times." Miles smiles, "If that is what you want to call it, those fights didn't last long enough to warm up my seat."

"Why was that?"

"Why Mister Guthrie knocked them fellers out almost as soon as they got into the ring, that's why." Miles continues, "They say his new bride made him quit the prize fighting game. Quite a shame, she must be some woman."

"Yes sir, she is." Moon studies the room then looks down at the agent. "Mister Guthrie says he will come in personally to sign your land lease before we start to build."

"I'll talk with the Council and arrange everything." Miles smiles at Moon. "The tribes will have to okay the lease before it is finalized."

Moon shakes hands with the Agent then looks about the Agency at the squaws and papooses walking up and down the aisles of supplies or lining the walls. He just happened to ride in on the day the Agent issues beef and supplies to the tribes. They divide the week up so each tribe comes in on a different day. The days of tribal warfare are too recent. Agent Miles is smart enough to know any minor insult can result in a killing, which in turn could cause a major uprising of the tribes.

"Who else is here?" Moon steps out on the porch with Agent Miles and studies the wide yard where horses and wagons stand about. The older warriors sit insolently near the wall of the agency. Still too proud to accept the white man's charity the Indian men send their women into the agency to receive their issue of beef and dry goods that they need so badly. They well knew the day of the buffalo, the warrior, and the war trail was forever gone. Now they must accept the white man's handouts, they do not like it but they all know their lives changed forever. They still have their pride but sadly, that was all. The white cavalry is too strong and too numerous for them to resist against further.

"U.S. Marshal Hank Vetter is here from Hays City by order of the government." Miles gestures over towards the big supply barn. "He rode in with two religious people sent here to help with the Indians."

"Religious people, here?" Moon is curious. "How are they going to help?"

The agent ignores Moon's question. "He's a Reverend and a young woman accompanies him, his sister I believe."

"I thought they had you educated agents for religious reasons."

"My dear Sir, I act in the capacity as the Indian Agent here only, all religious functions will be handled by the religious sects." Miles seems to look down on Moon even though he is much shorter. "I don't believe you'll find any Indian Agents anywhere that also teach religion to the tribes."

Moon glances over at the figure of Hank Vetter walking from the barn with a younger couple following close beside him. The Marshal's robust appearance is in deep contrast to the man who is average in height but very thin, almost a sickly thin like he has consumption or some other illness. Dressed in a brown suit and string tie, a derby hat sits atop the man's light hair. The woman is different; Moon can tell from where he stands she is a lively young woman. Her vibrant laugh as she looks up at the Marshal and her yellow hair blowing in the wind framing a beautiful face speaks volumes. He wonders what religion she is, most of the religious churches he was around want their women's heads covered with a bonnet.

Watching as the Marshal leads the couple towards the agency store Moon notices how the warriors openly stare at the woman. As she nears, he finds out why the closer she comes, the more beautiful she appears. Fine smooth skin covers the strong jaw and a delicate nose separates the bright blue eyes.

"Well I'll be." The Marshal is surprised to see Moon standing on the porch with Miles. "Grey Moon, it's been awhile since I seen you last."

Moon sticks out his hand and takes the extended hand of the lawman. "Marshal Vetter, it's good to see you as well."

"Ya'll have met Mister Miles but you haven't met this young man here." Vetter smiles as he introduces Moon. "This is Grey Moon, a wrangler that rides for a good friend of mine. Moon this is Mister George Barber and his sister Lana."

"Mister Moon." Barber sticks out his thin hand. "It's a pleasure."

"Just Moon will do, Mister Barber."

"Then you shall call me George." Barber smiles. "This is my sister Lana."

"Miss Barber."

The smile radiates her face making small lines crinkle at the corners of her blue eyes. "Mister Moon."

Moon looks over at Vetter uncomfortable, hardly knowing what to say to a creature of such beauty. He was around white women his entire life but none can compare to this young woman. The Marshal smiles at Moon's discomfort and comes to his rescue.

"Where is Will, I heard he left Hays when I passed through Shiloh Long's place a few days back."

"He's about ten miles west of here nearing the Canadian." Moon looks off to the west. "He's planning on building down in the breaks along the flats after he makes a deal with the Cheyenne and Arapaho."

"That's a good spot." Miles agrees, "Well it seems Marshal Vetter has a high opinion of Mister Guthrie, that's good enough for me."

"They don't come any better or upstanding Mister Miles." The Marshal smiles over at Grey Moon.

"That's good, I'll set it up he'll have to speak with Yellow Dog of the Arapaho and Charging Bull of the Cheyenne." Miles adds, "And their tribal council of course."

"You set it up then Agent Miles." Moon replies, "Mister Guthrie will ride in when you summon him, and before he starts building."

Lana looks at the tall young man curiously. Moon is tall and straight, his stance proud, his voice strong, and he speaks like an educated man. "You are of Indian decent Mister Moon?"

"Yes Ma'am, my mother was Northern Cheyenne, my father was black, a runaway slave from Georgia." Moon stares hard into the woman's eyes wanting to see her reaction.

She nods slowly. "A very proud heritage I'm sure."

"I'm proud of it, Ma'am."

Vetter clears his throat. "Moon tell Will, I'll see him when he comes in."

"I will give him your words." Moon nods. "Why have they sent you here Marshal?"

"I'm here to keep the peace between the new settlers coming here and the new army post being built."

"Settlers?" Moon is curious. "I didn't know there were settlers here."

"Not yet, but there will be one day, besides we've already got cowboys and hunters and they're already building a saloon over near the post." Vetter shakes his head. "You throw Indians, cowboys, and soldiers all together with spirits, to me that spells trouble. The government sent me here to keep the peace."

"The Indians will not be partaking of any spirits Marshal Vetter." Lana looks over at the tall man, "I forbid it."

"Yes Ma'am, that's fine but it'll be hard to enforce, they like their firewater as they call it."

George Barber takes the young woman by the arm. "I'm sure Marshal

Vetter and Mister Miles knows best about these things Sis."

"We will speak with Charging Bull about his warriors consuming alcohol." Miles interrupts the conversation.

Moon looks at the disturbed young woman wanting to tell her that she will be fighting a losing battle but the troubled look on her face keeps him quiet. Yet he can tell she is a strong-willed person, perhaps she will be able to stop the warriors from drinking, at least some of it.

"It was nice meeting you folks; I need to be riding." Moon looks over at the Agent then reaches for his reins. "I will take your words to Mister Guthrie."

Miles nods. "I'll send word when the council is set up."

The four people stand on the porch and watch Moon ride away from the agency. "He's a strange young man Marshal."

Vetter looks over at the woman. "I wouldn't say strange Miss Barber but I'll allow you he's different. Twenty years ago, he would have been a great warrior I bet."

They watch in surprise as a large warrior raises his arm and steps in front of Moon's bay gelding. Worried Miles starts to step from the porch thinking there might be trouble on the wind.

"It's okay Mister Miles, they're friends." Vetter stops the agent. "Moon and Two Dogs have been like brothers since they were little."

"Two Dogs is Kiowa and Moon is Cheyenne." Miles is in shock. "How do they know each other?"

"Moon's father Silam Moon found Two Dogs out on the prairie after he was stolen from his people by the Paiute." Vetter watches as the two men speak. "He raised Two Dogs for a few years until the Kiowa came and brought him here to live with some of his Arapaho Cousins."

"I have had trouble with Two Dogs on different occasions." Miles sighs. "He could be a troublemaker."

"Well, we'll tell the army to keep an eye on him." Vetter touches his hat and starts back towards the barn where he and the Barbers are temporarily headquartered. "I figure I'll get my horse and ride over to the new Fort to take care of that little chore right now."

Lana Barber watches as Moon rides away from the agency after speaking with the warrior. She is curious and never met anyone quite like him. Moon's long legged bay kicks up small puffs of dust as his hooves hit the ground lightly. Both man and horse appear as one as they disappear from sight. Her eyes turn to where Two Dogs takes his place beside the other warriors. She did not want to come out to this dusty wild land but she did not want her frail brother to come alone. She accompanied him and she was determined to make the best of the situation.

A strong iron-willed woman when she makes up her mind. She insisted on coming after he ordered her to stay in the east. She is here now and is going to help him convert the Indians to Christianity. However, looking over at the hostile and stern faces of the warriors sitting with Two Dogs, she wonders. This definitely is not going to be an easy chore as she first thought.

Locating Will and his large herd spread out across what earlier hunters call the Canadian Flatland; Moon sits his gelding and takes in the grasslands. The huge horseshoe bend of the Canadian River has grass that grows belly deep on a horse, all of it rich and green as a frog's back. Most cattle drivers would brag a horse or cow could get fat on the grass just by walking across it. Many a herd of Longhorns were held and fattened up on this range just before moving on to the northern cattle towns of Abilene or Dodge City. He wonders what the cattlemen will do when they find their valuable grass leased and no longer free-range for their trail weary cattle.

A mile distance he can see the smoke of the chuck wagon's fire as old Jumper has the crews supper on to cook. Moon feels his stomach grumble as he thinks about food. He aimed to find something to eat at the agency but when Lana Barber showed up, he forgot about eating. The mere thought of her brings a smile to his dark face; he had to admit she is a woman of rare beauty.

Kicking the gelding, he rides down to the campfire and dismounts as the old swamper walks from behind the wagon. "Well, look what the cats drug in the dogs wouldn't dare. Good to see you Grey Moon."

The Guthrie cook is the only man that calls him by his first name. "Jumper, where is everybody?"

"Most are out with the herd, trying to keep them from straying too far downriver until you got back here with a contract." Jumper kneels beside the fire. "You hungry young'un?"

Moon can only shake his head and smile; he knew Jumper since the Guthrie family took him in. The old man was grey headed when Moon arrived at the ranch years ago and he never seems to age. Jumper was responsible for teaching the young mixed blood many of the things most young white children already knew. They grew close over the years, two orphans one a half-breed and the other an old man, now they are like family.

"I best ride out and talk with Will."

"They'll be along pretty quick; it's getting dark they won't be able to hold the herd together after the sun goes down no how." Jumper spoons up Moon a plateful of beans and tortillas. "Unsaddle your animal and then come eat."

"Alright old man." Moon smiles.

"Old enough to tan your hide and don't you forget it." Jumper laughs and watches as his pride and joy walks away.

The old cook never had children of his own. The Guthries gave him a home so he took the youngster under his arm and he taught him everything he could. Most whites veer wide of a half-breed of any kind but not Jumper. He became the youngster's second father and mentor as he helped raise the boy. Will Guthrie insisted the boy get an education in the local one room schoolhouse. So on many a day he wiped Moon's bloody nose or cleaned the dirt from his face after a set to with the local children around Hays City. Over the years as Moon matured and grew into manhood, people around Hays came to accept and even respect the young wrangler's talent for breaking good horses and mules. Will Guthrie finally tired of seeing the boy sporting a black eye and bruises every day. Every evening after their chores were finished Will had both Munday and Moon in the stable punching away at a tow sack filled with sawdust or at each other. Not long after that, the town boys avoided them and their rock hard fists.

Moon hears the horses coming in at sundown as he finishes his second plate of food. Munday is the first to reach the chuck wagon and notices him sitting across the wagon tongue.

"Well now Mister Moon, you ain't riding for us anymore." The younger Guthrie snatches a plate from the wagon and waits for Jumper to fill it. "Hurry up old man and feed a real workingman."

"Keep your britches on boy, I'm getting there."

Moon studies the hotheaded Munday as the younger Guthrie frets and fumes. "I said hurry up."

"What's going on here Jumper?" Will and Alder hear Munday arguing with the cook as they walk up to the wagon from the picket line.

"Just Munday being Munday is all Boss."

Will looks over at the red face of his son and shakes his head. "Cool off Munday and eat your supper and then I want you to ride night herd."

"You what?" Munday whirls, knocking the plate of beans from Jumper's hand spilling it all over his own boots. "Damn you Jumper." The youngster's fist doubles up as he swears at the old cook.

"That'll be enough boy."

"Let the breed ride night herd, I've been in the saddle all-day."

"I'm telling you Munday to ride herd." Will steps towards his son. "After you pick up that plate and apologize to Jumper."

"I'll be dogged if I pick up anything." The younger Guthrie starts away from the wagon as his mother grabs his arm.

"Pick it up son then shut your mouth."

Munday knows better than to cross his mother. He knows his Pa will not tolerate any sass towards Alder Guthrie from anybody.

Dropping his eyes, he nods. "Yes Ma'am."

Will watches as Munday storms away towards where the remuda was picketed without his supper. "He's had a rough day Jumper; he didn't mean what he said."

Jumper does not back down as he serves supper. "He meant it boss every word, don't tell me he didn't."

Will looks hard at the old man and shakes his head. He carries his plate over to where Moon sits watching as the little episode plays out. "What did you find out at Darlington?"

"The agent wants you to come in and talk with a chief named Charging Bull about leasing this part of the river."

"Alright, I'll ride in come daylight."

"No, he said he'd send word when you were to come."

Will agrees, "Alright then, I'll wait."

"Two Dogs is at the agency, have him go with you to talk."

"It'll be good to see Two Dogs again, I've missed him."

"I talked with him; he will speak to Charging Bull for you." Moon sits his plate down. "But, Old Yellow Dog of the Arapaho might give you a hard time; he's a horse of a different color."

"Well, I'm thanking you Moon for setting up the meeting." Will nods between a bite full of food. "What about this Charging Bull?"

"Can't say, I don't know much about him, just the name."

"Well, I reckon we'll find out about him in a few days."

"What's wrong with Munday?" Moon asks.

"Like Jumper said, he's just being Munday tonight." Will exhaled air. "He got bucked off in front of the hands today and they all had a good laugh."

Moon laughs lightly. "That would set him off alright so who did he tangle with?"

"Nobody he couldn't, his mother was watching." Will smiles, "But you're right; it did set him off for a fact."

"May I join you two gentlemen?" Alder sits down beside Moon. "Or is this a secret meeting."

Moon looks up at the little woman who replaced his own mother and raised him with a strict and iron hand. Two things she never allowed and that was lying or showing weakness in any way. Moon lost many a fight to larger opponents who were picking on him but come morning Alder Guthrie was right behind him when he tackled the bully again. It might take a few days to get the bully whipped or run off but eventually it would happen. Moon laughs as he remembers once both of them being whipped right in the schoolhouse yard in Hays. The bully brought his own mother who outweighed Alder by several pounds and was at least eight inches taller.

The old schoolmarm, Misses Olsen, stammered and mumbled in disbelief as the fight continued until some local men broke it up. Both Alder and Moon had to admit they got the worst of the fight but come the next morning they were both at school and ready to continue. He never understood why she detested fighting so much when she was willing to fight a lightning bolt if she had to. He asked Will the same question only to see the man shrug his shoulders.

The next day Marshal Vetter approached the stable where Will was shoeing a horse. He asks Will to control his wife and if Moon wants to continue his schooling, he would have to stop fighting. At first Will was embarrassed that his wife was brawling in town like a Saturday night drunk but as the Marshal spoke Will started to laugh uncontrollably. Anyway, that was the end of Moon's formal education in Hays City; Jumper and Alder stepped in and took over. He learned writing and his numbers and the rest of it really did not matter to the fourteen year old. One thing came out of it, with Will Guthrie's coaching and Alder Guthrie's determination to never back down, Moon learned to hold his own in almost any fight.

"I'll carry Munday some supper."

Will nods as he watches Moon walk away with the tin of food. "Thank you boy."

Alder smiles. "You wouldn't know it to watch them two but they are just like brothers, maybe closer. Fighting one minute and then the best of friends the next."

Moon eases his horse up alongside the banks of the Canadian and studies the skyline above him. Whistling softly he waits until the same signal comes to him across the flats. Nudging the fresh bay gelding, he walks the horse off in the direction the whistle came from.

"You bring me some supper breed?"

Moon shakes his head and grins. "Yea, white boy I brought you some supper."

"Thank you Moon, I'm starved."

"I should have let you go hungry after the way you treated Jumper." Moon passes the tin bucket across to Munday. "Wasn't called for."

"Apologize to him for me, will you?"

Moon watches as Munday pulls the lid from the bucket. "No, you apologize to him. That old man has been good to both of us."

"I know he has." Munday wipes off his spoon. "I'll bring him back some sweets from the agency and apologize."

"I'll ride night herd if you want to go in."

"No, Pa would skin me alive but thank you anyway."

"I'll spell you about midnight." Moon starts to turn away then stops. "You ride with your Dad to the Agency when he goes; he might need you and Killian both."

"Alright Moon." Munday looks over curiously. "Are you expecting trouble?"

"No, but your presence with him will make him sit taller in the saddle I figure."

CHAPTER 7

RED RIVER CROSSING 1874

The banks of the wide river are deep sand but the trail across the Red River is well beat down from the thousands of longhorn cattle that crossed at the crossing. The herds and their punchers follow the age-old buffalo trails that lead down to this site. In good years with plenty of rain, the grass is plentiful. A small trading post sprang up by the Red River Crossing and it carries everything a drover would want from Winchester rifles to canned peaches.

Corrals line the ground around the large trading post, several Indian lodges stand in front of the store, and the place is littered with skinny Indian children and even skinnier dogs. A blacksmith shop beat out a steady rhythm on its anvil from daylight until dark repairing wagons and shoeing horses. The crossing has two saloons with their bawdy backrooms and their off-key pianos that would beat out their own noisy chatter to the singing of the drunken cowpunchers when a herd is in.

Clay and Bandy sit their horses and watch the slow movement of the murky water from the sandy bank. Across the wide river, they can see and hear the noisy settlement as it comes to life in the early morning hours. On the far bank of the Red, a mounted warrior sits his horse watching the two white men and then he starts across. The water comes up on the small Indian pony's chest as he nears midstream then grows shallow as he splashes onto the bank. A middle-aged warrior sits his horse and stares across at the two mounted men, his dark eyes piercing as they looks at them.

Dedrow raises his hand and nods at the warrior. "You speak English?"

"I speak plenty good white man talk, I know you Dedrow."

The foreman is in shock, he does not know the man. "You know me?"

"I ride with Quanah when we come to place you live many years ago."

Dedrow laughs and slaps his leg. "At the Running K when we had that little fight with a bunch of Comanche warriors. I'll bet a nickel that was where you seen me."

"I know you." The warrior repeats. "You shoot heap bang bang when we come there."

"Well, you're probably right about that old man." Dedrow hands him a sack of tobacco and some papers then turns to where Clay is sitting his horse enjoying the old warriors broken English. "I have a tendency to shoot at folks shooting at me."

"Is your friend big Chief Kincaid with you on trail?"

"He is and he'll be along pretty soon."

The warrior nods, then turns, and recrosses the river without a backwards glance. Clay turns to where the horses come into view behind the tree line that runs down to the river. "I better go see if Pa wants us to cross or hold them on this side."

"Yea." Dedrow studies the retreating back of the warrior. The old man sure has a good memory for faces, he did not say anything more, just took the tobacco and rode off. "I figure that old horse thief wants to see your Pa for some reason, let's go."

The day is young, Frank sends Clay across the Red to check out the pasture on the north side while he and the other wranglers circle the herd and let them graze while they wait. He paces beside the chuck wagon wanting to push on hard to reach the Canadian soon. The herd needs to be on good grass and settle in before the graze starts to turn brown in the fall. Frank also wants to get the herd to a location with good grassland before someone takes it. However, the colts need a few days rest and if the grass is good, the Red River Crossing and settlement is as good a place as any. He does not have the riders he needs to protect the large herd and the closer they stay to any kind of settlement, the better protection they have.

It is almost high noon when Clay comes loping back towards the chuck wagon. "There's grass enough over there to founder a buffalo herd."

"Let's cross." Frank waves his lariat rope and points north. "Lead'em out Clay."

"What about some grub?"

"Pull in your belt boy." Frank laughs, "You're getting fat."

Clay shakes his head then mumbles quietly to Dedrow. "In a pig's eye I am, if I pulled my shirt off you could see clear through me."

The stars shine bright overhead as the campfire sends sparks drifting skyward as the riders sit about the wagon on their bedrolls. The crossing was easy; the smaller colts float beside their mothers then buck and run as they exit the water. Frank sits his gelding and smiles as he watches the horses shake themselves, their hides glistening from the swim, as they wade ashore. The heavy chuck wagon follows the herd, the team of mules straining in their collars as they pull the wagon from the muddy water up the sandy banks.

"We'll go into the trading post tomorrow and resupply, then we'll pull out the following day after the colts are rested." Frank raises his familiar old battered cup.

"I've got me a list already made up husband." Emily leans back against him. "Maybe I'll have time to fix you some fried chicken and gravy."

"Sounds mighty good, Miss Em." Frank winks at her, "Mighty tasty."

Despite it being too early in the year for the cattle drives to reach this far north the store and the small settlement is alive with activity. Cowboys from across the Red in Texas cross to buy what they need at the well-supplied trading post. Several ranchers buy most of their supplies at the store saving the long ride into the larger towns on the Texas side of the river.

The Running K chuck wagon pulls up in the middle of the busy store yard and its occupants watch curiously as children, squaws, warriors, old people and dogs walk in and out of the store. Several cowboys sit about the porch letting their legs dangle down towards the ground watching the goings-on about them. Frank helps Emily from the wagon then follows her into the shady building. Walking up and down the long aisles inspecting the heavy stocked shelves filled with everything a man could think of he smiles, civilization is coming to the Oklahoma Territory.

The same old warrior from the river follows Frank up and down the aisle until the Rancher notices him and stops. "You need something old-timer?"

"Me Thunder Hawk; Kwahadi Comanche." The warrior thumps his chest. "Me same tribe, Quanah Parker, me know you big Kincaid."

Frank looks the old warrior over slowly and nods. "I know Thunder Hawk; I remember when you came to my lodge with Quanah many years ago."

"Me remember, you good man Kincaid."

"You look in good health."

"Thunder Hawk, sixty summers old, me feel good, like young man." The old warrior smiles. "Many squaw, many little ones, me happy."

Frank grins, he knows the Indian mind and the idle talk is leading up to something. "Where is Quanah?"

"Him hide far out on the Llano Estacado." The old man shakes his head. "Soldier Chief Mackenzie chase many days, maybe he catch, maybe Quanah catch white Chief."

"Why are you here Thunder Hawk?" Frank knows the warrior would not leave his people unless Quanah ordered it. "This is not Comanche land."

"Me come to this place see Charging Bull, then go Fort Sill see land white army want Quanah to live on." The old warrior nods. "Soon Comanche come to Fort Sill, maybe."

Frank is surprised at the old ones willingness to speak so openly. "Is Quanah going to surrender to the army?"

"Blue coat soldier Chief send word by white trader for Quanah to come in to this place and he would not attack the Comanche People." The warrior shrugs. "Him say if Quanah no come in horse soldier fight, much gun, much bullet."

"The blue coat cavalry has many men."

"White trader him bring many gifts of food and sweet rocks for young ones from Mackenzie; people hungry but not one take present just ride by trader and follow Quanah."

Frank knows the old warrior speaks of the hard rock candy that Indian children have a sweet tooth for. "It figures, the Comanche People are very proud."

Thunder Hawk shakes his head sadly. "Once Comanche greatest of all warriors, we rule everything. Now many of our best warriors are dead and gone. White man horse soldier chase us even out onto the great-staked plains like coyote chase rabbit. Quanah tired of fighting wants to come in, try to save his people."

"I agree with Quanah, in the long run the Comanche will have to quit the war trail and go on the reservation if they are to survive."

"This is something our council of elders have spoken of many times." Thunder Hawk nods. "There is no end to the white soldiers; they are like ants to honey."

Frank knows the old warrior wants something. "How can I help Thunder Hawk and the Comanche?"

The old warrior looks down at the sand floor ashamed to look the white man in the eye. "We come here to this place, white man get us drunk on white man firewater then we trade our horses for more whiskey. Very bad thing we do."

"How many are with you?"

"There is five of us; we trade three horses to whiskey man." Thunder Hawk is proud, he would steal a white man's horse without hesitating; this is the Comanche way but it is a lot to ask a white man to give him horses.

"The horses are yours; Quanah could have taken them all back in the old days." Frank smiles trying to erase a little of Thunder Hawk's shame.

Thunder Hawk smiles. "You have a good heart Kincaid; Quanah said this years ago when you did not kill our warriors."

Motioning to one of the younger clerks Frank nods at the old warrior. "Give this gentleman anything he wants and put it on my bill."

"Anything?" The clerk is not sure he is hearing right.

"Anything." Turning back to Thunder Hawk the Rancher smiles. "Get what supplies you need for your journey my friend, then come to my camp to the north of here."

"We will come."

Emily smiles as the wagon rolls across the grassland back towards their camp. She cannot believe the old warrior remembers them and the ranch after all these years. She well remembers the day Quanah rode his big black stallion so boldly into their front yard and waited patiently until Frank walked out the front door.

Five live roosters look out from the coop in the back of the wagon. "I'll get busy and we'll have a good supper for Thunder Hawk and his men when he arrives."

"You're gonna feed that old horse thief my chicken?" Frank pretends to act surprised.

"Yes I am, the same way you are going to give him three of our good horses."

Frank laughs as he hugs her to him. "You're something young lady, really something."

"Young, pssh I haven't been young in many a year mister." Emily smiles, "but thank you for saying so."

"You know Quanah could have made life pretty rough on us when we first settled on the Trinity."

"I know husband."

"We owe him."

"You paid him in full when his warriors were treated and let them live after they attacked our home." Emily spoke softly, remembering the affair. "He knew and that's exactly why he never raided the Running K again."

"I know but there was something else happened back then I never spoke of." Frank looks over at her.

"What?" She is curious now.

"You recall those five matching bay mares that mysteriously showed up in our front yard years ago?"

"I remember we never did figure who they belonged to or where they came from."

"I knew they were a gift from Quanah." Frank laughs. "Where he got them I don't know but they were beauties weren't they?"

"Yes they were."

"I figure they came from some Mexican Rancho down in old Mexico." He shakes his head. "Some Don woke up one morning and five of his best mares were gone."

"I hope Frank Kincaid you're just guessing and not a participant in horse stealing." Emily laughs.

"Why Missus, you know better than that." The rancher feigns shock.

Clay and Dedrow sit their horses and watch Thunder Hawk and four older warriors ride off to the west with three of their best geldings. "I knew the old horse thief wanted something yesterday at the crossing."

"I'll bet he was something in his day." Clay watches as the five Comanche Warriors ride out of sight.

"He was shucks, they all were." Dedrow nods. "That painted war shield the old horse thief gave your pappy last night tells his whole life."

"If they fight half as good as they eat, they were a tough bunch." Clay still cannot believe the chicken, gravy and biscuits the Comanche men put away.

"Don't doubt it for a minute; they were a brave bunch of men." Dedrow pulls out the makings. "Back then come a Comanche Moon, you had better keep a sharp look out and your powder dry."

Frank sits his horse and watches as the herd starts to move north following the beaten trail of the many cattle drives preceding them. The colts are frisky as the two days of rest rejuvenates their young bodies. He sends

Dedrow on ahead to the Darlington Agency to stake out pastureland for his large herd. Coming north to the grasslands of Oklahoma on the words of a few drovers is a gamble. They did it the same way back when they first settled on the Trinity Bottoms and started their Running K Ranch.

Dedrow rides into the newly constructed Fort Reno and reads the sign that hangs above one of the larger buildings. Sitting his horse quietly he stares up at the sign then looks around the compound. Soldiers dressed in blue tunics are busily building corrals and another building beside them he figures to be the post stable.

"Can't you read cowboy?" A young soldier smiles friendly like up at Dedrow. "It says Fort Reno, established 1874."

Dedrow nods and looks down at the young face. "I can read but thank you."

"Can I help you?"

"I came in looking for directions to the Darlington Agency but if I don't miss my guess that's it across the river."

"That's it alright, you got business over there?" The young man studies the far-off buildings of the agency. "That's all Indian across the river except for a few whites that run the agency."

Dedrow ignores the question then looks down at the soldier again. "Who's running this pile of sticks?"

"Well, right now Major West is in charge of building it but we got us a bona fide Colonel coming in next week to take over."

"I reckon he'll be doing the remount buying?"

"S'pect he will have the final say, although Captain Rains will probably be doing the actual picking out of the horses."

"Where might I find this Captain Rains?"

"Right over there Cowboy, he's the tall officer with the handlebar mustache."

"Thank you kindly." Dedrow nudges the gelding and rides down to where a tall light haired officer is studying a bundle of drawings. "Captain Rains?"

Turning, the officer looks up at the mounted man. "I'm Captain Rains."

Dedrow dismounts and sticks out his hand. "I'm Bandy Dedrow, I ride for the Running K Ranch and we're moving in around here somewhere. The reason I stopped to see you, my Boss wants me to tell you we've got plenty of good remounts for sale."

"Is that right Mister Dedrow, do you know what a good cavalry horse is supposed to look like?" The blue eyes of the soldier appear to twinkle when the man speaks. "Not a cow horse, a cavalry horse."

"Well sir, I'd figure they should have four legs and one tail."

The Captain smiles. "Forgive me Dedrow, I wasn't being rude, I just meant cavalry horses have to be a certain size and height."

"I understood your question Captain." Dedrow nods. "I rode with Jeb Stewart in the late war and yes, I know what a cavalry horse should look like."

"Jeb Stewart, we got the best of him at Malvern Hill but I'm afraid he got the best of us a lot more times."

"Yes Captain, he was a good officer but those days are long gone now."

"Yes Mister Dedrow, they are." Rains shakes his head. "Too bad."

"You like fighting and killing Sir?"

"Not especially but it does make a man feel alive."

"Or dead." Dedrow laughs and turns the bay he is riding sideways to the officer. "All of the Kincaid horses favor this one."

Rains nods as his blue eyes take in the fine lines of the animal. "Indeed, perhaps we will be doing business if your animals are all like this one."

"They are Sir; we'll be looking you up when we get settled hereabouts."

"How many horses do you have ready to be broke?"

"Maybe sixty in this herd but we'll be bringing in more from Texas." Dedrow steps nimbly back on the gelding.

"Come in and see me when you get settled, our commanding officer will be here next week and he's the one with the final say but I don't see any problem if it is as you say, your horses are all like this one."

Nodding Dedrow turns towards the river crossing and the Darlington Agency. He lived on the Texas Frontier practically his whole life and the presence of so many Indian lodges still makes his hair stand on end. As he rides nearer the buildings, he expects to see a mounted band of warriors charging straight at him.

Dismounting in front of the rough board building that has its own sign above the porch, Dedrow ties his gelding to the tie rack and looks around. He wishes he had brought Clay along to witness the countless Indians that loaf around the agency grounds. The youngster saw many Indians in his short life, mostly the ones that were shooting at him or running from them. However, the Indians here are where a man can see them without ducking.

"I reckon you'll be Mister Miles the Indian agent here?" Dedrow speaks to the little man who is busy issuing out supplies.

Hearing the question the man turns his attention taking in the dusty cowboy that stands before him. "I am John Miles."

"Bandy Dedrow, foreman for the Running K, owned by Frank Kincaid." Dedrow sticks out his hand.

"And you're wanting to lease land, if I'm not mistaken Sir?"

"Yes sir, you are correct."

Miles nods. "Well sir, as I told Mister Guthrie's boy last week the land is available but your boss will have to meet with the tribal elders to get a lease."

"Can you recommend a good piece of land for our herds?" Dedrow does not let on he heard the name of Guthrie once before.

"Horses?"

"Yes sir, cavalry remounts."

"The Guthrie people are downriver about ten miles west on the horseshoe flats." Miles walks to where a map hung on the wall. "My best suggestion to keep your animals separate would be for you to take upland to the east."

"Sounds reasonable," Dedrow replies. "Does the land east have the grass we need?"

"There's a place around the Yukon Mountains with good grass and water." Miles places his chubby finger on the map. "There, providing the tribal elders okay's it and I figure they will."

"That simple is it?"

"An old Comanche named Thunder Hawk stopped in two days ago and talked with the elders." Miles frowns. "It seems your Mister Kincaid has influential friends among the Comanche and Kiowa."

"We're a friendly bunch."

"That's good Mister Dedrow but you know the land around Fort Reno and this agency is Cheyenne and Arapaho range, not Comanche."

"Yes sir, I'm aware of that."

"Are you folk's friendly with them also?"

"Like I said Mister Miles, we're a friendly people."

"When will your herd be here?"

"Two days at most."

Miles nods. "Bring your horses here temporarily and hold them to the east until you have your council with the elders. I will draw up papers for your Mister Kincaid to sign."

"Yes sir, I'll be telling him." Dedrow turns towards the door then stops. "This Will Guthrie is he a rancher or something."

"He's a mule trader out of Hays City." Miles nods. "I met with him two days ago when he signed his lease."

"Is he a reputable man?"

"From all I've ever heard, he's an honest rancher."

Chapter 8

Canadian River 1874

The tribal council with the Cheyenne and Arapaho elders is over; Will Guthrie signs the thirty-year lease for thousands of acres lying along the Canadian River to satisfy the Indians and his own family. Timber is cut for the buildings that will be the new headquarters for the Guthrie Ranch. With the signing of the lease, Will drives in several head of beef and throws a huge banquet and barbecue in celebration of the event.

Three days later Grey Moon and Munday Guthrie sit their horses on the bank of the Canadian and watch as several hundred head of horses cross the water towards the Agency. Will sends them in to talk to Captain Rains about selling mules to the army.

"Horses, looks like trouble coming our way, Moon."

"Well, I don't know about trouble Munday but they're beauties for sure." Moon admires a beautiful, well-made horse more than anything.

"They're trouble; we may not be able to sell our mules."

Moon shakes his head. "Soldiers ride horses but they'll need mules to pull their supply wagons and pack with."

"They could pack a horse."

"You know better than that, the army ain't about to pay prime money to ruin a horse by using him to carry heavy packs."

"I still say them horses crossing the river are trouble."

"There's the man you want to talk to coming up river right now." Moon nods to the east.

Captain Rains stops his gelding on a knoll overlooking the Canadian and watches the large herd splash ashore and spread out on the abundant grass that lines the great river. Born in the great horse state of Kentucky the Captain is a born horseman, ramrod straight in the saddle, he looks at home and at ease on the back of his sorrel gelding. With his natural horsemanship, he has the keen ability to know a well-bred and sound animal, plus he has what many men didn't, he has a love for horses. People always say he should have been a horse breeder like his Pa and brothers back home but Rains also loves the Cavalry and being a Cavalry Officer he has the best of both worlds.

Turning in his saddle as Munday and Moon rein in beside him Rains smiles. "Well now gentlemen, I didn't expect to see you so soon after that party you folks gave the other night."

"Pa sent us in, Captain Rains."

Rains nods, "to sell the army some mules, is that it?"

"Yes sir, exactly."

"Well with Custer arriving at Camp Supply with the Seventh soon and fixing to move north against the Sioux and Northern Cheyenne, the army will be needing mules and horses." The Captain looks once again at the large horse herd. "How many head do you have?"

Munday looks over at Moon for an answer. "I'd guess about one hundred twenty head."

Rains looks at the dark complexioned speaker. "Are they broke to use?"

"Twenty are harness broke and will pull a wagon, another thirty or so are halter broke and the rest are pure green."

Rains laughs. "Well, if we buy them it'll give them lazy barracks loafers something to do won't it?"

Moon looks at the officer unsure of the man. "They'll weigh between nine and eleven hundred pounds and stand between thirteen and fifteen hands."

"Pretty good size mules." Rains is impressed.

Munday replies, "Pa owns the biggest mules to come out of Missouri."

"Good, tell him I'll be along in the morning to take a look." Rains looks over at Moon. "You're Cheyenne, I can see by the sewing on your shirt but what else?"

"Black." Moon never blinked.

"No offense intended youngster."

Moon nods, "None taken Captain, a man is what he is."

"Custer is looking for scouts, I just thought."

"I've got a job, thanks anyway."

Rains replies, "I understand you wouldn't want to fight against your own kind. Is that it?"

"What kind am I, Captain."

"I'll be along in the morning gentlemen." Rains turns away without answering then looks back over his shoulder. "Tell your Mother that was the best barbeque and mule lip pies I ever bit into."

Munday agrees, "We'll tell her Captain."

Rains looks curiously back at the two young men as he rides away. He watched them at the barbecue and they are close, as close as brothers. Waving his riding crop at the two, he rides on towards the Agency.

Raking his gelding hard, Munday hit a lope for the riverbank. He wades the Canadian and then heads towards the Fort. Reining up in front of the fresh rough cut lumber saloon that stands only a quarter mile from the posts front gates he dismounts and grins back at Moon. The brand spanking new sign proclaims to the world that Oney Thompson owns the establishment and all are welcome inside. Munday ties his gelding then motions for Moon to hurry as he starts for the porch.

"Your Pa said for us to get right back." Moon sits his horse shaking his head.

"Ah Moon, just one little old drink won't hurt anything."

Moon frowns as Munday's back disappears quickly through the swinging batwing doors. A wild cry of the Confederacy sounds out with a shrill rebel yell from inside. Shaking his head Moon dismounts and steps on to the porch. He heard that sound before and he knows what it possibly means; there are Yankee bluecoats inside.

Munday already sidles up to the bar and spread his elbows out across the wide wood slats. "Set me up two glasses barkeep and keep them full till I holler when."

Moon watches as the amber liquid spills into the glass. The barkeep looks the dark featured youth over with disdain then turns back towards the end of the bar without pouring another glass.

"I ordered two glasses barkeep." Moon watches as Munday slips loose the tie down on his pistol hammer then points his finger at the bar. "Two right here and right now."

The stocky barman turns slowly his features blank. "My name's Oney Thompson sonny and I say who drinks in here and it ain't Injuns."

Munday hands his full glass to Moon who sits it back on the bar. "I'll have me a drink Mister Thompson, now!"

The double-barreled shotgun appears as if by magic in the saloonkeepers hand and points it right at Munday's chest, cocked and ready. Thompson stands quietly as Munday grins as he looks into the face of death. At less than three feet, the scattergun cannot miss. "You might get me boy but this shotgun will spread you all over this floor."

Moon steps between the men and taking Munday by the shoulder turns him towards the door without a word. "Let's go home."

Furious the younger Guthrie shrugs loose and walks from the saloon.

"Wait a minute." Thompson pours a second drink and places it on the bar without taking his eyes off Munday. "You boys have a drink on the house before you leave."

Munday and Moon both look at the drinks then retreat out the doors as the noise of laughter sounds behind them. "No one laughs at me."

"Let it go, no one goes up against a coach gun like that in close quarters." Moon shoves Munday towards their horses, "And lives to tell about it."

"Tell that loudmouth to come outside."

"He ain't stupid, he won't come out." Moon pushes Munday again towards his horse. "Let it go for now."

"For now I will." Munday shrugs his shoulders. "Keep your half-breed hands off me."

"That's using your head Mister Guthrie; old Oney in there would kill you." Both Munday and Moon turn at the voice. Marshal Vetter who they both know well stands behind them smiling. "Take him back downriver Moon and keep him there till he cools off some."

Vetter watches the two young men ride side by side slowly away from Fort Reno. Breathing deeply he smiles to himself, he watched both Munday and Grey Moon grow into manhood since they were kids. He knew Munday was fast with a pistol and he has a temper to go along with his disposition. Only the double-barreled greaser in the close confines of the saloon kept the youngster from drawing on Thompson. Actually, Oney Thompson did Munday a favor; he could have shot the boy down where he stood and probably would never stand trial. Trouble is, then he would have Will Guthrie and his whole crew to deal with and Thompson knows how dangerous Guthrie can be. Vetter shakes his head as he knows the pride and temper the boy carries. He doubts the youngster will forget about the whole affair, someday he will catch Thompson without the shotgun.

Grey Moon is different, he is an excellent shot with a rifle but Vetter has never known the youngster to carry a pistol. Moon never looks for trouble, he will not walk around it but if he could, he would walk away from it. Slower to rile than Munday; Moon tries his best to stay out of trouble. Being a half-breed already makes him an outcast to some people. He knows causing trouble will only make public opinion about him worse. Vetter knows one thing though, if he has to have one of the boys mad at him, he would rather it be Munday.

Captain Rains watches the tail end of the great herd pass across the Canadian and then he turns his horse and rides over to the agency. He already talked to the Running K foreman so he knows the animals with the Running K brand on their hips are the horses that Dedrow talked about. His orders were to supply Custer with remounts by early fall. His task was just simplified, he sees several young geldings in this herd and they are old enough and mature enough to saddle break.

Dismounting, he ducks under the door jam and enters the busy store. Rains smiles to himself, today is his lucky day for sure. Behind the last counter, he finds what he is looking for, the honey blond hair of Lana Barber bobs back and forth as she waits on the waiting Squaws. From the very first time he laid eyes on her; he was smitten with love. On several occasions while out riding, he found his horse wandering in a semi-circle right back to the agency. Before the war back in Kentucky, he was interested in one of the local girls but nothing like this. He is infatuated with Lana Barber, working on his paperwork or out in the Fort's perimeter her smiling face materializes right before his eyes.

Rains tries his best to put her out of his mind. He tries to persuade himself that he is wasting his time but to no avail. He is smitten; all he can do now is try to win her affections. It is not going to be easy; Miss Barber seems to look right through him whenever he is around the agency. He thought about speaking with her brother but no, some brothers get a little riled when a man tries to pay attention to their sisters. The army sure would not put up with any shenanigans from a lovesick Captain of the Cavalry.

"Captain Rains." The soft voice speaks as she looks across the counter to where he is standing. "It's good to see you this morning."

"Miss Barber." Rains thinks his tongue is going to stick in his throat as he smiles back at her. "Thank you and how are you this fine morning."

The deep blue eyes study his dark tanned face for a second then turn businesslike. "Can I help you with something?"

There it is again, the coldness comes back into her voice. "Yes Ma'am, I'm here to pick up the papers on the Guthrie lease. Mister Miles wants me to put them in the Fort's safe and to tell you the Running K herd just arrived. I figure the Indians will be signing another lease soon with the Kincaid outfit."

"I met a gentleman a few days back that rode through here, would that be him?"

Rains frowns slightly, picking his words carefully making sure she does not read his mind or his thoughts. "He's the Running K foreman, name's Dedrow."

"He seems like a true gentleman." She read his thoughts, smiling slightly when he turns a shade redder. "From the south."

"Yes Ma'am, I reckon even the rebs can be gentlemen." Rains does not like their topic of conversation but at least he is getting to talk to her.

"I'll get the papers for you, Captain."

"Miss Barber." Rains hesitates.

"Yes." The long blond hair bounces as she turns to face him.

Clearing his throat slightly the Captain looks down at her. "I was wondering Miss Barber, would you like to go riding with me on Sunday?" She almost laughs, his face is beet red with embarrassment but at least he finally broke the ice and spoke to her about something besides business. "Ride a horse?"

"If you don't ride I can arrange a surrey."

"No, a horse would be nice; I haven't ridden in such a long time." She looks around at the Indian women waiting on her. "Before I can answer, I must speak with my brother."

"I'll come by tomorrow for the papers and his answer." Rains bows and hurries as he retreats from the store, hoping to not trip over his own boots.

Several of the squaws smile coyly at the Captain as they watch him leave. Seeing them smiling Rains blushes deeper, causing all of them to laugh.

"Him, great horse soldier." A tall younger Indian woman speaks up. "Many horses, this one."

Lana can hear the jealousy in the young woman's words. "I believe the horses belong to the army."

"Maybe soldier Chief belong to someone else too." The woman ducks her head and walks from the store. Lana is curious about what she means.

Turning to look at the other squaws Lana frowns as they turn from her and go back to their trading.

Frank Kincaid followed by Dedrow enter the Darlington Agency door and they wait until the agent notices them and approaches. Frank looks around, surprised at the well-stocked store and the mass of women and children that fill the isles.

Recognizing Dedrow from his previous meeting Miles sticks out his hand and introduces himself to the rancher. "Mister Kincaid I presume sir."

"Yes sir, I'm guilty." Frank takes the smaller hand of the Agent. "And you're Agent Miles."

"I understand Sir, that you have horses for sale."

"I do." Frank nods, "I've come here to lease land and a place to build some ranch buildings."

Miles smiles, "In our last meeting I explained to Mister Dedrow the restrictions and limitations of leasing Indian land from the Cheyenne and Arapaho."

"Yes sir, Bandy told me what you said."

"Good, I will set up a council with the tribes in two days, return then and we will have a meeting with the landowners themselves." Miles walks towards the front door and points. "Move your horses towards those far-off hills and graze them there until we settle your affairs with the tribes."

"Thank you sir." Frank replies.

Miles looks off towards the Canadian River. "You just missed Captain Rains, he's the officer in charge of the horse purchasing for the army out here."

Frank looks out across the flat lands. "We'll ride over and have a word with him when we come back in for the council."

"You do that Mister Kincaid." The agent turns. "If you need supplies step inside, we're well supplied for now."

"I can see you're shelves are loaded." Frank steps back into the yard among barking dogs and yelling children. "I believe we've got plenty for now."

"Don't let your horses stray past the knolls, Will Guthrie has mules ten miles east of here and we wouldn't want them to mix."

Frank frowns slightly at the mention of the name. The dead outlaw Fritch also mentioned that name before he died. "This Will Guthrie, what kind of man is he?"

"From what I've heard of the man from Marshal Vetter and the folks passing through here, they all say he is top-notch, honest as the day is long."

Kincaid nods. "Well, I hope you're right Sir."

"Have you heard something to the contrary?"

Frank declines to say more, shaking hands with the agent, he and Dedrow mount and turn their horses to the east. Neither man notices the squat cowboy sitting beside the agency door as they stand talking with the agent. Little Bit Dawkins draws in on his smoke and watches curiously as the two strangers ride away. Standing, he flips the burned down quirley into the yard then follows Miles back inside the store. Walking to the counter he looks across at the agent.

"Yes sir, can I help you?"

"Name's Little Bit Dawkins, I ride for Will Guthrie." The short cowboy looks about him then tosses a wadded up paper on the counter. "Boss sent me in to pick up a few things."

"Yes sir." Miles reads over the list then starts piling articles on the rough top counter. After several minutes, he hands Dawkins the list back. "That's everything I believe."

"Toss me on four sacks of Bull and some quirley paper."

Figuring with a short stub of pencil the agent looks across the counter at Dawkins. "That'll be eight dollars and fifty cents."

"Money sure don't go far these days, does it?" The short man tosses a ten-dollar bill on the counter.

"It's a long freight haul out of Hays City, costs money."

"Uh huh." The sarcastic reply hit a sour note on the little agent's nerves.

"Well cowboy, you can ride two hundred miles north and get them supplies cheaper I suppose." Miles voice turns cold.

Dawkins looks over at the twinkling blue eyes of the agent then grabs the cotton sack, cussing as he left the store. "Dang smart aleck."

Lana walks over to where Miles stands watching the departing back. "Unhappy customer?"

"Seems like he was at that."

Frank pushes the herd into the rolling foothills south of the Yukons then orders to build a temporary camp. They will move the herd several miles farther to the east after the signing of the lease but for now, they will hold the horses here in the knolls. The news of the large mule herd west of the agency is disturbing to Kincaid, not that the mules would interfere with his horse sales, they are two different work animals. No, the problem with mules being in proximity with the horse herd is the huge Missouri Jacks can smell the mares for miles. If the two herds mix, the Jacks will cross breed with any of his open mares and he sure does not want any mule colts. One man riding herd will have to watch over the mares day and night until they move farther east into the Yukon.

Sitting his bay gelding Frank looks over the country, the grass and rangeland is all the Jingle Bob Wranglers said it would be. Tomorrow they will ride into the agency and sign a grass lease with the tribes then they can begin pushing the herd east and begin building their new ranch. Kincaid is satisfied, he found exactly what he hoped would be here in the Nations, good graze and a good market for his horses.

Little Bit Dawkins rides into the noise and bustling of the ranch buildings being built and dismounts. Unsaddling, he turns his gelding into the hastily erected corral and carries the cotton sack over to the chuck wagon where Alder is busy helping Jumper prepare supper. Handing the sack to her, he looks around for Will.

"Thank you Little Bit."

"Yes Ma'am." The rider tips his hat. "Where's the Boss; Misses Guthrie?"

"He's hauling logs over from the river."

"Well, reckon I better get to work before dark."

Dawkins locates Will dragging logs across the flat ground and walks to intersect him. The timbers are heavy making the mules strain in their collars, not hard enough to strain their shoulders but they sure have to pull a load.

"Good team of mules Boss."

"Yes they are." Will stops the team next to where the log house is going up. "Make it alright?"

"Yes sir." Dawkins fidgets.

"Something wrong Little Bit?"

"Maybe, maybe not." The short cowboy rolls a smoke and offers Will the sack of Bull. "There's a new outfit moving in east of the agency."

"I already heard." Will takes the tobacco makings. "Well, there's plenty of grass out here for everyone."

"Yea, I know but your name was mentioned at the agency, kinda like they were trying to get the deadwood on you."

Will strikes a match to his smoke. "How was I mentioned?"

"Nothing much, they just wanted to know if Miles knew anything of you." Dawkins shrugs. "It was just the way they asked, nosy like."

"What else?"

"They'll be meeting with the Indians in two days." Little Bit tosses down his burned smoke. "I figure they'll be another big hoedown like you and the Missus threw last week."

"Maybe we'll ride in and get acquainted with our new neighbors." Will unbuckles the collars and pulls them and the chain harness from the mules. "That way Mister Dawkins, we can answer any questions they have about us in person."

"Yes sir." Little Bit grins from ear to ear.

Chapter 9

Horses and Mules on the Canadian

Frank Kincaid, Clay Kincaid and Bandy Dedrow saddle up right after breakfast. They head east to the Darlington Agency for their meeting with the Cheyenne and Arapaho Tribes that control the land along the Canadian River. Frank rides his favorite trail horse, a medium built bay that can fox trot a hole in the wind. With a horse like the bay under him, a man cannot help but enjoy the dawning of the early morning. Crossing the never-ending grasslands where birds of every kind fly up before them as they pass. Frank slaps his rein absentmindedly against the geldings shoulder as he breathes in the pleasant smell of the grass. The early morning sun causes the heavy dew to sparkle brightly on the sweet smelling blades of tall grass. Frank breathes in deeply and smiles as the pure clean air fills his lungs.

"You want a smoke Boss?" Dedrow offers a quirley.

Shaking his head Frank declines the offer. "No thanks."

"What you got on your mind Pa?"

"Nothing son, just enjoying the morning is all." Frank motions with his hand. "This is a beautiful, clean pastureland."

"Yes sir." Clay points as a whole covey of quail flies up at their passing. "Should have brought my shotgun."

"I've never smelled air as fresh."

Dedrow blows smoke to the wind. "You like this land better than the Trinity River Bottoms?"

"Texas is my home Bandy, nothing can ever take its place but this country is a new beginning for us all." Frank looks across the swell of the grass. "We can sell horses here."

Only the squeak of saddle leather and the sound of their horse's hooves hitting the sandy ground, make a sound the rest of the way to the agency. Not one of the three speak, each one keeps their thoughts to themselves as they enjoy the solidarity and quietness of the early morning. With the sighting of the agency and farther off across the Canadian the new walls of Fort Reno; Frank reins in and sits the bay.

"This is a big day for the Running K." Frank is speaking more to himself than Clay and Dedrow. "I believe if we get the lease we'll be here to stay."

"We'll get the lease Pa, according to Mister Miles; that old rascal Thunder Hawk spoke for us to the Cheyenne and Arapaho Tribes, almost guaranteeing that we'll get it."

Dedrow is curious about Frank's remark. "What do you mean we're here to stay?"

"Just that, this Oklahoma land is vast." Frank waves his hand. "There's no way the Yankee government is going to let the tribes control this much land forever."

"But it's theirs by treaty."

"Ugh huh, how many times have we heard that before?' The rancher shakes his head. "No sir, one day this land will be opened up for settlement and I'm going to latch onto some of it now, before that time comes."

"And just how do you plan on doing that?"

"Easy, I aim to buy it." Frank smiles and waves his arm pointing across the rolling grasslands. "As much as I can."

"Do you think the Indians might be willing to sell?"

"If they figure to lose it they just might."

Marshal Vetter watches as the three riders ride slowly towards him reining up their horses in front of the Agency store. All three focus on the badge that decorates the front of his vest. Stepping to the edge of the broad porch away from the noise of the Agency doorway the Marshal studies the three men.

Frank looks nervously over at the Marshal then back at Clay. "Good morning Marshal."

"You boys must be the Kincaids?"

"You asking for a reason?"

"No." The word comes out slow. "My names Vetter, I'm here for a spell to keep the peace. Just wanted to get acquainted with all newcomers is all."

"I'm Frank Kincaid," Frank dismounts but does not offer to shake the Marshal's hand.

"I understand you're here to sign a lease on the land east of here?"

"I am."

Vetter nods. "That's good; we need new people around these parts. This land needs to be settled and civilized."

"You greet every one that passes through Marshal?" Dedrow looks hard at the lawman. "Or are we privileged?"

"If they're of interest to me I do." Vetter's eyes focus on Clay. "I reckon you're the young gun hand that downed Red Hooper?"

Clay nods calmly. "That's what I'm accused of Marshal but it weren't me that did him in."

"Who was it then?"

"You a friend of Red Hooper?" Dedrow dismounts.

Ignoring Dedrow the cold slate blue eyes of the Marshal turns back to Clay. "I asked you a question Mister."

"Bill Longley, I got one in ol'Red but the one that did him in was fired by Longley."

Vetter nods. "That's fine young man but I'm telling you only once to keep that fast gun of yours holstered unless you're shooting at a rattlesnake."

Clay agrees, "Oh I will Marshal, unless I'm shooting at a snake."

Vetter starts to turn then looks back at Dedrow. "Heard you been asking about Will Guthrie?"

"That right?"

Again, Vetter looks at Frank. "They're a good law-abiding family but they can get rough if necessary."

"Well Marshal." Frank looks into the hard eyes of the man. "We're law abiding too and if we have to we can get rough too."

"Ugh huh." Vetter steps from the porch and starts towards the barn then stops. "Let's just hope you don't have to."

The lawman perches atop a bale of hay and watches as the three men follow Miles across the flat sandy grounds towards a large council lodge. He studies the younger Kincaid, he is young and polite but the look in his eyes are of an older man. The youngster walks with the proud bearing of a typical gunman, slow and deliberate throwing out a challenge to all comers yet not saying a word. Vetter knows if provoked he figures this young man could be very dangerous, he can sense it. He was a Marshal almost all of his adult life, he can read a bad man, and Clay Kincaid fit the bill.

"How did a Kansas Marshal find out about a killing in Texas?" Dedrow mumbles as they follow the agent.

"You've heard about the long arm of the law haven't you Bandy?" Frank shrugs. "They've got their ways, that's for sure."

"He didn't seem too interested in me."

"Just give him time Clay my boy, give him time." Dedrow laughs and slaps the younger man on the back.

The lodge is already crowded with the elders and head chiefs who gather to hold council with the white men. The three whites along with the Indian agent Miles take their places before the gathered warriors and sit down. They are Cheyenne and Arapaho: northern plains Indians that Frank is completely unfamiliar with. The dark eyes of the warriors study the newcomers with interest. They heard much about this big white man with the grey eyes from Thunder Hawk.

Charging Bull, Yellow Dog, Crooked Leg and Red Tail are just a few of the head chiefs present at the council. Every warrior present has their dark eyes focused on the three men. Frank always heard a red man could sit for hours staring at an anthill and never once reveal their true thoughts. Watching the gathered warrior's blank stares, he is beginning to believe whoever said it.

John Miles stands and is about to open the council when Yellow Dog stands and opens his hand for quiet. "This white man Kincaid will have the land he wants near the Yukon Mountains."

Miles turns to where the Chief is standing and clears his throat. "Yellow Dog does not want me to explain the terms of the lease to these men?"

"No, this white man is a friend of Quanah, he is a friend of Satank and Satanta. We wish him to be a friend of the Cheyenne and Arapaho People." Yellow Dog looks about at the other Chiefs for confirmation. "The land is his, if he wishes to sign your paper so be it. For us, his word is good enough."

Frank listens, as the broken English of the Arapaho is translated clearer then nods. "I wish to sign the lease for all to see and know we have treated in good faith with our friends the Cheyenne and Arapaho."

Several heads bob up and down. "This is good." Yellow Dog nods.

Frank heard about the large barbeque Will Guthrie threw for the tribes after his lease was signed. He wants the Running K to set a good example of peace also. "In three days you will all be my guests here for a feast, all are welcome."

The gathered warriors make the lodge come alive speaking loudly, nodding their heads, and smiling at the invitation. Normally a stoic and subdued people when among strangers, this morning they come alive welcoming Frank and the others into their country.

"Thunder Hawk of the Comanche People told us of you Frank Kincaid, Satank, and Satanta has spoken of you also." Charging Bull stands straight as an arrow before the assembled whites. "Here in this place you are welcome, if anyone rides against our brother they will be sent away from these lands."

Frank nods. "My friends the Cheyenne and Arapaho are always welcome to my lodge in the Yukon's."

Miles looks across at Frank as the council breaks up and everyone walks outside. "You have great influence among these people Mister Kincaid."

"I've always try to treat any Indian I've ever met fair in my dealings."

"Well that is good." Miles appears a little agitated; maybe it is jealousy, Frank cannot tell. "The Yukons will be yours. I will draw up the papers, good day Mister Kincaid."

"Good day Mister Miles." Frank studies the short man as he walks away towards the Agency. "Thank you."

"Are we going to ride over to the new Fort and talk with Captain Rains?" Dedrow nods towards the Canadian. "We told him you'd be over to talk with him after the council."

"Alright, let's go see the gentleman."

Fort Reno with its new fresh smelling buildings, it's well laid out parade ground, and stables are quite a remarkable sight as the three men ride past a sentry standing guard near the entrance to the large compound. The American Flag pops in the slight breeze as the red, white, and blue waves high on the flagpole looking out over the Fort. Soldiers work on an earthen wall to the west while some parade across the field. The ringing of the blacksmith's anvil under a brush arbor take their attention as they watch a heavily muscled soldier strip to his waist as he beats on a red-hot horseshoe.

"Quite an impressive place." Frank reins up in front of the blacksmith shop and sits his gelding. The blue uniforms chaff him some but he has to admit whoever is in charge of the work is a good man.

Dedrow nods. "They've sure been working like beavers since I was here last."

"Say soldier, you know where we could find Captain Rains this morning?"

The heavy hammer stops in midair as the small eyes of the blacksmith look over at the mounted men. "Yes sir, that'll be him, riding through the gates right now."

Turning to where an officer rides towards them at a slow trot all eyes focus immediately on the woman riding beside him. The officer is straight as an arrow; impressive as he sat the sorrel he rode but the blond headed woman riding beside him takes the younger men's attention. The smith stops what he is doing and steps up beside them grinning. "That'll be Miss Lana Barber; she is the local bible pumper for the tribe's civilization."

Clay's jaw nearly unhinges as he looks at the beautiful woman. "She's a preacher?"

"Nah." The smith spit a stream of tobacco. "Her brother does the preaching and she does the consoling and singing."

Dedrow laughs. "Well sir, I could use some consoling for sure."

The smith laughs lightly then starts back towards the anvil before the Captain comes near. "Don't let the Captain here you Reb, he's mighty taken with the young lady. Just might sour any horse sales you boys got planned."

Frank frowns over at Dedrow shaking his head. "You boys know better than to speak about a lady, any lady."

"Just having a little fun with the Yank is all." Dedrow grins. "Sure didn't mean anything against the lady."

Either Captain Rains does not see the three riders at the stable or he chooses to ignore them as he rides over to the sign that reads Sixth Cavalry Headquarters. Frank motions with his chin then rides towards where Rains is helping the girl dismount. Reining in as the Captain and Lana step up onto the porch Frank tips his hat to her as they turn.

"Captain Rains, I believe."

"I'm Rains Sir and this is Miss Barber."

"Captain, Miss Barber." Frank bows slightly. "I'm Frank Kincaid, my son Clay, and my foreman Bandy Dedrow."

Plainly agitated at the interruption of his plans, good manners and military etiquette forbid the Captain from dismissing the men. His eyes went naturally to the men's horses, sweeping over the three geldings, taking in their conformation and small-refined heads. Above all Rains is a horseman, he appreciates a well-bred horse and these three are picture-perfect. The only thing a man would want to change about them was, if the rider prefers to ride a palomino, sorrel, appaloosa, or paint.

The cavalry rides all colors but it prefers bays or sorrels. Working cowboys do not give a hang about the color he rides as long as the horse can head a cow and pull from the horn. Most prefer a horse that would pitch a little on a frosty morning they say it warms up their blood.

Rains looks over at the smiling face of Lana and shrugs. "You gentlemen light and tie, then we'll get down to business."

Frank knows the officer would much prefer to be talking with the young lady and the price of his horses could verge on his mood. "No sir, we're going over to the saloon and see if we can get us a bite to eat."

Bowing, Rains thanks Frank with a smile. "Perhaps we can talk some other time."

"In a couple days we'll be giving a barbeque to seal the deal on our new land lease." Frank smiles, "Perhaps we can conduct our business then."

"That'll be fine, we'll talk then."

Clay looks into the deep blue eyes of the girl then tips his hat. Smiling back at him, she holds her gaze for several seconds then turns away before Rains notices but not before Dedrow notices. Slapping his hat against Clay's leg, he smiles from ear to ear then winks at Clay. Touching his horse Clay races towards the nearby saloon before Dedrow could open his mouth and get him in trouble with Frank.

"I believe she took a shine to you young'un." Dedrow pushes through the swinging doors looking back to see how far away Frank was. "You see the way she looked at you?"

"Pa hears you talking about her; he'll skin both of us." Clay warns.

"The Boss is too old fashioned."

"Pa's just Pa, now shut up about it."

"Just trying to help you."

Clay shrugs his shoulders and walks towards a near table. "Help me out and order us a good meal."

Munday Guthrie, Grey Moon, and Little Bit Dawkins push the doors open and walk into the cool of the saloon stopping at the long bar. From where he sat eating, Dedrow's sharp eyes recognize the short squat rider from the Agency. The short rider walks up to the bar with two other men. Focusing back on his meal the tall man notices as Little Bit turns and nods at their table. Kneeing Frank and Clay both under the table Dedrow gets their attention while never missing a mouthful of food or uttering a word.

"That wasn't half bad." Dedrow leans back in his chair casually as he unhooks the tie down holding his pistol.

Frank laughs easily. "You want another steak Bandy?"

"No sir, reckon not."

The floor squeaks lightly as Munday with Little Bit siding him walks over to their table. Dedrow rolls himself a smoke then blows smoke craftily towards the two men.

Munday braces his feet and looks at the men. "Heard you men were asking about my Pa?"

"And who might your Pa be young man?" Frank looks over at the youngster.

"Will Guthrie."

Frank can see the twitching fingers and the anxious stare as Munday throws out the name. "No harm meant youngster, just heard the name once so I was asking about it is all."

"Who spoke it?"

Both Dedrow and Clay turn in their chairs and look up at the tall slender young man. "Jack Fritch was what he called himself just before he expired."

"Fritch is dead?"

"He looked pretty dead last time I seen him."

"Who killed him and when?"

Frank stands up slowly, never letting his grey eyes leave Munday's face. "He a friend of yours?"

"No, but like I said Will Guthrie's my Pa and I want to know why you're asking around about him?"

"Go home son and leave me be."

Moon walks over to the table stepping in front of Munday. "Leave it be Munday, if your Pa wants to take it up, these folks will be nearby."

"Get out of the way Moon, I'll handle this." Munday tries to push Moon out of the way.

"Let's go home." Moon grabs Munday's pistol in the scuffle. "Little Bit get the horses."

"I'll see you again." Munday waves his finger in Frank's face. "Next time, old man."

"I'm not old." Clay steps sideways away from the table. "Give him his pistol."

Frank looks across the table at Clay. "Leave it be boy, I believe this gentleman has it under control."

Munday shrugs away from Moon's grasp. "Gimme my gun, Moon!"

"No, let's ride out." Moon pushes Munday towards the front door where Little Bit waits holding the horses.

"Let's take them Moon, we can do it." Munday whirls as he steps out onto the porch.

"Why, we don't even know them."

"I told you yesterday, their horses are gonna be trouble." Munday tries to move around Moon. "Let's finish it now."

"You planning on killing anyone you don't like?" Moon shakes his head. "You start trouble here and your Pa is gonna skin you alive."

"They wouldn't be any trouble." Munday cusses as he steps up onto his buckskin. "Danged horse thieves."

"If you and your temper get your Pa and his mules kicked off this range, you're gonna be in real trouble."

Captain Rains and Lana Baxter trot their horses slowly past the saloon as Moon, Munday, and Dawkins race away towards the west. Waving at the girl Moon turns once in the saddle then rides to catch up with the others.

"You know that breed?" Rains' eyes follow the running horses.

Lana replies, "Yes, I met him a few days ago at the Agency."

"I see, he seems very friendly."

"Well I hope so Captain, I wouldn't want him mad at me."

"That wasn't exactly what I meant Miss Lana."

Lana smiles softly. "I know what you meant."

"I didn't mean any disrespect Miss Lana but folks out here could start talk." Rains looks at her. "A white woman doesn't associate with a breed out here."

"I can assure you Sir; merely speaking civilly to Mister Moon at the Agency is not association."

Rains shakes his head. "Some would think so."

Clay stands on the porch outside the saloon watching the girl ride out as he waits for Frank to pay their bill. He waves at her as she takes a fleeting look backwards at him and smiles. He knows one thing; she is definitely a very beautiful girl.

"A woman that beautiful is sure gonna cause trouble for someone hoss just make sure it ain't you." Dedrow strikes a sulphur on the porch railing.

"Bandy, old friend a woman that beautiful is worth a little trouble, maybe a whole lot of trouble." Clay smiles, his straight white teeth shine by his tanned face and cold black hair making them seem even whiter.

"Boy, you've been fairly warned."

"What's he being warned about Bandy?" Frank steps out on the porch and heard the last of the conversation. "The blond headed woman riding with the Captain?"

Dedrow turns, surprised. "No not that, I was just telling him to always check his cinch before climbing aboard."

"Sure you were." Frank's eyes look off towards the Canadian. "If he ain't learnt that by now, we're all in trouble."

Chapter 10

Barbeque on the Canadian

John Miles watches from the agency porch as warriors from the Cheyenne and Arapaho People chase the five head of steers across the flats near their village. The Running K hands drive the fat cattle into the Darlington Agency early in the morning for the much anticipated council. There will be a feast with dancing later in the afternoon and into the night.

"Why are they torturing the poor beasts?" Lana watches in horror as the warriors ride their little horses expertly after the frightened steers.

Miles smiles. "They're not torturing them Lana, it's just the way they prepare the animals before killing them."

"Why it's terrible!"

"It's just their way, the way they chased the buffalo during the great hunts." Miles watches the warriors as they circle the animals back towards where the waiting squaws hold their skinning knives. "They want their blood rushing through their veins and muscles. They say it makes the meat tastier and softer."

"How awful," Lana turns from the porch. "I'll not eat a bite of the meat."

Miles laughs as she turns. "This is the west Lana; you're no longer back east."

"Perhaps I should be."

"You'll get used to it and the barbeque will melt in your mouth young lady."

"I'll not eat a bite."

Miles smiles trying to comfort her. "Everyone that comes west Lana, has to learn new ways or they won't survive."

Clay and Dedrow sit their horses and watch from a distance as several warriors bring the steers down practically in front of the waiting squaws. The short strong bows of the racing warriors send silent death into the sides of the terrified cattle. A particularly well-muscled Cheyenne releases his arrow with such force that it goes clean through one of the steers killing the animal in mid stride before it hit the ground.

Clay shakes his head in disbelief. "Did you see that shot Bandy?"

"I seen it." Dedrow spit. "I've seen them do the same to some of my friends in the old days."

"Those were Comanche, they fancied the long lance." Clay can sense the coldness in the foreman's voice. "These are Cheyenne."

"They were Indians, same as these."

Clay laughs and kicks his yellow gelding towards where the gathered warriors were chasing the cattle sat their horses. Reining the horse to a stop in front of the warrior that sent his arrow so powerfully through the steer Clay nods then pushes his hand forward in the traditional greeting on the plains.

"Any of you speak English?" Not a word comes forth from the curious warriors as they watch the young white. "Reckon not." Clay motions at the dead steer then acts as if he is shooting an arrow. Reaching into his saddlebags he pulls out a bowie knife encased in a fringed leather scabbard then kicks the gelding two steps forward and hands the knife to the warrior.

Watching the surprise spread over the warrior's dark face as he admires the knife Clay nods and backs his horse a few steps backwards. The warrior pulls the razor sharp knife from its sheath and tests it across his finger. Clay watches as blood runs from a cut the warrior does not feel. Nodding, the warrior smiles over at Clay then unties a leather string from around his neck that holds a flint arrowhead and rides his horse closer.

Clay holds the arrowhead up inspecting its well-formed shape. Tying the leather around his own neck, he nods. "Thank you."

"I am Strong Bull, I thank you white man for the knife."

"My name is Clay Kincaid and that was some shot you made on that steer."

Strong Bull looks to where the women are butchering the cattle. "Thanks to your people we will eat and celebrate tonight Clay Kincaid, you will honor my father and come to his lodge later to eat."

Clay is surprised they invite him to the warrior's lodge. "I will come, and I thank you."

"This is good; I will come for you later."

"Looks like you made a friend." Dedrow falls in beside Clay as they ride back towards the Agency.

"Can't hurt anything."

"Didn't hurt your Pa none over the years."

"Was he really a friend of Quanah?"

Dedrow looks back to the swarm of activity going on around the cook fires and lodges. "Friends, no I wouldn't say that but they had a mutual respect for each other alright."

"Well for some reason old Thunder Hawk sure helped us out here."

"He did that for a fact." The two men dismount lightly and ground tie their geldings. "Let's get us come crackers, I'm hungry."

Lana Barber fixes her eyes on Clay as he passes through the doors slipping gracefully around the squaws and babies lining the aisles. She smiles to herself as he pushes his Stetson hat back letting several locks of black curly hair fall from under it. She is intrigued, bar none he is the most handsome man she has ever seen, she cannot take her eyes from him. Besides being handsome, he has the strong ruggedness that marks him as a leader of men. As she watches, he moves quietly along the busy aisles towards where the cracker-barrel sits beside a large slab of cheese. She cannot remove her eyes; he fascinates her, making her skin tingle, and her heart pound faster.

"May I help you Sir?" The soft friendly voice along with the bright blue eyes of the girl startle him for a second as she approaches the round barrel.

"Agh, yes Ma'am, agh." He is at a loss for words even forgetting why he walked back to the cracker-barrel and cheese counter.

"We need some crackers and a little cheese Miss." Dedrow pushes the stammering Clay aside. "I'm Bandy Dedrow and my tongue-tied young friend here is Clay Kincaid."

"Well." She smiles making her eyes appear a darker blue. "It's nice to meet you gentlemen. I'm Lana Barber. I believe we met once or twice before."

"Yes Ma'am, we saw you riding with Captain Rains a few days back."

Lana looks over at Clay openly. "I remember both of you from both days."

Clay takes the wrapped up crackers and cheese from her slender hand. Accidentally grazing her hand with his own, he felt the softness of her skin. Embarrassed even more, he fumbles with his money until Dedrow takes it from his hand and pays Lana.

Clay turns bright red making his suntanned face seem even darker as he listens to Dedrow talk easily with the girl. "Are you coming to the barbeque this evening Miss Barber?"

"Oh yes, I've been told how good the beef will be and I wouldn't miss it." Lana does not see Miles shaking his head from where he is standing. "And the army will have a band there too."

"Do you like to dance Ma'am?"

"Love to." She smiles sweetly. "My brother doesn't approve though."

Dedrow smiles, "Well anything in moderation couldn't hurt."

"According to my brother, dancing is temptation and any temptation is a sin if one allows it."

"Yes Ma'am, well we'll see you at the dance later." Dedrow slaps Clay with his hat.

"Good day Miss Barber." Clay tips his hat.

"Mister Kincaid, I hope to see you at the dance." Lana drops her eyes coyly. "Maybe we could have a dance."

"Yes Ma'am." Clay smiles, "Just call me Clay, my father is the only Mister Kincaid I know."

"Okay Clay, tonight then."

John Miles shakes his head in amusement as the two men exit the store. "I thought you weren't about to eat the beef tonight."

"Isn't he something Mister Miles?"

"Who, the young one or the older one?" Miles baits her.

Staring towards the front door wistfully, she inhales deeply. "Don't be silly, you know perfectly well who I mean."

"What about Captain Rains, I believe you told him you'd go to the dance with him."

"The Captain is nice too and I will be going with him tonight." She sighs deeply and smiles as she walks away then whispers under her breath. "But he isn't as pretty."

"But Clay Kincaid is nicer?" Miles calls out thinking he heard her say something.

"Umh huh, he is very nice."

Miles shakes his head then taps the counter loudly getting her attention. "Be careful Lana, this is the west something like this can cause a shooting real easy."

Smiling over at him, she flips her blond hair sideways and walks away. Miles worries, he knows she is just an innocent young girl but Rains and now this young Kincaid has an interest in her. Miles heard what Marshal Vetter said about Clay Kincaid being a gunfighter.

"Mister Miles is right Miss Barber." Marshal Vetter stands behind a counter listening to the conversation. "Be careful you don't stir up a hornet's nest."

"Whatever do you mean Marshal?" Land asks innocently. "They're both so nice."

"Yes Ma'am, Captain Rains is an old time southern gentleman who was raised settling his disagreements by duels. Your young Mister Kincaid last month killed one of the most dangerous gunmen in Texas."

"I don't believe it." Lana is in shock. "He couldn't have murdered anyone; he's so nice and polite."

"Believe it Miss Barber." Vetter shakes his head. "But, I said killed not murdered."

"What's the difference Marshal?"

"Well Miss, for one thing you don't hang for killing a man in a fair gunfight." Vetter grins over at the shocked girl. "But now, if you murder someone you possibly could get your neck stretched and I'm sure you wouldn't want that to happen to our young Mister Kincaid."

Will Guthrie pulls his best suit coat on and studies himself in the mirror. He intends to talk with Rains today and set a price on his mules but the coat is for the barbeque and council that will come later. He hates dressing up but he wants to look his best when he appears at the Agency. Both Munday and Moon gave him a report on what happened at the post saloon two days ago. Both stories varied slightly, now he is looking forward to meeting the Kincaids. Alder Guthrie appears in the doorway wearing her new green dress with matching shawl and bonnet.

"My my, you look handsome Mister Guthrie." She smiles, "I haven't seen you in a suit in years."

"No, you haven't." He is perplexed as he buttons the suit coat. "Am I getting fat?"

Taking his neck, she pulls him down to her and kisses him. "No husband, you're certainly not."

"The coat feels tighter than it did the last time I wore it."

"Now how would you remember how tight it was back then?" She pushes him towards the door. "Let's go, the boys are outside waiting."

"I remember alright." Will smiles, "I remember something else woman, I've never seen you looking so beautiful."

Munday, Moon, Killian, and Jumper sit their horses alongside the wagon as Will helps Alder onto the seat. Knowing it is a long dusty ten miles into the agency, Alder wishes she were horseback instead of riding on the bouncing wagon but in a dress that would not be practical.

Will looks sideways at the mounted riders. "I ain't telling you boys but one time; keep them shooters holstered and your mouths buttoned up."

"That could be hard to do Pa." Munday grins sarcastically.

"No it won't, I'll lick anyone of you myself that starts a ruckus of any kind, for any reason."

"Yes sir." Munday pulls at his reins, embarrassed.

"Giddup." Will slaps the lines gently against the backs of the matching grey mules. "We're going in as good neighbors and to sell mules, nothing more."

Frank Kincaid stares in disbelief around the Agency grounds. Where did all the wagons, saddle horses, and people come from? Looking over at Emily, he questions. "I hope we brought in enough beef to feed this bunch, I didn't know there were this many people in all the territory."

"Quit your fretting husband, we did." Emily smiles, "With the loaves of bread, potatoes, corn, and all the pies and cakes they'll be plenty for all."

"I've always been told by the old buffalo hunters that Injuns could eat their way through a whole buffalo in one night."

"Yes my love and those same hunters told me more than once that it was broad daylight when it was pitch-black outside."

"They did?" Frank smiles, "How about that."

"They would swear with a straight face that we were having some kind of eclipse or something." Emily laughs. "They were the worst lying bunch of no goods that you ever let hang around the Running K."

"They were the ones that explored this country for the rest of us." Frank grows serious. "We owe them."

"Well maybe so but not anymore." She frowns at him. "We fed them for years and some are still hanging around freeloading at the stable back in Jacksboro."

"Ugh huh, well we best get busy."

"Mister Kincaid, Misses Kincaid." Miles comes up behind Frank and doffs his derby hat, turning to the couple following closely behind him. "May I present Mister and Misses Will Guthrie from Hays City and our new neighbors and ranchers here at Fort Reno."

Frank looks at Will Guthrie with a mild curiosity then removes his own Stetson before extending his hand. "It's my pleasure to meet you folks."

"I have heard you have a beautiful herd of horses Mister Kincaid." Alder smiles and bows slightly.

"Thank you Ma'am." Frank smiles down at Alder. "We're proud of them."

Will studies Frank closely then decides to say nothing of what the boys told him. Kincaid seems unconcerned so there is no reason to question him and maybe stir up any kind of trouble. Besides, by all accounts the man only asked if Miles knew the name Guthrie.

Frank nods again and takes Emily by the arm. "It was very nice meeting you folks maybe we can talk later at the barbeque but right now I've got guests to see to."

The sun is going down and the huge bonfires are belching smoke and cinders into the evening sky when the iron dinner bell sounds its call for the barbeque and eating to begin. Lines form as everyone carries plates or pots of every size towards the racks of beef that turn slowly over the spits.

Clay watches as Rains walks arm in arm with Lana towards the nearest table laughing as he looks down at her. Something from deep within stabs at him as he watches her walking with the Captain. She looks so content with him. Smiling and laughing she looks so happy, so vibrant and with her long blonde hair and slender form, she is so beautiful. Sensing someone at his shoulder, he turns to find Strong Bull beside him staring at the girl himself.

"She is indeed very beautiful Clay Kincaid." The young warrior smiles, "You look at her as the Cavalry Captain does."

Clay agrees. "Yes, she is beautiful."

"Two warriors and one beautiful woman." Strong Bull clicks his tongue. "My people have a saying about such things."

"They do?"

"My people say when two men want same woman they become blind and soon there is only one man and one woman."

Clay looks over at the serious warrior. "What happened to the other man?"

"My people did not say." Strong Bull shrugs.

Looking at Lana as she laughs, Clay nods. "Sounds like a good idea to me."

"Come, we go to my father's lodge to eat."

"What is your father's name?"

"He is Charging Bull, Chief of the Cheyenne."

"I have heard of this great Chief, Thunder Hawk of the Comanche spoke of him." Clay takes a last look at Lana then follows Strong Bull.

Strong Bull introduces Clay to his family and they treat him with respect as they seat him in the place of honor at the Chief's left side. He actually enjoys himself as they tell many stories of fights and mythical beings. The food the women bring in is abundant. Strong Bull translates the words of his father and the other gathered warriors as each one tells their story.

Removed to Oklahoma Territory, the Cheyenne were unhappy in their confinement to the reservation but the whites were too strong and too numerous. It was futile to resist further in their faraway homelands. They know the Sioux and the Northern Cheyenne still fight the cavalry to the north. Charging Bull is a wise and strong leader who wants to save his people from starvation and extermination so he had to succumb to the will of the whites.

A trumpet breaks the silence outside signaling the start of the music and dancing. Clay and Strong Bull excuse themselves and leave the lodge walking to where a crowd is watching the Indian dancers perform their tribal dances. Finally, the Fort Reno Band starts playing and a few whites take to the board dance floor that was prepared for the dance. Emily laughs as several soldiers act the part of the women as the soldiers dance. Spending most of her time alone on the ranch, she is having the time of her life tonight.

Lana's blue eyes center on Clay as he walks from the Cheyenne Village with a young warrior making their way towards the dance floor. She is mesmerized and she cannot help but stare. She never saw a young man with his natural charm and eye-catching looks. He walks with the proud grace and carriage of a southern gentleman, yet at the same time, he has an unspoken hardness that leaps forward from his eye when they center on you. The huge forty-five pistol that hangs from his low-slung holster takes her attention as she remembers Marshal Vetter's words about him being a gunfighter. It intrigues her; she cannot take her eyes from him.

"Would you like to dance?" Rains looks down at her.

"What?" Her attention is brought back to him.

"Dance young lady, I fear you haven't heard a word I've said." Rains looks over to where her attention was and frowns.

"Yes, of course." Lana feels her face turn red as her thoughts are discovered. "I would love to dance Captain."

Clay watches as the couple take the floor among the other dancers. He has to admit Rains is an excellent dancer gliding across the floor holding Lana lightly in his arms. Dedrow steps up beside Clay and Strong Bull and watches the dancers.

"You eat your fill?" Clay glances over at Dedrow.

"You bet that beef we snagged out of the brush has me stuffed like a tick on a dog's back." Dedrow pats his stomach and nods at Frank and Emily as they dance past. "Your folks are good dancers."

"Yes they are." Clay smiles; he never learned to dance. Now seeing Lana out on the floor so gracefully he wishes he had. Perhaps he would have his mother teach him.

Dedrow can hear the tone of Clay's voice. "What are we doing here?"

"You got any better ideas?"

Clay notices as a slender Indian woman looking coyly at Strong Bull. Finally the warrior smiles at Clay and follows the woman away from the white dancers and over to where the Indian dancing is going strong.

"Anything beats standing here and watching others have fun."

"Like what?"

"I hear the saloon at the Fort just brought in a few women to work." Dedrow follows Clay's eyes as the dancers swing around the floor. "What say we ride over there and have us a look-see."

Clay looks over to where Lana and Rains stops dancing. They are standing over a punch bowl laughing, absorbed only with each other. "Let's ride."

Turning, the two walk away, weaving their way through the crowd that stands watching the dancers. Breaking free from the throng of people, they finally are able to make their way towards the corral where their horses are tied. Clay never turned or looked back; he never saw the blue eyes of the girl following him sadly away from the agency.

CHAPTER 11

RANCHING THE CANADIAN

The old piano was beating out a lively tune as Clay and Dedrow push their way through the saloon doors. Soldiers, hunters, and a few cowboys line the wooden bar or sit around the poker tables. True to his word, Dedrow points out the heavy powdered women that laugh as they serve the raucous loud soldiers. Dedrow was a soldier during the big war between the States. He knows well the hard, lonely life of a post soldier.

"Watch yourself in here youngster." The rider whispers lightly. "These boys can play awfully rough, ain't quite like Trinity Country."

"I'm in the mood to play a little rough myself." Clay shoulders his way through the crowded room towards the end of the bar.

Pulling out chairs the two sit down after getting their drinks they study the smoke-filled room. "Roll me a smoke Bandy."

"Why, you don't smoke last time I looked."

"Roll me one and look again."

Dedrow shrugs as Clay takes a long pull on his warm beer. "Better take it easy on that stuff too, it'll get to you if you ain't used to it."

"If I wanted babying I would have brought Ma along with me."

"Boy, there's nine women in here that I count." Dedrow looks about the room. "Grab one and dance and forget about that yellow haired Agency girl, she's pure dynamite and I believe the lady is already taken."

"For tonight she is." Clay seems to smile and frown all at once. "There's always tomorrow."

"My old Pappy used to tell us boys to ride an ugly horse, that way no horse thieves would try to steal it away from you." Dedrow quips.

"What's that supposed to mean?"

"It means my young friend; marry an ugly woman, that way you don't have to worry about anybody stealing her." Dedrow laughs. "Shucks boy, my third wife Matilda was so ugly I couldn't even pay somebody to take her."

"Bandy, I swear I ain't never seen you ride an ugly horse in my life."

"True enough and I ain't planning on getting married to an ugly woman either." The foreman laughs out loud then hollers at a young bar woman passing by to bring them another beer. "But it is good advice."

"Funny Mister Dedrow, very funny."

"Shucks Clay my boy, look at her, she's downright pretty herself." Dedrow nods at the younger woman.

Returning, the girl places two full mugs on the table then picks up Dedrow's money and smiles down at the men. "Thank you, gentlemen."

"What's your name Miss?'

"Connie." The girl answers Dedrow but never removes her eyes from Clay. "I just arrived here today for the big doings across the river."

"Where did Thompson get ya'll from?"

"Hays City by way of St Louis." She smiles at Clay. "What's your name honey?"

"Clay Kincaid."

Dedrow laughs. "That's him Miss and he needs some special care, he's lost his best girl."

"Kincaid!" She looks sharply across the room where four men sit playing cards.

Dedrow catches the tone in her voice. "Is something wrong Connie?"

"Watch yourselves; I heard your name mentioned several times by the younger one over there." Connie cut her eyes towards Munday Guthrie. "He's drunk enough to be mean."

Dedrow blinks, they saw the youngster she pointed out at the barbeque eating just awhile earlier in the evening. Now here he is with three others swilling down warm beer as if it was creek water.

"Thank you Ma'am." Clay smiles up at her. "I'm fixing to get that way myself."

"How'd you lose a girl in a forsaken country like this?" Connie laughs. "There's not any women out here."

"Oh there's one." Dedrow laughs. "Yes Ma'am, there's certainly one."

"Well Clay Kincaid." The saloon woman takes his chin in her hand. "Any woman that would dump a good-looking young man like you is bound to be crazy."

"Hey girl, we need some drinks over here." A big soldier yells at her. "Cut them babies loose and come over here with real men."

Dedrow grabs Clay by the arm as the younger man starts to rise. "Let it go, you heard your Pa, he'll skin us alive if we start anything tonight."

"He ain't here."

"This is army ground boy; they don't cotton much to civilians, especially southern gentlemen like us." Dedrow holds his arm. "You start something with this bunch and they'll stomp us into next week."

"So?"

"So, just have your drink and keep your eyes on the table."

A loud boisterous yell went up in the saloon coming from a table where several soldiers sit drinking. Turning, Munday looks across the room at the noisemakers and grins as he recognizes Dedrow. Motioning to Killian across the table, he points at the table where Dedrow and Clay sit.

"Don't start trouble Munday, you heard your Pa." Killian grabs Munday by the sleeve. "I don't care if they are the Kincaids."

"I ain't starting nothing." Heavy with drink Munday stands shakily and walks across to where the big soldier making all the noise is sitting.

"What's he up to?" Little Bit is curious as he watches the young Guthrie speak with the soldier.

Killian shakes his head. "Trouble, I figure, I believe that's the Kincaid riders sitting over there."

Munday barely wobbles back to his seat when the big soldier stands up and makes his way to where Clay and Dedrow are sitting. Connie just finished sitting two more mugs of beer on the table when the drunken soldier grabs her from behind and sits her bodily behind him.

"I told you girl, don't waste your time on these babies." The soldier picks Clay along with his chair from the floor and flings him into the wall as if he was a feather.

Slapping his knee, Munday laughs aloud then takes a long swill of beer to chase his whiskey. "That'll teach them boys to question folks about us again."

Killian shakes his head. "Your Pa's gonna beat you half to death for this."

"For what?" Munday snorts, "I ain't done nothing."

The fourth rider sitting at the table frowns at Munday then stands up. "You boys are on your own, I like my job."

"Where you going Jace?" Munday paws at the man's sleeve.

"Home."

"Oh let him go." Little Bit slurs his words as he watches the big soldier start after the littler man who is trying get untangled from the chair and wall.

Rolling to his feet Clay comes up swinging as the big soldier bull rushes into him crushing him back against the wall. Suddenly the heavy body of the soldier seems to sag against Clay as the forty-five slams into the soldier's head. Wheeling Dedrow turns the cocked pistol on the drunken soldiers that started to rise from their seats.

"You boys just set back down and finish your drinks, it's all over."

"That it is." Oney Thompson comes from the bar with his familiar scattergun cocked and ready.

"We ain't letting him get by with that." Another well-intoxicated soldier starts forward. "He can't pistol-whip one of our'n and get away with it."

Thompson waves the shotgun and points it at the door. "I'm fixing to blow a hole all the way to the front door if you boys don't make a path."

Slowly grumbling their defiance, the other soldiers finally make a wide berth to the front doors. Motioning with the scattergun towards the front Thompson follows Clay and Dedrow out the door.

"You boys have enemies, best watch your backs." Oney spoke as they reach the porch, then turns back inside.

"Thanks Thompson." Dedrow nods at the man's back. "We owe you one."

The saloon owner hesitates. "No, you don't owe me anything."

"Got any more ideas Bandy?" Clay steps near his horse and pulls the cinch tight. "I was just warming up in there."

"Yea, it looked like you had that big ox under control alright."

Clay grins and feels his back. "Well, I was working on it."

"Did you see what happened back there boy?" Dedrow looks back at the closed saloon doors. "Those boys from Guthries done sic that soldier on us."

Shaking his head slowly Munday watches as they help the soldier back to his seat. "Well that was a wasted ten dollars. My Pa always said if you want something done right, do it yourself."

"You paid ten dollars to have that soldier jump on the Kincaid kid?" Killian shakes his head. "Your Pa's gonna kill you."

"Now how is he gonna find out?" Munday looks across at the foreman. "You gonna tell him?"

"No I ain't gonna tell him." Killian stands up disgusted. "I swear boy you're a piece of work, let's go home."

"Home? Shucks that's a long ride." Little Bit shakes his head. "Let's just pull us up a spot over at the stables."

Munday looks over to where Connie is removing empty glasses from a vacated table and smiles. "I reckon I'll be staying awhile longer."

Standing up, Killian finishes off his beer then looks down at the younger Guthrie. "No you ain't boy; we're heading home before your Pa skins me alive. There's not gonna be any more trouble tonight, now is it gonna be the easy way or the rough way."

Munday doubles up his fist but he is just sober enough to know he is too drunk to fight the rough foreman tonight. "One of these days Mister Tom Killian, I'll be running the Guthrie Ranches."

"Yea, you probably will Munday boy." Killian motions towards the door. "When that day comes, I'll let you make your own decisions and probably get your head blown off."

Outside it takes Munday three attempts before his foot finds the stirrup, then he pulls himself drunkenly into the saddle almost falling off the other side. The coal oil lamps from the saloon porch send their eerie shadows out into the flat ground in front of the porch as the three men turn. Blinking in shock all three pull their horses up and stop in surprise as Clay and Dedrow materialize out of the shadows right in front of them. Killian notices the revolver in Dedrow's hand and the slight grin on the tall rider's face.

"You other boys just sit tight." The sound of the revolver cocking sounds out across the few feet that separates them. "These two boys need to have a few words."

"What's the problem mister?" Killian kneed his gelding in front of the others. "There's no reason to pull a gun on us."

"I told you mister to stay put." The voice grew cold and hard. "I won't be a telling you again."

Killian pulls in and looks across at Dedrow. "And I asked you what the problem was?"

"Your young friend there put that soldier on us back in the saloon." Dedrow points the pistol at Munday. "You denying that?"

"Nope, he did that for a fact but he's too drunk tonight to defend himself." Killian looks back at the grinning Munday then across at Dedrow. "We'll let them settle this some other time."

"Nope, right here and right now." Clay slowly dismounts and drops his reins. "He was sober enough to sic that soldier on me. Get down!"

Grinning Munday slid clumsily from his horse falling backwards on the ground then unsteadily regains his feet. "Where'd you go?"

"Turn around Guthrie, I'm back here."

Turning Munday squints at the blurry figure before him then grins. "You looked kinda funny flying through the air back there."

The punch sounded like a pistol crack as Clay lands a hard right to Munday's unprotected jaw knocking him backwards into the dirt. Stepping forward quickly he catches the prone youth with two more quick punches before he can rise then kicks him hard in the ribs. Killian starts forward to help the drunken Munday but a warning from Dedrow freezes him in place. Standing over Munday as he tries his best to get to his feet Clay waits ready to land another blow when the sound of horses and a harsh voice call out.

"That'll be enough, what's going on here?" Captain Rains looks down from the buggy. He saw Clay knock the man backwards into the dirt but did not know the reason for the fight.

"Nothing Captain just a friendly little disagreement, nothing more." Dedrow holsters his pistol. "We were just fixing to ride out."

Rains nods, "This is government property you're on; I'll have no fighting on this post, now break it up and head for home."

"Yes sir Captain, we're going." Dedrow motions towards Clay. "Mount up, let's go."

"From now on, if you boys want to fight stay on the north side of the Canadian or I'll take it personal." Rains watches as Killian helps the bleeding Munday to his horse. "I've got business with both your Fathers. So let's keep the peace, alright?"

"Yes sir Captain, we were just leaving." Dedrow repeats himself as he turns his horse towards the river with Killian and the others following.

Clay steps up on his horse and looks across at the buggy where Lana is sitting next to Rains. Tipping his hat to the frowning girl, he kicks his gelding and rides away from the fort.

"Ruffians." Lana speaks softly to Rains, then smiles slightly.

"That they are my dear." Rains smiles to himself smugly. "Cowboys are just delinquent children, mostly unsavory characters to say the least but very dangerous."

Almost across the Canadian, Munday falls out of his saddle as he tries to reach down for some water to wash his face. Feeling himself pulled from the shallow water, he looks up as he grabs the extended hand.

"Well Mister Kincaid, I reckon I deserve this one, you definitely got the best end of it but it's far from over." Munday wipes his face, grinning as Clay helps him from the water. "We'll have this conversation again sometime when I'm sober."

Clay nods. "Whenever you say, it'll be my pleasure."

"Maybe it will and then again maybe it won't." The water soaks Munday as he lies on the sandy bank where Clay deposited him and looks up at the stars. "Anyway, I'm a thanking you for pulling me from the river and not letting me drown."

Two days later after the barbeque, Captain Rains sits on a small knoll and looks over the geldings that mill around the small pasture. "Well Mister Kincaid, there's not a blemish on anyone of them."

"If there were, they wouldn't be here in this herd." Frank looks at his horses. "What's the army paying?"

"Sixty a head for this bunch." Rains figures mentally in his head. "I count fifty two head here that the army will buy."

"That's correct, some are broke and some ain't never been touched." Frank looks over his pride and joy. "They're yours."

Motioning for the squad of mounted cavalry, he brought with him, to drive the horses to the fort, Rains smiles. "Come in when you're ready and the money will be waiting."

"We'll be there tomorrow."

Rains watches as his men start the herd towards the fort. "Mister Kincaid, there's one other thing."

Frank knows what is coming; Dedrow already filled him in on the trouble at the fort. "Come in alone tomorrow, I would appreciate it if you would keep your foreman Mister Dedrow and your boy away from the fort; give them time to cool off some."

"And the Guthrie boy?" Frank looks at Rains. "I understand he started the trouble at the saloon."

"I'm riding out to see Mister Guthrie tomorrow." Rains slaps at a horsefly. "I'll demand the same of him."

"Is that an order Captain?" Frank questions the officer. "The boys are pretty much used to going wherever they want."

"Yes sir, if you want to sell horses to me it is." Rains knees his gelding and smiles to himself as he rides off. "Good day sir."

Frank watches as the small herd disappears upriver then motions for his riders to follow him. Today is a good day; he sold more horses this morning than he had in months. He just cannot understand Rains taking a small petty fight so serious. "Sell horses to me?" Frank repeats Rains words. "Not sell horses to the army."

Dedrow rides up beside Frank and reins in. "Well, I reckon we're out of work until we grow off some more of the young stuff."

"No, we've got at least a hundred more two year olds back on the Trinity River Bottoms in Texas." Frank looks over at Dedrow. "You're gonna take Clay and Lebo and go after them."

"That'll leave you mighty shorthanded here until we get back."

"It'll also keep Clay and the Guthrie boy apart." Frank shrugs. "I want more horses here for the cavalry before Custer arrives at Fort Supply later this fall. Besides there won't be any work to do now, with no horses."

"Rains told you something didn't he?"

"Yep, told me to keep you boys out of Fort Reno."

Dedrow frowns as he throws his leg over the swells of his saddle. "For how long?"

"Indefinitely I reckon." Frank shrugs. "He didn't say."

"And the Guthrie boy?"

Frank nods. "Same order I reckon, funny thing the army doesn't like fighting."

"It ain't got a thing to do with the fight those boys had." Dedrow shrugs. "Not a thing."

"What are you saying Bandy?"

"It's simple." Dedrow rolls himself a smoke then looks through the smoke at the man. "It's over that blond headed agency woman, I'll guarantee it."

"What's Miss Barber got to do with the fight?"

"Nothing, she hasn't done one thing herself." Dedrow pushes his Stetson back. "Fact is the girl showed a little interest in Clay is all, flirting and flashing her pretty blue eyes."

"And?"

"I figure this is the good Captains way of getting him out of the picture."

Frank nods thoughtfully. "Could be you're right, I seen her looking at him myself."

"Now I ain't saying nothing against Miss Barber, she's a lady and hasn't done a thing other than turn her eyes at Clay and be friendly. It's just the

Captain's way of clearing the field for a while you might say."

"You may be right." Frank kicks his gelding. "But, it sure won't hurt to keep those two young roosters apart until they've cooled down.

"You still sending us to Richardson?"

"Let me think on it some."

"Jorge could go; you need me and Clay here."

"For what?" Frank grins. "You're both shirkers, sure can't get no work out of either one of you."

Dedrow grows serious. "This is still dangerous country Frank; I've heard some rumors about that horse thief we killed back on the Red."

"You mean Fritch?"

"Yep, and if his partner Galt takes it in his head he may try to pay us another visit." Dedrow flipped his burned down stub. "I hear he's been laid up nursing a gunshot wound. I also hear he's got a pretty rough bunch riding with him and he considers this his private running range."

"You saying he was part of the bunch with Fritch that raided us on the Red." Frank rubs his jaw. "I figured Fritch was running that show."

"That's what I heard, and I figure he'll round up more men and come looking to even the score on account of Fritch."

"Were they that close?"

"Can't say, they rode together for years but I remember Galt had a pretty big ego and he has that reputation to protect." Dedrow straightens in his saddle and follows Frank. "If people think he's getting soft they might turn on him right quick. And there's still our horses he wants."

"You may be right, I'll send Jorge back to the Running K and he can hire a few hands to help push the rest of the young stuff back here."

"Now that's a load off my mind." Dedrow grins.

"It may be a load off your mind Bandy but it's sure gonna be a load on your back for a few weeks."

"What's that supposed to mean?"

"Well, with a house to finish, barns, and corrals to build, not to mention fences and a well to dig I figure you two are gonna be mighty busy." Frank laughs as he kicks his horse and rides away from the complaining foreman.

Captain Rains walks around the dusty corral watching as the wranglers sort out the mixed herd of mules ready to break, mares nursing colts, and a few saddle horses. He is here to buy pack animals for the Cavalry and he wants only top quality mules. Pointing at each animal he wants to inspect closer, he watches as the heavy gates open and close behind the mules. They send the mules down a long chute and hold them enclosed where they cannot jump or kick a man's head off as they inspect them.

Several times Munday passes by where Rains stands but each man avoids eye contact with the other. Neither forgot the fight that took place at the fort but not a word is spoken.

All morning Will Guthrie pushes and prods the mules as Rains picks the ones he wants and they herd them into a larger corral. Blacks, grays, reds, zebra legged every description of mule mills about the sandy corral ducking quickly whenever they move too close to the men sitting atop the log rails. The off corral already holds several heavy mules for pulling a wagon, then lighter ones for packing.

"I'd rather have all horse mules Mister Guthrie but we may have to let a few of the bigger molly mules through to fit my quota." Rains stands on a lower rail looking over the herd.

"There's seventy-five head in the lot now Captain."

"I'll take them all." Rains steps down and slaps his leg with a riding crop. "On one condition."

"And that being?" Will looks over at the Captain waiting for his terms.

"I understand that young hand of yours Grey Moon is the best horse breaker in Kansas."

Will nods, "I believe he is but I'm prejudiced."

"I want that little palomino mare you've got standing over there and that bay horse mule there gentle broke with a good handle on them." Rains points out the animals. "I'll pay for the horse and mule but the breaking will be free."

"Well, I figure I know why you are wanting the mare but who's the mule for?"

"You're right on the palomino mare Sir; she'll make Miss Barber a beautiful wedding present." Rains knows the rancher figures the palomino is for Lana Barber. "The mule is for General George Crook, an old friend of our family and the man that sponsored me for West Point."

"Well, congratulations Captain, when is the big day?"

"Well now, that I can't rightly say, I haven't asked the lady yet."

Will is curious. "A General riding a long eared mule?"

"Believe it or not the General prefers a mule over a horse, he always has."

"Really and why is that?"

"Yep, says they're a lot more dependable, surefooted and hardier on a long trail."

"I expect some people would argue that, reckon it depends on what side of the fence you're on." Will replies, "I think we can come to some kind of understanding Captain but what are you offering for the mules?"

"Forty dollars a head."

"Fifty."

"Forty-five and you'll gentle break the two I mentioned, at no charge."

"Done." Will looks over at the palomino mare. "She'll cost you an even one hundred dollars."

"That's a lot of money."

"Yes sir it is but that's a lot of horse."

"I agree Mister Guthrie." Rains smiles, "That powder face with the long mane and tail sure makes her classy alright."

"Her and Miss Barber will be something to behold going through the fort."

"It's a deal." Rains looks over at the chuck wagon then around at the start of the new buildings under construction. "Soon, you'll have a nice ranch here Mister Guthrie."

"For a few years anyway." Will adds, "Until our lease runs out."

"Yes sir today was a good day; we'll do more business when Custer gets here with the Seventh." Rains studies the little mare and smiles. "A real good day."

Ewen Galt sits huddled, wrapped up in a wool blanket next to a small fire. Several others circle the fire drinking coffee and smoking. Galt moves stiffly as he tries to reposition himself against a rock. He took two bullets in the botched horse-stealing raid back on the Red River; both are painful but not fatal.

The sound of a slow walking horse materializes out of the dark then the sound of squeaking leather as a man dismounts. "How's the side Ewen?"

The outlaw leader turns his head slightly and nods at the newcomer. "It's mending Pine, long as it doesn't break open again."

"Yea, another inch over and you'd be lying back there with poor old Fritch."

"I believe it."

"I seen him when he got it, Jack never knew what hit him." The lean rider reaches for the steaming coffeepot. "Bad luck all around."

"Water under the bridge now, he's gone under."

"Yea, it's a shame, we rode many a trail together." The rider called Pine sips at the hot coffee. "Many a mile."

"The luck of the draw, in our business you take your chances, you know that." Galt changes the subject. "What did you find out?"

Pine looks at his coffee mug then around at the other men. "Anybody got a smoke?"

"Here." He tosses a sack of makings across the fire.

Quickly rolling a quirley, he blows smoke into the air and returns the sack of Bull. "You wouldn't believe the place, the new Fort is almost finished and there's two ranchers moved in on the grass up and down the river."

"Did you get any names?"

"Will Guthrie you already know, the other one they call Kincaid, from Texas." Pine blows smoke. "Kincaid's bunch is the ones who shot us up so bad back on the Red."

Galt shakes his head. "Yea, I remember Fritch saying the name. Funny it was Guthrie he was worried about and the Kincaid bunch got him."

"The new Fort is bringing in more people."

"Vetter still hanging around?"

"He is, still as crusty as ever." Pine nods. "He stays mostly over around the agency; the Fort is controlled by the Yankee Cavalry unless some civilian gets out of hand.

"He see you?"

Pine laughs lightly. "I'm here in one piece ain't I?"

"Soon as I heal, we're going in after those horses like we planned." Galt pokes at the fire absently. "We might just take Guthrie's stock too."

"The army has been buying horses and mules from them ranchers." Pine adds, "Just might be bad business to rustle those herds."

"You turning yellow on me Pine?"

"Not many men would dare call me yeller Ewen." Pine looks across the blaze at Galt. "No it ain't that, perhaps I'm just a little smarter in my old age. We sure don't need the Cavalry hot on our heels."

"Then why don't you mount up and ride out." Galt cusses then turns to the fire. "You're starting to sound like Fritch."

"I'll study on it for a spell Mister Galt." Pine tosses his burned-out stub into the fire. "Don't dig your spurs into me or ride me to hard Ewen, I ain't Fritch."

"I owe it to Jack."

Pine snickers. "Bull, you don't give a dang about Fritch getting himself wasted, you just want revenge for them Kincaids beating you is all and you know it."

Galt smiles wickedly. "For once you're right; we can't afford feelings in this business."

"How long you figure it'll be until you can ride?"

"Two weeks." Galt feels the bandage against his side. "Rest up a day then take Paddy and Moss and ride back to the fort."

"For what, I done told you all I know?" Pine grins. "Except one thing."

"What's that?"

"Oney Thompson brought in some women for his new saloon." Pine grins. "A bunch of them."

Galt frowns. "Right now until this job is finished we'll stay out of saloons."

"You're the Boss."

"Lie around the Fort and get the lay out." Galt rolls himself a smoke. "When you've got the deadwood on the place send Moss back here and we'll come on."

"I'll do it." Pine pours himself some coffee. "You know that nosey Marshal will be a problem."

"Stay out of his sights."

"I'll do my best." Pine nods. "Vetter is sneaky and slippery as a greased pig."

"I'm hitting both ranchers." Galt builds himself a quirley and smiles. "I ain't scared of Mister Guthrie, like Jack Fritch was."

Pine shakes his head. "I don't figure Jack was scared of Guthrie, I just figure he didn't want the man trailing him all over creation."

"I want them animals Pine, one good job and I'm retiring out west." Galt feels his side. "It's getting overcrowded around these parts."

"If we do get them Ewen, what then?"

Galt sucks in his breath when he tries to sit up. "North, we'll take them north into Missouri or maybe Ohio and sell them."

"Sounds good, I'll ride out at sun up."

Chapter 12

The Preacher

Grey Moon stands off to the side of the agency porch inspecting a set of work harness as Pine Johnson and two others ride in and get down from their dusty horses. His black eyes take in the trail dust and wore out horses as the three men disappear inside the building. Looking towards the end of the porch where Munday is talking with Lana Barber, he walks over to where they are standing.

"Miss Barber."

Smiling she nods. "Mister Moon, it's good to see you."

"Yes Ma'am, it's good to see you too." Moon nods. "Could you find out how much Agent Miles wants for the harness?"

"I will." The girl walks away her wide skirts whipping around her legs.

"Thanks Moon, we were just getting acquainted." Munday is perplexed.

"You see them riders that just rode in?" Moon wants to get Munday alone.

"I did but I had more important things on my mind than to look at cowhands." Munday grins. "What about them?'

"They are not mere cowboys." Moon glances over his shoulder. "The short one is Pine Johnson, he rides with Galt and Fritch."

"Just Galt, I hear Fritch turned up his toes and is growing wild flowers." Munday looks off across the flat ground of the agency. "Leastways that's the talk."

"Johnson is a bad one." Moon catches the figure of Lana returning. "Hold it for now."

"Twenty-five dollars for the set." Lana smiles brightly, her snow-white teeth shining in the sun.

"Fair enough, we'll take them." Moon looks over at Munday. "Pay the lady."

"Pa wants an extra pair of collars size twenty." Munday starts to count out the money when Lana stops him.

"I'm sorry Mister Guthrie but you'll have to pay Mister Miles inside."

Moon watches the irritated young man disappear inside the store then turns his eyes on Lana. "You enjoying yourself out here Miss Barber?"

"I am enjoying myself immensely." The blonde hair bounces as she turns her head and looks about the Agency. "At first, I didn't think I would but now I love it."

"It is a beautiful country down here in the Nations." Moon looks around at the people milling about the Agency. "Where are you from Miss Barber?"

"Originally we were in Philadelphia, then St Louis." She smiles. "My brother has a wandering foot since our folks passed."

"You've seen a lot of this country then?"

"I have."

"Will you be staying here?"

"Perhaps, Captain Rains has asked my brother to open a store over near the Fort." Lana looks out across the bottoms. "And he has his Church."

"Won't that interfere with the Agency Store?"

"I don't think so; the soldiers rarely come over to this side of the Canadian to buy anything."

"You've been seeing a lot of the Captain." Moon remembers the night he seen her with Rains after the barbeque. "I've seen you with him several times since you've been here."

"He's a gentleman and I enjoy his company." She smiles sweetly. "The same as I enjoy talking with you and Mister Guthrie."

"And Clay Kincaid?"

Lana nods then blushes slightly, "and Mister Kincaid."

"The Captain might just get jealous," Moon smiles.

"Why don't you call me Lana?"

"No Ma'am, I don't believe that would be appropriate."

"I see." She blushes. "Because you're Indian?"

"Something like that Ma'am."

"No matter, you can if you wish to."

"Thank you Miss Barber."

"Tell me Mister Moon." Her tone was crisper than usual. "You do not approve of Captain Rains?"

Moon looks down at the girl and thought about the Palomino mare he was breaking for Rains, a gift for her. Her hair and the little horse's mane would match closely. He knows Rains is doing anything he can to win her.

"Captain Rains may be a good man but the man himself I do not know Miss Barber." Moon looks away. "It's not for me to judge him."

"I'll make a deal with you Sir." The girl persists. "Tell me and I won't ask again."

Moon looks over at the girl slightly embarrassed. "Why do you want me, a half breed to tell you about the man you're planning to marry?"

"Marry!" Lana laughs aloud. "I think sir, I have given you the wrong impression and now you are the one jumping to conclusions."

"From what I have seen and heard, he is a good man Miss Barber."

"Thank you Mister Moon."

Munday walks back onto the porch and interrupts the talk between Moon and the girl. "We're finished here Moon and free to ride."

Lana watches as the two men ride from her sight then smiles. Moon has her marrying Captain Rains, she knows he is a good pick but there is another of interest to her that he did not mention, Clay Kincaid.

The long table inside the newly built ranch house of the Kincaid Ranch is a hub of activity as all the Running K hands are busily eating breakfast. Frank looks down the table at his men and most trusted friends.

"Jorge, you will ride out today." Frank picks up his old coffee mug. "If he will come, bring back Henry Sloan."

"What do you want that old bandit for?" Dedrow looks down the table.

"Because he's my partner and I want him here." Frank laughs. "Only reason you resent old Henry is he horn swaggled you on that wind broke Claybank Gelding a few years back."

"Horn swaggled my eye, he done cheated me that's what." Dedrow frowns. "Run that horse ten feet and he sounded like a bellows a blowing hot air."

"You bring him Jorge."

"Si Senior, I will bring him." Jorge smiles as he bit into a biscuit. "But I think, Senor Sloan he no come here."

"If he don't oh well but bring back every head we've got left on the Trinity."

"Si Patron."

"Be careful Jorge and return with haste." Frank looks around the table. "Check on Craig and his wife and tell them we'll be in touch."

Frank walks from the house and watches a lone rider riding in from the west from the direction of Fort Reno. He steps down from the porch as the rider, a soldier, wearing the hated blue of the north reins up in front of the ranch house.

Nodding his greetings the soldier can see the cold and unfriendliness emitting from the rancher. "Mister Kincaid?"

"I'm Kincaid."

"I'm Sergeant Harvey Ray." The Sergeant reaches into his horn bag and withdraws two letters. "Captain Rains sent me here with these dispatches Sir."

"And what would that be soldier?"

"I believe sir, it's an invitation to the dance the Colonel is putting on to celebrate the Fourth of July and the completion of the Fort."

"Thank you Sergeant." Frank reaches for the extended dispatch and opens it slowly.

"Will there be a reply Sir?"

Frank read the well-written note slowly then nods. "Tell the Captain, my family including my son will gratefully attend his dance and thank him for me."

"You don't like us much do you Mister Kincaid?" The soldier looks down at the rancher.

"No sir, I don't." Frank looks at the man. "You Yankees have never given us much reason to."

"Well Sir, the war's over now."

Frank studies the soldier. "You're right Sergeant, my apologies, bad manners are inexcusable."

"Yes sir they are and I volunteered for this ride solely to apologize to your son for attacking him without provocation a while back at the Fort."

"You were the Sergeant in the saloon?"

The Sergeant drops his head and grins slightly. "That I was but I think I got the worst of that little set to."

"You also got me banned from the Fort." Clay steps from the house and looks over at the soldier.

"I was drunk, that's no excuse but that's all I have young man."

"Well Sergeant, there's no real harm done."

"The Colonel sent this dispatch to you personally Mister Kincaid." The Sergeant hands over a second dispatch to the younger Kincaid.

Clay opens the letter and read the words to himself. "Seems your Colonel Blalock has overruled Captain Rains and now I'm invited back to the Fort any time I wish."

Frank nods, "Thank you Sergeant for bringing the invitations and we will attend the dance."

"Have the Guthries been invited?"

"They have and I'll be happy to hold your coat." The Sergeant laughs. "I don't like being made a fool of while I'm under the weather. I make enough of a fool of myself without help."

"There won't be any of that." Frank frowns, "Good day Sergeant."

Will Guthrie backs his gelding stretching the young mule out between him and Munday as Little Bit buckles the leather halter securely around the mules head.

"Why do they always try to take off a finger or two every time you start breaking them?" Little Bit dodges the mules snapping teeth.

Will laughs as Little Bit steps back from the mule and hands him the lead rope. "Get the ropes off him and let him up."

"Watch him Boss, he's a fighter."

Little Bit did not lie, releasing the ropes that were holding his head and feet the mule comes up pawing and rearing backwards trying to free himself from whatever monster that is holding his head. The mule charges forward at the man sitting on the horse. The young mule intends to take a bite out of something but only the hard foot of a human kicking his tender nose is all he tastes.

Turning the heavy gelding, Will starts dragging the sulled up mule around the soft ground of the corral making little furrows in the ground.

"He's a tough little nut Boss." Little Bit laughs from the top rail of the corral. "We could plant corn where you're plowing with his feet."

Will keeps his eye on the mule knowing it would only take a split second for the mule's huge teeth to plant themselves in his leg. Finally, seeing the futility of pulling back or fighting, the mule starts to walk after the gelding. First, in slight jumps then he finally gives up completely and starts following the gelding around the corral without setting back.

"Get a saddle on him boys." Will pulls the mule's head tight up against his leg then reaches over and ears the youngster down. Even with the heavy bull hide chaps protecting his legs, he knows if the mule gets a chance to bite he can leave a good bruise on his leg.

"Look out for them long legs." Munday hollers as a hind foot barely grazes him.

Will laughs as Little Bit and Munday work carefully around the young mule making sure to dodge both front and hind feet. "He's a fighter boy, look out for them feet."

"Looks to me like he's half alligator and half snapping turtle." Little Bit takes a hard kick to his leg. "Dang Boss that felt good."

Finally, after the saddle is cinched down with the breast collar and britching in place, Will nudges his snub horse and starts leading the pitching mule again. Munday and Little Bit laugh and holler their encouragement as the mule turns upside down and falls on the ground trying to remove the strange thing on his back. Now most of the fight is out of the wringing wet mule as he follows the horse around the corral no longer fighting the saddle or the rope.

"He's ready boys, who's gonna do the honors?" Will looks over at the corral fence. "Get a sideline on him and whoever feels lucky get a leg over him."

Munday shakes his head. "Where's Moon, he's supposed to be our bronc rider?"

Will looks around then shrugs. "He ain't here but you two are."

"Ug huh." Munday grins. "You cripple me up before the dance and I ain't gonna be happy Pa."

Will laughs as the mule takes a swipe at Munday as he pulls up the off leg so he would not get kicked as he mounts, then swings quickly into the saddle. The extra weight in the saddle sends the mule into one last bucking frenzy as he tries to dislodge the human on his back. Will knows most horses will not buck when snubbed to a lead horse but a mule is different, hardheaded most mules will try their best to fight until they finally give it up and settle down. On two occasions, he was leading the mule when it jumped clear over him and the snub horse.

Munday stays with the mule clinging to him tighter than a tick until he finally gives up and quits bucking. Relaxing a little, Munday smiles over at Will. "He's gonna make a dandy."

"You ready for him boy?"

"Cut us loose and run for your life old man." Munday laughs as Will flips the lead rope across the mule's neck.

"You're on your own, hang on to him."

The young mule follows the horse a few steps as Will moves out of the way then stops and sulls again. Munday pulls down his hat and waits expecting explosion. The animal is tired having already put up a good battle but he is young, full of vinegar and stout. Expecting the mule to buck Munday is taken by surprise when he takes off in a dead run around the corral.

"Open the gate and turn him out." Munday has the mule's head pulled all the way around to his left knee to no avail. After several turns around the corral, he knows the animal is not going to quit running. Finally giving up on trying to stop him, Munday yells again at Little Bit.

Slipping from the corral rails Little Bit throws the big gate wide open just as the runaway spots the opening on his next pass and races through it. "Hang to him boy, see you soon I hope."

Will watches as the lunging mule races across the ranch yard and takes off east along the Canadian. "Man Little Bit, that mule can run a lick."

"We might pick up a little extra cash running him at the Fort." Little Bit looks sideways at his boss. "Those soldiers are suckers for a horse race."

Will dismounts and hands the reins to Little Bit. "You better ride out and catch him before he runs clear back to Kansas."

Alder steps from the porch and watches as Little Bit leaves the yard in a hard run. "The way he left here, the boy might not get back in time for the dance."

"Don't let that worry you none, he would never miss a shindig for any reason."

She laughs. "I know he kinda takes after his Pa that way."

"Supper ready woman?"

"It's ready." Alder takes him by the arm and walks back to the porch. "What time we leaving tomorrow?"

Will looks across the flat where Little Bit and Munday were riding back towards the ranch. "Midafternoon I reckon."

"And after the dance?"

"We'll stay the night so you better pack the wagon with blankets."

Smiling she looks back at him as they pass through the door. "You know it's been a while since we danced."

"We danced last Christmas."

"That wasn't a dance Mister Guthrie, it was just a party." Alder laughs and whirls happily. "This is gonna be a real dance with a band and all the trimmings."

"You know how I like dancing." Will frowns.

"I know husband, so you go talk mules and horses and I'll find me a handsome officer to dance with."

Will smiles, "You know the rules Misses Guthrie, you're free to do what you want to at a dance but you come home with the man that brought you."

Alder smiles and hugs him. "I'm a lucky woman my husband, the luckiest in the world and I know it."

"And Misses, I'm an even luckier man." Will smiles, "See that you only dance with older married men, they're safe."

"Why Mister Guthrie, whatever do you mean?" She laughs causing Will to laugh and hug her to him. "Are you jealous of this old woman?"

Looking down into her bright eyes, he nods. "A man would be a fool if he wasn't."

Supper dishes rattle as Grey Moon steps into the heated kitchen and removes his hat. Smiling over at the woman that is like a mother to him, he pulls out a chair and settles his tall frame into it.

"You hungry young man?" Alder walks to where he sits and places her hand on his shoulder.

"Yes Ma'am, I'm pert near starved." Moon looks up at her. "But we've got company and it'll have to wait. Where is everybody?"

"Will's at the barn loading the wagon." She pulls a plate from the shelf. "The rest of the boys have already turned in for the night. What company are you speaking of?"

"They're outside; I'll bring them in directly."

Alder places a steaming pot of potatoes and steaks on the side of the stove and turns to where Moon was sitting. "Munday was riding a rough mule today and got shook up a little."

"How bad?"

"Not bad, just pulling hard on a runaway mule, probably strained his arm a little."

Moon nods, "Must have been a tough mule?"

"He was."

Standing up Moon starts for the door. "Hold supper for three Ma'am, we'll be back shortly."

"You hurry up young man." She grins as he ducks out the door.

Walking into the barn Moon finds Will rubbing saddle soap on a set of brass knobby harness. He is proud of his mules and always has his team shining and looking sharp whenever he went to town.

"You gonna have so much grease on that harness the mules won't be able to carry it." Moon jokes; he knows Will's weakness about his mules.

"It's good to see you back son." Will sits the soap down and shakes hands with Moon. "How was your trip?"

"Good, no rain, just sunshine and a blue sky all the way."

"You get him bought?" Will starts for the corral.

"I did but he cost you a little more than you figured on paying." Moon follows Will. "Maybe a lot more."

Will stops and turns, "How much more?"

Moon motions outside as he starts forward with Will now following him. A spring wagon sits beside the corral where the biggest Stud Jack he ever saw stands docile next to the palomino mare Captain Rains bought for Lana Barber. A man and woman stand next to the wagon waiting as Will and Moon walk towards them.

"Mister Will Guthrie, meet Mister and Mrs. Dan White." Moon introduces the young couple and nods at the tall Jack. "They're part of the deal for that Missouri Jack there."

Good manners prevent Will from questioning Moon about the couple in their presence but he is curious. Sticking out his hand, he greets the newcomers welcoming them and then he focuses on the new Jack he just purchased from Missouri. "Man alive Moon, he's a big'un."

"Sixteen hands and twelve hundred pounds of solid muscle."

"I've never seen anything like him in all my days." Will is impressed. "Have you Mister White?"

"Yes sir, I'm proud to say I have." The tall man smiles, "I helped raise him and have several more like him back in Missouri."

"You must be related to Abraham Ricketts?"

"I am Sir, he's my great-uncle."

"By any chance were you the young boy that I met when I came to your Uncle Abrahams Farm many years ago?"

"I am the same boy, just grown up some." The tall man smiles, "But not enough to please my uncle it seems."

Unsaddling the mare, Moon puts her in a stall in the barn then turns the Jack in a tall corral by himself. Will cannot take his eyes from the animal as he talks with the Whites. He knows in the corral stands the makings of his new herd of mules. The larger draft mules will be in great demand as settlers travel west and prefer mules to horses.

"Well now, he is a dandy." Will smiles, "Now, what's this extra fee you said something about?"

"The Whites are the extra charge I spoke of." Moon turns and motions towards the house. "I'll explain inside over supper; I know Misses White is hungry and very tired."

Will makes his apologies for being a poor host but the size of the Jack completely took his attention. "You two go along with Moon, I'll unhitch your team then I'll be right in and we'll talk."

"Thank you Sir."

Climbing to the top of the corral Will let his eyes slowly take in the huge animal. Men who prefer draft horses will think the Jack ugly but to him the animal is beautiful. Size and weight means strength and pulling power and this big Jack when crossed with heavy mares is sure going to throw some big mules. He can visualize the huge teams he will have for sale and the farmers coming with their money to buy them.

Alder is taken by surprise as Joy White enters her kitchen. Her place has always been beside her husband, the only woman on the ranch or prairie wherever they happen to be. The company of another woman is always a welcome reprieve from the boredom and loneliness of the prairie. Ranch women on the remote prairies are hungry for the latest news from back east. The newest bonnets or latest fashions in dresses are always the first and main topics of conversation. Moon makes the introductions then sits down at the table with the Whites.

"May I be of help Mrs. Guthrie?"

"No Ma'am, you've had a long trip, now you sit and enjoy some hot coffee while I get you some supper." Alder looks at the young woman. "You sit right there and tell me everything, all the latest news from the big cities."

"Yes Ma'am."

"Her bite's a lot worse than her bark." Moon laughs.

"You watch your mouth young man." Alder waves a spoon at Grey Moon and then turns back to the stove.

Moon grins and winks at the Whites. "Told you."

"Where's Mister Guthrie?"

"Outside I figure, drooling over that new Jack that we just brought in."

"Hope he don't turn his back on old Thimble Legs." Dan grins.

"Why?' Alder is curious. "Is he mean?"

"Yes Ma'am a little mean, that Jack has a bite like a Louisiana Alligator and he kicks like a mule."

"He must be a dandy." Alder laughs as Will walks into the kitchen and pours himself a cup of coffee before taking his place at the head of the table.

"Mister Guthrie and Thimble Legs will get along fine then."

"Who's Thimble Legs?" Will looks over his cup at the visitors.

"The new Jack." Alder grins.

Will smiles. "Are you folks getting enough to eat?"

"Yes sir, we are." Dan smiles between bites. "Thank you."

"Now, what is this extra charge all about?"

"It's about me and the missus I reckon."

"How's that?"

Moon looks over at Dan White waiting for the man to speak. White sets his cup down and shrugs. "It's simple Mister Guthrie, we go with the Jack."

"You mind explaining that?" Will looks down the table at the young people.

"Well Sir, my Uncle Abraham has great respect for both you and your wife. He has seen you fight in the ring, now he's getting older and we're his only heirs. He sent me here to work for you until he feels I am capable of taking over his breeding farm in Missouri."

"And what do you think of this arrangement Mister White?" Will is slightly confused at the man's words.

The tall man smiles, "I look forward to it Sir, you're a great mule man and I can learn a great deal here."

"What can you learn from me that your Uncle Abraham can't teach you?"

"To fight for one thing Mister Guthrie."

"To fight!"

"Yes sir, since the war we're up against a lot of border trash, former soldiers and frankly I'm not much of a man to fear." Dan shrugs flatly with no emotion. "My Uncle knows it and so do I."

Will looks over at the young woman who seems embarrassed for her husband but impressed at his honesty. "To fight, you wish to learn to fight?"

"Yes sir, my Uncle feels I am a weakling and will not fight to defend his farm and mules against the thieves and ruffians after he passes."

"And what do you think Mister White?"

"I don't know." The young man shrugs and looks away. "Perhaps I am weak."

"No!" The young woman speaks up. "My husband is no coward; he's just a gentle person that wants to be left alone. He was bullied back home since we were children and Uncle Abraham is ashamed of him."

Will is perplexed for once, he does not have an answer. Looking over at Moon, he shakes his head as the breed ducks his head and starts eating. In all his life, he has never heard a man admit to being weak, especially in front of his own wife.

"Mister White, a man that doesn't know whether he is afraid to fight or not is a curious thing." Will shrugs, "Perhaps I can teach you to fight but I can't put the fight inside you. Are you sure this is what you want?"

"Sir, it's not that simple." Dan looks over at his wife. "If I don't prove to my uncle that I am willing to fight and defend our family's honor he'll disavow me. I'll lose the farm and perhaps something more important."

"Well sir, I've heard it all now, around the Guthrie Ranches the problem isn't getting a man to fight, it is keeping him from fighting." Will looks over at Moon. "You ain't said a word Injun."

The dark eyes of Grey Moon rivet on the table and his plate. He has grown to like the quiet Dan White but the man is soft, not so much in muscle but in temperament. He shakes hands with the tall quiet man and his grip is powerful, Moon believes his uncle might be underestimating his nephew. He does not want to say so in front of his wife but perhaps he is a coward. However, it is not his place to say, in the Cheyenne Tribe no man is considered a coward until he does something to show he is.

"Nothing white man." Moon laughs as Will smiles.

Alder clucks her tongue at the two, as she knows they are just having their fun. Will always calls Moon an Injun but he loves the young man as his own son but today they have company. "You two stop it in front of company. Never mind these two."

Moon shrugs. "I think the food is good." The words brought a snort from Will and a burst of laughter from Alder.

"Well Mister Dan White, it's your nose and head that will suffer but if that's what you're a wanting, then I reckon we can show you a few things."

"I can assure you sir, it's not what I want but I have no choice in the matter."

Refilling their coffee cups Alder looks down at the handsome young man then over at Will. "A man always has a choice Dan."

"Not with Uncle Abraham, no Ma'am, he don't." Joy White speaks up.

"And just what would you like to do Dan?"

"I've always wanted to be a Preacher." Dan looks around the table. "And raise mules."

Moon thought Will was going to choke on his coffee as the words slip out. "A man of the cloth raising hardheaded mules?"

"Yes Sir, I thought that would be a helpful thing to be."

Alder starts laughing and has to sit down until the fits of laughter finally stop. "A Preacher!" The words start her laughing again.

"Did I say something wrong Ma'am?"

"No Dan, it's just that Mister Guthrie's daddy was a Baptist Minister and the only man that could whip my husband in or out of the ring." She laughs again. "Yes Mister White, his old daddy would dispense both the words of the good book with one hand and a sound whipping with the other hand."

Looking over to where Will sat, Moon smiles. He just learned something new. "I let him win those fights; a man can't beat-up his own Father."

"Ugh huh." Alder wipes her eyes and retreats to the stove.

Moon looks up. "We've got a Preacher at the agency, maybe you can learn from him."

"To fight or preach?"

"To preach Mister White."

Dan shakes his head. "No sir, I just said I wanted to be a Preacher, no I'll settle for raising mules and maybe a little boxing."

"Well Mister White, tomorrow we have a social engagement at the Fort, the day after we will see about starting you in the fisticuffs business." Will smiles, "You are invited to go with us."

Chapter 13

The Dance

The wagon lumbers down the banks of the Canadian shaking its passengers as it bounces in and around the small animal burrows along the river. The Guthries did not travel the trail enough to mark it as a road so the wagon is rolling over virgin ground for the most part. Will added another board covered with thick blankets making a seat for the Whites.

Talk and laughter ring out from the wagon as everyone is in a good mood and looking forward to the dance. Grey Moon and Munday flank the wagon but keep their thoughts to themselves. Killian rides ahead with the other hands to get a head start on the festivities at Thompson's Saloon before the dance.

"We're gonna have us a hot time in the old house tonight." Munday has his leg thrown around his saddle horn and his eyes focus on Joy White. "You're gonna save me a dance I hope Miss White?"

"That's Mrs. White." Moon corrects Munday with a sharp glance of warning.

"My apologies Mrs. White." Munday doffs his hat and pulls at the rope hatband that dangles from it. "But you will save me a dance?"

Joy looks over at Dan then smiles. "I will save you one dance Sir."

"Wonderful, I'll look forward to it." Munday smiles, not seeing the slight frown that covers her husband's face.

Frank Kincaid pulls the wagon up outside the Agency barn and steps to the ground. Helping Emily down he looks over to where Clay and Dedrow were sitting their horses. The rancher frowns; the pistols strapped around their waists look like cannons to him.

"You boys try to stay out of trouble, if that's possible."

Dedrow laughs, "Now Boss, we're perfect little angels, you know that."

"You heard me, we're here to stay and we're gonna get along with our neighbors or I'm gonna know the reason why."

"We ain't looking for trouble Pa." Clay looks down at his Mother.

"You boys don't have to look, it comes looking for you." Frank shakes his head. "You attract trouble like honey attracts bees."

The Agency is a hubbub of activity as people pass in and out of the large building. Clay follows along behind Dedrow to the store and enters the busy establishment taking care to not step on any of the cradleboards that line the floor. It always amazes Clay that none of the Indian babies ever cry or make noise. Their big dark eyes follow them as they pass but not a peep comes from any of them.

Bobbing up from behind the counter Lana smiles as she notices Clay. "Why Mister Kincaid, it's good to see you once more."

Clay removes his hat and nods, he still remembers the frown on her face the night he saw her with Rains at the saloon. "Yes Ma'am, it's good to see you too."

"Are you and your family here for the dance and festivities this evening?"

"We are." Clay nods, "I guess you'll be going."

"Yes of course." She hands a package over the counter. "Maybe we could have a dance together?"

"I doubt Captain Rains would approve."

A slight flush crosses her face. "Captain Rains does not control what I do."

"Really." Clay bows slightly then turns to walk away. "In that case I will look forward to this evening and our dance."

Watching him walk away through the crowd of bodies, his shoulders straight and proud, a slight smile touches at the corners of her mouth. "Sister you're being a little flirt again."

"I am not; he needs a little encouragement is all." She turns to where her brother stands listening.

"Peered to me like you were the one that got the encouragement."

Lana smiles, "He is something ain't he?"

"And Captain Rains, what is he?"

"For one thing he's my date for the night and he's a gentleman, not a ruffian brawling in the dirt like a child."

"Really?" Barber smiles, he knows his spoiled little sister and he knows her moods. She is the only daughter and with her beautiful yellow hair and big blue eyes, their parents doted and spoiled their only daughter. She always got whatever she wanted but now in this young man she may have run up against someone who will not jump at her every whim. Lana is not a mean person, she is very kindhearted but she never learns she cannot always have her way. "I've been told your Captain Rains was involved in several duels where men were killed and I understand some of the duels were over women."

Lana frowns. "Oh you can hear all sorts of rumors out here."

"Perhaps but be careful little sister." Barber hugs her to him. "You wouldn't want to be the cause of another duel."

Turning she looks out the doorway and watches as Clay and Dedrow walk across the open ground towards the barn. Fingering a pencil absently she smiles to herself then returns her attention to the Indian women lined up to buy supplies. Barber stands back watching his sister knowing full well the man that eventually wins her will have to rule her with a strong hand. Strength is all that she respects.

At dusk, the Kincaid's wagon crosses the wide Canadian; Frank pulls up beside the new corrals at the fort leaving Clay and Dedrow to unhitch and feed. Entering the mess hall they find it is huge, bigger in size than any of the other buildings. Decorated for the dance, the floor is covered in a light dusting of sawdust for the dancers and the refreshment table is completely filled with drinks and sweets. Civilians and soldiers, both officers and enlisted men, and something almost unheard-of, the working women from Thompson's Saloon were invited so the men would have dancing partners. One soldier with Marshal Vetter makes sure every man carrying a weapon checks it before entering the building.

Captain Rains with Lana grasping tightly to his arm are almost the last to appear in the dining hall. Rains wears his dress uniform while Lana wears a yellow flowing dress that she sewn herself. The dress set off her beautiful blond hair and the deep blue eyes. Rains calculates that arriving almost last they will be the center of attraction. He is right, every eye in the dining hall focuses on the handsome pair as they walk to where Colonel Blalock and his wife wait in line to greet their guests. Tall, ramrod straight through the shoulders as most West Point graduates are, Rains is a perfect match for the beautiful and graceful Lana Barber.

From where he stands against the wall trying to stay away from the prying eyes of everyone attending, Clay cannot keep his eyes from straying across the room at the girl.

"She's a beaut ain't she?" Dedrow slips up beside him and tilts his punch glass pointing it towards Lana.

"Never said she weren't." Clay agrees. "You better go slow on that stuff, we might need you sober."

"Why, they done made me give up my hog leg." Dedrow looks down at his side. "Yes sir Clay boy, she's like a China Doll I seen once in a store."

Clay studies the smug face of Rains as he presents Lana to the Colonel and his wife. The man is proud and arrogant but he has to admit the Captain has a right to swagger a bit. Education, money, breeding, and the girl on his arm give him that right; he is a mighty lucky man. He cannot blame Lana Barber; the Captain is the most eligible bachelor in the Nations.

The post band starts taking their places as the people gathering are growing impatient, ready to dance. A waltz starts the dance and Clay is mesmerized as Rains gallantly bows then swings Lana onto the dance floor. He has to admit they dance beautifully. Raised on the hurricane back of a bucking horse he never learned the art of dancing. Clay looks down at his worn high heeled riding boots. He knows the clumsy shuffling of his feet dancing as he does with the saloon women will be scoffed at here in the company of real dancers.

He smiles as his folks move out onto the floor. Not as graceful as Rains and Lana, nevertheless Clay is proud of them.

"Who is that?" Clay motions at Will Guthrie and his wife who joined the dancers.

"I believe he's the mule man from Hays." Dedrow drains his glass. "Leastways Munday Guthrie came in with them and that other young couple while you were staring at Miss Barber."

Clay nods. "He looks like he could be rough."

"They say he use to prizefight back east; looking at his mug I believe they were right." Dedrow studies Will Guthrie. "If you tangle with the young Guthrie look out, his old Pappy might have taught him to box pretty well."

Studying the bulldog jaw of the man, the thick trunk and heavy legs, and the muscular arms Clay is inclined to believe him. It is the face covered in scars, a nose that looks like it was run over by a boulder, big cauliflower ears, and scars that show where the man was stitched up many a time. There was no doubt; here would be a very tough man to tangle with.

Clay looks over to where the younger Guthrie stands beside the young man with the dark complexion that rides for the Guthries. He watches as another young couple takes the floor and moves slowly away. He never saw the couple before around the Fort or Agency. The way the young woman looks up at the man with adoring eyes, he figures she is his wife. The dance hardly commences when Munday Guthrie moves in and taps the man taking the young woman in his arms. Clay can see the man is not happy but he relinquishes the dance floor and moves back against the wall. He can almost see the whipped dog look in the man's eyes and the longing in the woman's eyes as she looks towards him.

Stepping out onto the floor as Munday and Joy pass, Clay taps and takes the woman in his arms as she lets go of her dancing partner. Dancing the woman clumsily over to where the man stood he turns the woman back into his hands.

She smiles as she turns from him. "Thank you Sir, you are a gentleman."

"You're welcome Ma'am, glad to be of service."

Held tightly in the Captain's arms, Lana watches over his shoulder as the drama plays out. She sees Clay Kincaid dance the woman back to the man who is waiting against the wall, and she watches the hard redness settle on the face of Munday Guthrie.

Munday starts forward but the viselike grip of Grey Moon holds him back. "She's a married woman; she's a lady and our guest."

Shrugging loose Munday glares across the room to where Clay was talking with Dedrow then whirls and takes Connie by the arm. "I only wanted to dance."

"Just for once don't cause trouble and embarrass your Pa."

"Yes Sir, Mister Moon." Munday pulls Connie onto the floor roughly, as she happens to pass where they are standing. "Whatever you say breed."

Looking over, Moon catches the eyes of Clay staring at him, nodding he walks towards the refreshment table. Moon pours himself a glass of punch and turns as Clay moves close to him.

"I thank you Sir for heading off trouble."

"I didn't do it for you Mister Kincaid; I don't want his folks embarrassed in front of these people."

"I understand completely, my name's Clay." Moon looks at the extended hand for a second then shakes briefly.

"Moon."

"You ride for the Guthries don't you?"

"You might say that."

"No sir, you might say he's my adopted son." Will sticks out his huge hand and shakes hands with Clay. Never has Clay felt the raw power as he now feels in the man's grip. "My name's Will Guthrie."

"I'm Clay Kincaid." Clay looks into the friendly eyes of the man. "Word is you used to be a prizefighter."

"Not anymore, I've been through with all that for a long time."

"We had a fighter stay with us one winter down on the Trinity; he had a fight set up in Fort Worth that spring."

"The Englishman, Jo Jo Johnson." Will smiles, "He was a rough customer, too bad he up and got himself killed, he would have been champ one day."

"Yea, he was a rough man." Clay agrees. "I was just a kid when we got word he was killed."

"Well, let that be a lesson to each of us, don't mess with another man's wife."

Clay looks over at Will. "Is that what he got killed for?"

"Yep but it wasn't true, the husband thought it was." Will shakes his head sadly. "Well I'm getting that look, nice meeting you Clay Kincaid."

"Yes sir, its nice meeting you too." Clay was being honest; he likes Will Guthrie at once. "He's a nice man."

"Yes he is." Moon agrees as they watch Will move onto the dance floor with Alder.

Moving close to Clay as he stands leaning against the wall, Connie smiles, "Would you like to dance cowboy?"

"I ain't much of a dancer Ma'am but if you're willing to get stomped on?"

"Dancing is easy; just let yourself roll with the music." Connie laughs, her voice soft and pleasant, as she moves smoothly into his arms.

Two times around the floor and Clay is getting the rhythm of the music down and he starts to relax and enjoy himself. Connie was right; dancing is fun and easy to learn. She is light on her feet, laughing easily as she looks up into his dark eyes.

"You know, if you were to take your spurs off, you might find you won't get them tangled up so much." Connie quips as Clay stumbles slightly.

"Yes Ma'am, but my spurs are part of my boots; they haven't been off since I bought them back in Fort Worth."

"You don't sleep in them do you?"

"Why yes Ma'am, I even take my Saturday night bath with them on." Clay looks at her with a deadpan gaze.

"I have always heard you Texans knew how to stretch the truth." She laughs as he moves her around the floor. "But just how far, they didn't say."

Munday watches as Clay and Connie circle the dance hall several times then move onto the floor and taps him on the shoulder. "My turn Kincaid, you've had her long enough."

Clay looks behind him then down at Connie. "I reckon that's the custom?"

"It is but there's always the next one." Connie frowns slightly.

"She just might be taken for the rest of the night." Munday nods over to where Oney Johnson stands. "Ask him."

"Don't press your luck Guthrie."

Munday grins. "I'm pressing but it'll have to wait until I've used up my hundred bucks for the night."

Clay looks at Connie then back at the grinning Munday. "I'll be waiting out back when you're ready."

Walking away Clay stops beside Thompson. "You sell him all of her dances for the night?'

"I did for a hundred dollars and young man that's a lot of money." Oney nods over at the other bar women. "There's more women out there, take your pick."

Shaking his head in disgust Clay rejoins Dedrow at a far table and sits down. "What happened boy?"

"Nothing, I just got outbid is all."

"Not yet you ain't, the Captain had to leave for a few minutes." Dedrow eyed the yellow dress as Lana walks to their table. "Time to shine youngster, time to shine."

Stopping before their table, Lana smiles down at Clay. "I believe this is my dance Mister Kincaid."

"Yes Ma'am, at your service."

Clay moves slowly around the dance floor trying his best to not step on Lana's toes. Halfway embarrassed and the other hand half elated as the beautiful girl asked him to dance. He smiles down into her face unaware of the looks he is getting from Captain Rains who returned to the dance.

"You lied to me." Lana pretends hurt feelings.

Clay looks down at the blond confused. "I lied, lied about what?"

"You said you didn't know how to dance."

"I'm a quick learner." Clay made eye contact with Connie. "I sure ain't in your Captain's league."

"You ever heard Mister Kincaid that an ounce of try is worth more than a pound of do sometimes?" The blue eyes seem to blaze momentarily, "And he isn't my Captain."

"Yes Ma'am." Clay is about to say something when he feels a tap on his shoulder.

"Let's switch." Munday Guthrie stands grinning. "I'll take her."

Clay looks over at the embarrassed Connie. "Not this time."

"Dance rules Mister Kincaid." Munday smirks and shoves Connie roughly forward. "I insist you take this one."

"You take this one." The hard right landing on Munday's left eye sounds like a clap of thunder knocking him across the floor. Clay is in shock when Munday rolls nimbly to his feet and starts forward. "Not bad Kincaid but you'll have to do better than that, I ain't drunk tonight."

"Here, you men stop that." Colonel Blalock steps between the two. "Take it outside."

Lanterns are hurriedly strung about the parade ground as a ring of half-drunken soldiers eagerly surround the two combatants eager to see a good fight. Neither Will nor Frank speaks a word or tries to stop the impending fight. Will is furious as well as embarrassed but if he stops it, he would embarrass Munday and himself even more. He was watching Munday all night and knows he was picking at the Kincaid boy right along.

"Like I said, I ain't drunk tonight pretty boy." Munday wipes a trickle of blood from his eyelid. "And I'll let you have the first punch free."

"You stay calm boy and get your licks in." Clay looks to where the whispered words came from, Sergeant Ray smiles. "Remember young'un, it ain't the size of the dog in a fight, it's the size of the fight in the dog, and I think you've got lots of fight in you."

"You're fixing to get your tail stomped in front of the entire settlement."

Munday bobs around in front of Clay flicking out quick jabs.

"You gonna talk me to death or fight Guthrie." Clay moves forward right into two fast jabs from the rock hard fists of the taunting Munday. "How's that feel Kincaid, does it feel like I'm talking now?"

Circling slowly, Munday keeps up the fast jabs as Clay tries to close unsuccessfully with him. Both men are a match in size and strength but Clay is quickly finding out he may be outmatched as a boxer. Munday is fast and he hit hard, his face is already beginning to swell where the hard fists landed.

"That all you got boy?" Munday laughs aloud as he baits Clay, something he was instructed by Will never to do. Taking his eyes off Clay momentarily to grin at the watching crowd, he never sees the charge Clay makes as he rams headfirst into his stomach. Gasping for air, Munday goes to one knee where Clay's boot catches him hard in the ribs. Shaking his head, Munday gasps and rolls to his feet slowly.

Holding his side, he moves away from the stalking Clay as he tries to regain his breath. "That was kinda sneaky old boy."

Clay has to admit despite the fact Munday is a bully and loudmouth, he is not about to quit. The Guthrie youngster may be many things but a coward he is not. The boy has guts and lots of them. Closing with a rush the two forgot the boxing. They just went at it tooth and claw, swinging with all they had.

Munday was winning the fight but being a show off, his horsing around let Clay get in a couple hard blows turning the fight into an even match. Munday is protecting his right side. He knows the kick from Clay broke his ribs and he can feel them moving about as tries to throw his jab.

Stepping back, Clay looks at the painful look in Munday's face then over at Will Guthrie. "I've had enough, let's call it a draw for now."

A funny look comes over Munday's face, he knows Clay is letting him off the hook so he can save face and not take a whipping in front of his folks. "Sounds good to me, for now."

Everyone filed back into the dining hall, even the band members who were outside watching the fight. Clay follows Dedrow over to the water trough and sticks his head beneath the water washing away the blood and some of the burning sensation from the many blows Munday landed. Dedrow looks up at the long porch as Rains takes Lana by the arm and forcing her back inside. Clay is holding a towel up to his face and did not see the worried look on her face as she walks away.

Opening his eyes, he is in shock to see Connie standing beside him. "You hurt Cowboy?"

Smiling he shakes his head. "No Ma'am, just my pride a little."

"Your pride, why? You won the fight."

Clay shakes his head and smiles. "No Miss Connie, I didn't win the fight."

She smiles lightly. "Well, it was a draw then."

"Let me tell you something, if old Munday hadn't started showing off he would have whipped me to a frazzle. That boy can hit hard and he knows how to fight."

"I'm proud of you Clay Kincaid." Connie touches his face gingerly then kisses him on the cheek before turning for the dance hall. "You were put in a bad situation in there but you are a gentleman and you handled it well."

Looking at her, he smiles. "Thank you Miss Connie."

"You're welcome; we'll finish our dance anytime you say."

"I'd like that Ma'am."

Dedrow shakes his head as she walks away. "That takes the cake."

"What takes the cake Bandy?"

"Here I stand the most eligible and prettiest bachelor around and who are all the women after?" The older man frowns, "A kid."

"Well, you are getting pretty feeble old man." Clay dodges as Dedrow slaps playfully at him.

Pulling their cinches tight, Clay and Dedrow cross the river and ride towards home. The foreman looks over at the youngster and smiles. "You remember that big old boar coon we caught last winter down on the Trinity?"

Clay nods over at the man curious as to what is coming. "Yea, what about him?"

"That coon caught himself, all he had to do to get loose was turn loose of that piece of glitter paper inside the trap and he would have been free."

"What's the point about that old coon, Mister Bandy?"

"No point, I was just thinking yellow hair and blue eyes attract a man like that piece of shiny metal attracted that old coon."

"If you saying I'm caught, you're crazy?" Clay shakes his head. "She's all wrapped up in her Captain."

"Is she?" Dedrow lights himself a quirley. "Seems to me, she was awfully worried about you at the fight. The good Captain had to force her back into the dance hall and I seen her watching you as we rode out."

"I didn't see her come to check on me."

"You mean like Connie did?"

"Maybe."

Dedrow laughs. "Connie is a bar woman, she doesn't have to protect her reputation as a lady like Miss Barber has to."

"Does that make her less of a woman?"

"No it don't, it just makes her less virtuous."

Clay nods. "You're saying Connie isn't a prim and proper lady?"

"Give the man a dollar, he just guessed right." Dedrow grins then pulls out the makings for another smoke. "This old coon don't think you'll ever turn the virtuous girl loose for the barmaid."

"She may not be true-blue virtuous Bandy but if you want a woman that'll stand behind you, Connie is the one."

Bandy smiles. "You're learning hoss."

The horses splash belly deep in the water drinking deeply before Clay's gelding starts to paw the water wanting to lie down and roll. Spurring the horse hard he rides him onto dry ground.

"I ain't a coon and I sure ain't caught by anyone." Clay frowns at Dedrow. "Neither Lana nor Connie."

Dedrow blows smoke and laughs. "Yea you are, you're like that old coon, you're caught and just don't know it, caught by a small piece of glitter."

"Where we headed?"

Dedrow laughs. "To the bunkhouse and some sleep!"

Will Guthrie stands beside the wagon and watches as the post surgeon wraps Munday's ribs with a strong cloth bandage. "You're lucky young man, your ribs are broke but it's a clean break."

"I don't feel too lucky." Munday grimaces. "They burn like fire every time I move or breath."

The surgeon grins. "They will for quite a spell I reckon."

"How much do I owe you?" Munday reaches into his pocket for his money pouch.

"Nothing, young man that was a good show ya'll put on out there." The surgeon smiles, "I sure enjoyed it."

Munday shakes his head and hands the man five dollars. "Wish I could say the same."

Grimacing in pain as Will and Dan White help him into the wagon, Munday looks up at his mother sitting on the high seat. He knows her feelings about making a scene in public, especially when her son is the culprit who started the trouble.

Will looks in the back of the wagon at his son and at White. "I hope you both learned a lesson from what just happened. The Kincaid boy could have taken you apart but he let you off the hook."

"He just got in a lucky punch is all."

The slap sound like thunder as Will's big hand raps his son's face. "I told you, no trouble tonight. Moon told you no trouble and I've told you more than once not to fight a man with your mouth."

"I'm sorry Pa." Munday seems genuinely sorry. "I had him whipped and turned my head for a little fun."

"No you didn't have him whipped; you're a better boxer because I've made you one. That boy has the heart of a grizzly, you were winning but you sure didn't have him whipped by a long shot."

"Yes sir."

Moon rides up to the wagon leading Munday and Killian's horses as Will steps up onto the seat and clucks to the team. Looking down at Killian as he mounts he can only shake his head. Munday has always been wild, getting into one thing after another around Hays. Moon was raised by the same people and by the same principles but he avoided trouble. Most folks said it was just plain bad blood in Munday. Moon knows better, many of the boy's problems come from Tom Killian.

Marshal Vetter steps from the shadow of the long barn and stops the team, looking up at Will. "I had to cross the river to check on the Agency and was a little late getting back here Mister Guthrie but this place is carrying the same law as Hays for civilians. You best control your wildcat there or I will."

"Nothing serious Marshal, just a little fisticuffs is all."

"Folks here are trying to civilize the tribes." Vetter motions at Munday. "He's not teaching them much civilization."

"You're a little out of your jurisdiction on this side of the Canadian ain't you Marshal?" Munday speaks up from the bed of the wagon.

"Shut your mouth boy" Will nods at Vetter. "It's a long way home Marshal, I best see to the boy."

"You do that Mister Guthrie." Vetter backs away. "Save me the trouble."

Will Guthrie looks across the breakfast table at Dan White. "You ready for a few lessons in boxing today Mister White?"

"Yes sir, I reckon." Dan nods. "Ready as I'll ever be."

"Good, you go on to the barn and I'll be right along."

"Yes sir."

Killian watches from the bunkhouse as Dan makes his way slowly to the barn. "You boys look at that."

"What is it?" Slim and Moon walk to the door.

"Will said he was gonna give that young man a few lessons this morning." Killian sneers. "I reckon the fun is fixing to start, he already looks like a whipped dog."

"I wouldn't sell him short if I were you." Moon feels sad for the tall young man as he drags his feet seemingly walking towards an unknown fate.

"Look at him, a sissy from the east." Killian walks out on the porch. "He ain't got the gumption to fight a biscuit."

Slim takes Killian's arm and turns him around. "Leave the boy be Tom, Will ain't gonna like it if you jump on him."

Shrugging loose Killian grins. "A softie like that with such a beautiful wife, it just ain't right. Sides you heard him yourself, he wants to learn how to fight. I might just oblige him a bit."

Moon watches as Killian follows Dan to the barn then looks over at the house to see if Will is coming. "I better go over and keep him off the young man."

"Leave it be boy." Jumper spit a stream of tobacco on the ground. "Killian's been raring for a fight ever since last night, let's see if Mister White has any fight in him or if he is what they say, a coward."

"I've got five dollars says Tom Killian might just be a fixing to run into a hornet's nest." Slim tucks his shirt into his pants and tightens his belt. "Let's go watch."

Dan turns as Killian enters the barn thinking it was Will. "Oh, it's you Mister Killian; I thought it was Mister Guthrie."

"You always so polite pilgrim?"

Dan looks behind Killian as Moon, Slim, and Jumper enter the barn quietly. "Well Sir, I don't know of any law against being courteous to a friend."

Killian frowns. "I ain't your friend mister."

"Well Sir, I'm sorry to hear that."

"You're sorry alright and I think you're yellow." Killian steps closer to the taller man. "Tell me, how'd you ever get a pretty little thing like her all by yourself?"

"She's my wife Mister Killian; I'd rather you didn't speak of her that way."

"You'd rather I didn't speak of her." Killian mocks. "Why don't you send her over here to a real man White? I'll bet she is a real Joy alright."

"I told you, don't say another word or else."

"Or else what?" The slap sounds like a clap of thunder as Killian backhands the younger man. Moon starts forward until Jumper takes his arm and shakes his head, pulling him back.

"Stay out of it Moon."

Will steps into the barn and witnesses the slap. He looks across as Dan feels the blood running from his split lip. He drops his head ashamed as the young man just stands there bleeding. Perhaps Uncle Abraham is right, the boy is soft.

"You yellow pup, she is too much woman for you." Killian turns away shaking his head. "I'll bet she's sweet tasting."

Will blinks in shock as a scream rips through the barn. Dan grabs Killian and physically lifts him from the dirt floor and tosses him halfway across the barn. Pointing his finger as Will and Moon start forward, he warns them to get back.

"I asked him polite to leave Mrs. White out of this, now nobody better interfere." Dan looks around, his face a mask of rage. "Nobody or else I'll kill them!"

Killian rolls to his feet and bull rushes the taller man only to collide with the rock hard fist of Dan coming down on top of his head. Down on one knee, Killian shakes his head as he is lifted bodily again in a bone crushing bear hug. Screaming in agony, he punches at Dan's face trying to free himself. Again, he feels himself being tossed through the air as if he was a feather. Landing against a stall door he barely looks up when the hard fists of White come down on him one after the other. Rolling to his stomach, he covers his head trying to dodge the heavy blows. Then Killian feels the viselike grasp of the powerful arms as they encircle his neck in a strangling chokehold.

Kicking with both feet as he is lifted again in the air, Killian tears at the arm that holds his throat while his feet flail in the air. He is having the life choked out of him. Slowly blackness engulfs his mind as the pressure on his throat tightens and his legs go limp.

"Turn him loose Dan, you'll kill him." Slim and Jumper jump in trying to free the crazy man's arms from Killian's throat. Turning loose with one arm, Dan tosses the two men across the barn floor as if they were rag dolls.

Seeing Killian's face turning blue Moon knows the man will soon be dead. Pulling his pistol Moon is about to hit the enraged man across the head when Joy White steps between them and places her hand on her husband's arm.

"Turn him loose Dan." The voice is soft. "I said turn him loose now."

Killian collapses as the strangle hold on him is released. Turning from the down man, Dan looks across to where Will stands with a shocked look on his face. The tall man is in a trance or something as she leads him across the barn floor towards the door. Staring down at his unconscious foreman, Will shakes his head, all his life he was around fights and fighters and he never saw a man go as crazy as what he just witnessed. If he did not see it himself, he would not believe a pleasant young man as Dan White could become an enraged killer.

Jumper and Slim roll Killian to his side as the man gasps to get air through his bruised windpipe. Will and then Moon follow the Whites out into the bright morning sun. Dan still in a trance, he wilts as the adrenalin rush from the fight and his temper evaporates from his body leaving him spent.

Jumper walks out to where they stand beside the corrals. "He'll be alright Will, he's coming around. Just can't talk well right now."

Dan White looks around at the staring faces then swipes a hand over his own haggard face. Seeing them all standing around and the disheveled look of Dan from the window, Alder walks out onto the porch and over to where they are all standing.

"What's happened?" She can see the disbelief on every face.

"Killian jumped on Dan here and almost got himself killed." Jumper speaks up first.

Listening from the doorway, Munday steps painfully forward. "Get out of here, you're joshing."

"Go see for yourself boy." Jumper growls over at Munday then cocks his head towards the barn. "You might learn a lesson from this yourself."

"Get our things Mrs. White, we'll be leaving."

Joy nods and starts to turn then stops and looks at Will. "Uncle Abraham is wrong, has been wrong for many years. My husband isn't weak or a coward as you can see. He just doesn't like trouble and you can see why now."

"I can see why alright." Jumper mumbles to Moon.

"There's no reason for you folks to leave." Will tries to stop them. "You're still welcome here."

"Yes there is Mister Guthrie." Dan straightens his clothes. "It's time for me and Uncle Abraham to come to an agreement. Me and Joy will probably be heading back east."

"You're not staying to raise mules with your Uncle?'

"No Sir, I'm going into the Ministry, I guess you can see why." Dan nods slowly. "Today just made me realize I must. I hope your foreman is okay."

As Dan walks away, Will takes Joy White by the arm. "Has this happened before?"

Nodding she drops her head. "Twice and both times it was over me. That's why my husband doesn't want to fight anyone; he'd rather be called a coward."

"Sometimes it takes a stronger man to walk away from a fight Misses White." Will smiles.

"As you can see Sir, Dan White is a strong man." Joy smiles and hugs Alder. "In spite of everything, I'm very proud of him."

Everyone waves and watches the surrey out of sight as Dan and Joy White turn east. "Would you have ever thought it?" Slim laughs and slaps his thigh. "I had me a feeling about that one, I sure did."

"Someone better check on Tom." Will looks towards the bunkhouse.

"Not me." Jumper starts away. "He got what he deserved and more this time and that forty-four of his didn't help him none at all, no sir."

"I would have never believed it." Munday shakes his head. "And I missed it."

"You're lucky it wasn't you last night Munday Guthrie in front of the whole fort." Moon nods. "I've heard men get stronger when they become enraged, now I've seen it."

"I could have handled it."

Moon laughs, "He would have had you for lunch, just like he did Killian."

Chapter 14

The Comanche

It is late afternoon when Moss Shadrack pushes through the saloon doors. He looks around Oney Thompson's Saloon until he spots Paddy Murphy sitting alone near the back of the saloon. Ordering a beer from the bar, he walks over and pulls out a rickety chair.

"Good to see you Paddy, what's going on?"

"It's good to see you Moss. I was getting a little jittery." The squat Irishman looks nervously around the saloon then over at the new arrival. "Marshal Vetter has been in here two times already, I think he's got word about us, he's on to something."

"Us?" Moss studies the room nervously. "I thought he didn't have jurisdiction here on the Post grounds, sides he don't know me."

"He's a U.S. Marshal and he knows me for sure, Pine's lit out, he's been lying low across the river, Vetter knows him on sight." Murphy picks up his beer. "He told me to wait here until someone showed."

"I showed, now let's ride." Moss swallows his beer without putting the mug down.

"Where to?"

"Galt's outside the Fort waiting, we'll pick him up and go find Pine." Moss starts to rise when Vetter walks through the doors.

"Crap! Paddy drops his hat turning his body to block the Marshal's view of Moss. "It's Vetter, you sure he doesn't know you on sight?"

"He doesn't know me." Moss shakes his head. "What about you?"

"He knows me alright. He had me and Pine Johnson in jail when Galt got shot up." Paddy eases his pistol out and cocks it. "I put a slug in him once back in Hays."

"You did?" Moss swears, "Great, how'd ya'll get out?"

"Escaped and I did for a fact shoot him; trouble was he put two in me." Paddy mutters, "Dang near settled my hash for sure."

"Well here he comes." Moss nods towards the Marshal. "You want to run or fight?"

"Is he looking our way?"

"He can't miss us if he keeps coming this way."

Paddy drops his head letting his hat cover his face while holding the cocked pistol in his lap. Only ten more steps and Marshal Vetter will be no more.

"Let me know when he gets real close."

"Marshal Vetter." Oney Thompson stands at the end of the bar and hails the lawman. He was watching Paddy and another man he did not know for several minutes. He knew Paddy from El Paso in the old days and he knows Vetter is walking unaware straight into a shooting scrape with at least one bad man, maybe two, that do not mind killing. "Can I have a word with you?"

Vetter turns and walks back to the bar as Paddy and Moss seeing their chance make their way hastily out the back door. "What can I do for you Mister Thompson?"

Oney watches as the two disappear then smiles. "Just wanting to buy you a beer is all."

Vetter turns only to see an empty table where the two men were sitting. "Who were they Oney?"

"Now Marshal you know that ain't professional, even if I knew who they were." Oney pushes the full beer over to the lawman. "I expect I just saved your bacon for a fact."

Vetter pushes the beer away and starts for the door. "Goodnight Oney."

"Don't thank me Marshal." Oney watches Vetter disappear out the door.

"Don't aim too; be glad I don't close you down here and now."

Ewen Galt with four men from the original gang since running in with the Kincaids, sit their horses a mile outside the Fort as Moss leads Paddy back to where they were waiting.

"Let's ride Ewen." Paddy never slows his horse as he passes the waiting men.

"What's the hurry?"

"Vetter might be following us."

A few miles downriver, a small stand of live oaks surrounded by deep grass for the horses make a natural camp for the outlaw and his men. Off saddling and hobbling the horses the men kick a fire together and start coffee to boiling.

Galt eases himself down and looks over where Paddy is tossing a pile of limbs together. "Where's Pine at, back in jail?"

"He's probably been watching us since we left the Fort; he'll be along pretty quick."

Galt leans back slowly against his saddle and puts a burning brand to his quirley. "You boys got anything for me?"

Paddy settles beside the fire then looks over at the man. "We think we have a plan."

"Spit it out."

"Here's Pine boss." One of the other riders spots a lone rider coming in at a slow walk. "Let's wait on him."

The thin man they call Pine Johnson dismounts and greets Galt and the rest of the men. Pine takes his time pouring himself a cup of coffee.

Paddy nods and turns his attention back on Galt. "We heard Guthrie bought himself a real high dollar Jackass, imported all the way from Missouri."

Pine chimes in, "Yea, he paid some big bucks for him."

Galt draws in on his smoke. "A Jackass, what would I want with a stud jack?"

"Guthrie's kid was bragging his Pa wouldn't take any amount of money for the animal."

"For crying out loud, what are ya'll getting at?"

"It's simple, we grab the Jack, then let one or two men lead him deep into the Nations. Mister Will Guthrie will follow and leave his herd wide open for the rest of us to run off with."

"You sure he thinks that much of the animal?"

"I figure he does." Pine agrees. "His men say that's all he talks about."

"What about the Kincaid herd?"

Pine looks over at Galt and draws in on his smoke. "We don't have the men to hit both herds at once."

"If we don't get the horses and mules at the same time we'll never get another chance." Galt exhales, "Sides, I've got some more men on the way, some of the old gang."

"That's close to four hundred head to push out of here before the army can get on our trail."

"The army will be too busy to worry about us."

"What you got in mind?"

"Come morning you'll see." Galt looks into the fire. "Now have you thought of a way to get Kincaid out of the way?"

"We've got that planned out too." Pine smiles, "We weren't sure which herd you wanted to go after."

"Tell me."

"We got word at the Fort that Kincaid sent a Mexican named Jorge across the Red to pick up the rest of his horses." Paddy looks down at Galt. "If Kincaid thinks his men could be in danger or his horse herd could be raided he might ride out and leave his place unprotected to go warn the men coming up from Texas."

"It might work at that." Galt tosses his burned-out smoke. "That means we'll lose the horses he's bringing up."

"Greed will get you caught every time." Pine shakes his head. "We'll have more than enough if we get lucky and get both herds."

"It could make you rich Pine." Galt grins, "Think small and you wind up old and broke."

"Ugh huh, well I'll take being small and alive if I have to pick."

"You're sure the horse herd we raided is owned by this same rancher Kincaid?" Galt heard the name already but he cannot believe it is the same rancher.

"You mean the ones ya'll tried to raid?" Pine tosses the dregs from his cup. "Yea, he's the same man, it was his men that killed Jack and wounded you."

"Where is his place?"

"Upriver about ten miles, due east on the north side of the Canadian. He started building a place over in the Yukon." Pine looks over at Galt. "What are you thinking now?"

"Nothing much, just that one less man to watch over the horses wouldn't hurt none." The outlaw gives an evil grin. "What does this Kincaid look like?"

"Big man well over six foot, biggest in their outfit, and strong looking with grayish brown hair."

"You ride for Guthrie's place and take Paddy and Moss with you."

"And?'

"Grab the Jackass and get them headed south with him, then wait around and see what Guthrie does."

"Alright, are you gonna stay camped here?"

"I'll be right here." Galt pulls on his smoke. "When Guthrie is far enough away come get us and then we'll swoop in and take his herd."

"Alright Boss, you're running the show." Pine stands up slowly. "Think about this, if you kill Kincaid before he takes his men out the rest may not go to Texas."

"Take one of the other men with you and drop him off at the Agency so he can round us up some supplies." Galt ignores the warning. "We're getting low on coffee and smokes."

"You sure you'll be here?" Pine smells a skunk. Galt is up to something.

"Now where would I go?"

Galt watches Pine and the three men mount up and listen as they ride slowly back through the twilight. Throwing out night guards, he calls a lanky rider over to where he sat trying to get himself comfortable. The swarthy-skinned man with long black hair falling from under his hat kneels beside the fire and stares quietly.

"Ride to Snake Shields Camp and tell him we will strike soon." Galt looks over at the breed. "Tell him to be ready and tell him he will be paid many horses, many rifles."

"Where do you wish Snake Shield to strike?"

"Just tell him to stay put until you return and tell him what to do."

"I go."

"If you see any of our other men, you know Suds Adell, he will be leading them, point them this way."

Galt watches as the half-breed swings nimbly into his saddle and whirls the gelding cruelly away. Charlie Tom is half Tonto Apache and half Kwahadi Comanche; how that cross ever presented itself Galt has no idea. The Apache and Comanche hate one another; he figures the breed's mother must have been a Comanche Captive, Mexican slave or something.

The breed rode with him for three years now, bloodthirsty and cruel as they come. He is still one of Galt's most trusted men. Completely fearless, the breed was a loyal follower ever since Galt saved him from a lynch crazy posse who thought Charlie stole the horse he was riding. The half-breed always rode the fastest, best-looking horse he could find and that was almost his downfall. He would not have escaped the ambush at the horse herd if the breed did not hold him on his horse during their retreat.

Lying back Galt grins into the fire, everything is in place, now all he has to do is wait until he gets word from Pine then it will all come together. Lighting a quirley he let the smoke drift and float around his bearded face as he studies the blaze.

Looking around for a smaller rider the outlaw leader whistles. "Saddle two horses Tate, mine and yours."

"We going somewhere tonight?"

"We're riding upriver and pay a visit to Mister Kincaid." Galt pulls himself slowly erect. "Bring your rifle."

Munday moves slowly out to the corral and finds a seat where he can watch Moon work with the yellow mare and the mule Rains swapped with his Pa.

"That mule reins like a well-trained cow horse." The injured youngster repositions himself trying to get comfortable. "Ma said the Captain was coming after them today, he should be pleased."

Grey Moon nods as he backs the mule several steps then dismounts. "He sent word he'd be down about noon."

Munday nods, "That's why she's baking huh?"

"Probably, how's the old ribs?"

"They're mending." He raises his arm slowly. "Slow but sure, Kincaid done a job on them."

"When are you gonna grow up and stop making trouble for yourself?" Moon looks through the corral rails. "You asked for it.'

"I don't know brother; it's just something I can't help." Munday grins, "It's just in my blood I reckon."

"Grow up." Moon steps up onto the Palomino. "Quit listening to Killian."

"He's my friend and Pa's foreman."

"He's trouble." Moon pats the yellow mare on the neck. He grew fond of the horse, maybe because of the girl. He put many extra hours in on the horse. He wants the Palomino to make Lana Barber a fine mount for years to come. "I figure he puts you up to most of the trouble you get into."

"Now, why would he do that?"

Moon shrugs, "Ever since you were little he wanted you to be the toughest kid in town."

"Is that so?"

"It is and you know it." Moon nudges the mare lightly. "Down here in the Nations, these men don't play; someday it could get you killed."

"It ain't killed me yet." Munday speaks to the air as Moon lopes the mare out of earshot not wanting to argue.

Grey Moon heard the last remark and shook his head. He and Munday are almost the same age and they were raised together. He knows Munday and he knows the wildness in him, something that will only be tamed by maturity or death. Moon wonders, will Munday outgrow his wild ways or will someday he meet someone tougher?

Munday looks out across the flats where a lone rider is coming downriver at a high lope. As the horse and man nears, he recognizes Slim Jennings by the way he set a horse.

"Old Slim's in a hurry." Moon reins the palomino mare over to the fence and waits as the skinny man approaches at a hard run.

"Where's the fire at Slim?"

Dismounting from the blowing gelding, the rider removes his Stetson and wipes his brow. "Trouble boys that horse rancher east of the agency, Frank Kincaid, was shot and there are reports that some of Quanah's Comanche have been seen in these parts."

"Kincaid's dead, Quanah's in this area?"

"Didn't stick around so I don't know for sure how bad he was shot, when I got word that hostiles were in this area I come back on the fly."

"Who shot him, the Comanche's?" Moon questions the rider as he takes a long pull on his canteen.

"The soldier that came in with the word didn't say, he just rode on to the Fort to report to Colonel Blalock and Captain Rains."

Moon stiffens, Rains and Lana are to be at the ranch by midday for dinner. "You didn't pass Captain Rains and Miss Barber on your way back?"

"Sure didn't Moon but I took the shorter route across the breaks. It's a lot rougher but I wanted to get back as quick as I could."

"Moon looks off towards the west then down towards the river. Patting the mare on the neck, he looks down at the two men. "I'll give them an hour more and then I'll ride out."

"You think there's trouble about?"

"When Comanche's are out, there's always that possibility." Moon replies, "Slim get a fresh horse and ride out to the herd and bring Mister Guthrie in and tell the others to stay awake and on their toes."

"I'll do that Moon."

Lana and Captain Rains trot their horses slowly across the flat prairie heading west to the Guthrie Ranch. Grey Moon sent word to the Fort two days earlier that the General's mule and Lana's palomino mare were finished; gentle broke and ready to go home. Charlie Tom was squatting near the Agency Door blending in with the other Agency Indians. He overhears Rains telling Lana of his plans to ride out with her in two days to pick up a surprise for her. Quickly mounting his long legged gelding the breed rides at a hard lope to Galt's camp with the news.

Galt smiles cruelly and looks over at the breed. "Now's the time, ride and tell Snake Shield to intercept our two lovers. That'll get the army on the move with their army man dead and a white woman taken captive. Tell the old devil to let the Cavalry follow him clear back to Texas."

"Snake Shield will want his payment." Charlie Tom grunts. "Him no get guns, him plenty mad at this one."

"Just tell him you'll bring them to him down on the Red in four sleeps."

"Will I do this thing?" The breed looks over at Galt. "Charlie does not want to break word to Snake Shield."

"You scared of that Comanche?"

"Him very bad man." The half-breed nods. "You betcha this one scared of Snake Shield."

"You will have the rifles to take him." Galt pulls on his smoke. "You have my word."

Two days later Rains picks up Lana almost at daylight. The sun is coming up over their shoulders as they ride and talk. They enjoy the early morning with its bright rays of sunshine casting out over the land. Passing through the tall waving grass Rains is in no hurry. He has the prettiest girl in the Nations for company and he sent word ahead that he would be at the Ranch around noon.

"Are you going to tell me what your big surprise is Mister Rains?" Lana can hardly sit still in her saddle, she is busting with curiosity. He got her out of her warm bed before sun-up and headed them west along the Canadian without her morning coffee or breakfast. "After all I didn't even get breakfast."

"You'll see and I guarantee it'll be worth missing out on one breakfast."

Rains smiles over at her then suddenly he stiffens. Five miles from the safety of the Fort and almost halfway to the Guthrie Ranch several mounted warriors appear off to their left flank closing in on them at a hard run. Slapping her gelding hard with his gloved hand Rains hollers. "Run Lana, kick him out and stay due west along the river."

The Captain has been on the frontier since the end of the Great War. He knows the different Indian tribes and he knows the warriors closing in on them are Comanche. They are a tribe that still raids and kills on the Texas side of the Red. Quanah and his Comanche warriors were feared along the Texas border and into Oklahoma Territory, raiding and murdering then retreating back out into the Llano Estacado. Rains can hear the defiant screams of the warriors. He knows his and Lana's safety depend on the fleetness of their horses and staying ahead of the Comanche until they reach the Guthrie Ranch and hopefully safety. Rains looks back over his shoulder; the warriors are closing the distance. Riding almost naked and bareback, their horses are carrying less weight that on a long run it gives them the advantage. The horse Lana rides had to be gentle for her since she was not a good rider so it is an older and slower gelding.

"Keep going Lana, I'll try to slow them down." Rains pulls his service revolver as the warriors close the gap drawing nearer. "Ride due west don't look back, stay low, and whip him hard."

Fifteen Comanche warriors are charging towards him. Rains slows his racing gelding and fires at them, hoping they would slow down and give her time to get away safely. Spurring his horse away as a warrior raises his rifle Rains hears the report of the rifle then feels his horse jerk and stumble causing both horse and rider to fall to the ground. Slightly stunned, he staggers to his feet as the warriors bear down on him. Rains fires his pistol until it is empty then he feels a burning pain in his side as he is hit and shouldered aside then trampled by the charging mustangs.

Two miles further along the slow moving river, Lana lashes at her tiring gelding frantically as she tries to force more speed from the blowing horse. Looking over her shoulder, she cringes in fright as a large warrior with his long hair streaming out behind him, closes in beside her. The coiled body of a serpent was painted on the small shield that he brandished using it to push away her feeble attempts at slapping at his hand. Reaching for her Lana screams as he lifts her bodily from her faltering gelding then drops her bodily onto the hard ground. Dismounting quickly he stands over the frightened girl and glares down at her.

Pushing her back to the ground as she tries to rise he laughs then stands staring at her long yellow hair. Scooting backwards along the ground as the warrior pulls his knife she screams in fright as he cut off a lock of her hair and holds it up for the others to see. Physically lifting the hysterical Lana onto the horse in front of him, the warrior leaps lightly up behind her and points to the Northwest. Speaking in a guttural voice the warrior kicks his small mustang into a slow lope along the river.

Rains rolls sideways and tries his best to dodge the running horses as they pass over him. One warrior fires point-blank into his face then races after the others in pursuit of the fleeing girl. Staggering slowly to his feet Rains feels the powder burns on his face and the blood oozing from his left side. Lana and the pursuing warriors disappear from his sight as he stumbles a few feet after them. Reeling he staggers and plunges back to the ground.

Reining in the palomino near where Munday sat, Moon turns and cocks his ear. "Did you hear that gunfire?"

"I sure heard something off east of here."

"It was too much shooting for a hunter." Moon turns the mare towards the gate. "Open up."

"I'll go with you." Munday hobbles towards the gate.

"No, you're in no shape just send your Pa and Killian after me when they get here and tell them to hurry." Moon looks off to the east as the gate opens slowly. "You better get to the house and check the rifles. Keep your Ma inside until I see what's going on out there."

"You ride easy and keep your eyes open." Munday yells trying to tell Moon he does not have his rifle that the scabbard is empty but he is already out of hearing range on the racing mare.

Grey Moon turns the little mare to the east alongside the Canadian in a hard run. The shots were faint; he knows they came from several miles away. Needing to save the mare for a long run, he pulls her down to a lope and studies the landscape carefully as he rides. Looking down and noticing the empty scabbard he cusses himself, in his haste to go see if someone was in trouble he failed to bring his own rifle with him. He knows there has to be some kind of trouble or danger ahead as too many shots were fired for it to be a mere hunter.

Pulling the palomino to a stop, he surveys the grassy prairie then kicks the mare and moves forward cautiously. Nothing shows on the horizon as far as he can see. Riding slowly Moon rides to a small mound and pulls the mare in again. Two hundred yards below him in a flat, he sees a prone man crawling in the grass. Kicking the mare hard he races forward and reins in beside where the man lay.

"Captain Rains!" Moon slides to the ground and rolls Rains over. "What's happened to you?"

The blue eyes open briefly then the confused Rains tries weakly to fight. Moon grabs his wrists and restrains the Captain until the wounded man stops slapping at him. Recognizing Grey Moon the Captain ceases to resist. "Lana, they've taken Lana."

Moon is not quite sure that he heard right. "Who's taken Lana?"

"Comanche!"

Moon looks around him then back down at Rains. "Comanche here in Cheyenne land, no." Slim said there were sightings of Comanche but Moon cannot believe they would dare raid this far north of the Red.

Rains grabs Moon's buckskin shirt. "They've got her Moon. We were headed to your place when they jumped us."

"You sure they were Comanche?"

Rains tries to rise shaking his head weakly. "I know what they are lad, they are Comanche; we've got to go after her."

"We will Captain but first I've got to get you home." Moon packs the gaping hole in the Captain's side trying to stem the flow of blood. "You're hurt bad but you'll have to ride."

"Then leave me, go after her."

"Can you get up to your feet?" Rains is a big man, Moon doubts he can lift the deadweight of the big man into the saddle without help.

"I can try." With Moon's help, the Captain slowly stands up then pulls himself painfully onto the green broke mare as she spooks sideways from the smell of blood.

"Whoa mare." Moon steadies the palomino then gets Rains onto the mare and straighten in the saddle. Groaning as the mare starts forward Rains grits his teeth and grabs the horn with both hands. "You okay Captain?"

"Don't worry about me, just hurry." Rains hisses through clenched teeth. "They've got her."

Moon leads the mare for almost a mile before he spots Will and Killian riding like the wind heading for them. Waving his hat, he waits where he is steadying the weak man in the saddle.

Will reins his gelding in hard and looks over at Rains. "It's the Captain from the fort. What's happened boy?"

"He said Comanche's shot him and took the girl."

"You mean Lana Barber?"

"Yes sir looks to be about fifteen or more warriors in the bunch." Moon looks at Killian's horse. "I'll need your horse."

"Where you going Moon?"

"After the girl, before the Comanche get too far ahead." Moon hands the reins of the mare to the foreman.

"You want my pistol?" The foreman starts to unbuckle his sidearm.

Moon looks at the Winchester in the scabbard. "Your rifle loaded?"

"It is and there's more shells in the saddlebags."

"I'll go with you." Will looks at Moon.

"No sir, you get the Captain to the house then send someone to the fort, tell them what happened."

Will shakes his head. "Son, you can't go alone."

"I'll be alright, get the soldiers on their trail." Moon nods. "And watch your tail feathers as they may still be close. They could hit the ranch."

Will watches as Moon turns the big bay gelding back along the river and races out of their sight. "Stay with the Captain, I'll go get a wagon."

"They've got her." Rains mumbles feebly.

Clay and Dedrow sit on the steps of the Post Hospital and Chief Surgeons office and watch the parading soldiers as they march back and forth across the flat parade ground.

"I thought these Yankees were supposed to be horse soldiers?" Dedrow puffs on his quirley, his eyes rivet on the soldiers.

"Reckon they have to know how to walk too." Clay nods then looks behind him as the door opens. "How is he Ma?"

"Same as yesterday, he's in a lot of pain but the Doctor says he'll be fine." Emily sits down tiredly. "Bullet broke his leg but passed on through without hitting any blood vessels."

"What about his arm?"

"It's just a scratch."

Flipping his burned-out smoke Dedrow shakes his head. "Well, someone was sure trying to kill him."

"Yes, but who?" Emily looks over at the foreman. "Frank doesn't have an enemy in the world, never has."

Clay is about to answer when a running horse passes the saloon and races into the compound pulling up before the Post Commander's building. Recognizing the tall form of Slim Jennings as one of the Guthrie riders, Clay and Dedrow stand up and start towards the building. They know something is wrong. The horse was run nearly to its limit, something no horseman would do unless it was awfully important, a matter of life and death.

Stepping into the office, they catch the tail end of the rider telling Colonel Blalock of the Captain being shot and Lana Barber taken. As the Colonel starts hollering orders, Clay takes Slim by the arm and pulls him aside.

"Where did all this happen?"

Slim shakes his head. "Maybe two miles east of the ranch, down along the river."

"You plumb sure it was Comanche?"

"You've been here and heard the rumors yourself." Slim rolls himself a smoke with shaking hands. "I've got to get back."

Clay grabs his arm roughly. "Which way did the warriors ride after they took the girl?"

"Looks like right towards the ranch, due west and north across the river." Slim jerks loose from the steel grasp. "That's why I've got to get back."

"Your horse is done in, take that bay gelding there." Clay points at Dedrow's horse.

"That's my horse."

"You stay with Ma and keep her safe. I'll feel better if I know you're here with them."

"I'll take care of her boy." Dedrow pulls his saddlebags and rifle from the bay as Slim ties his on.

"Take care of my horse would you cowboy?" Slim pats the blowing gelding. "I rode him pert near to death."

Dedrow nods gruffly. "I'll see to him."

"Thank you Sir." Slim nods then looks over at Clay. "I'm headed back to the ranch, I may be needed there."

"I'll be riding out with you mister." The ice in Clay's words did not leave room for argument.

"You going after Miss Barber son?" Emily Kincaid steps beside him.

"I'm gonna try, you know better than anyone what she's in for if we don't get her back and quick."

"I know son, you be careful and make sure and keep your hair on. You hear?" Emily hugs him then steps back. "You come back safe."

Clay hugs the woman then looks at Dedrow. "I'm counting on you Bandy."

"I'll see after them."

Clay mounts then looks over at Slim. "We'll ride to the Agency, get some supplies and shells, and let Agent Miles know what's happened."

Crossing the Canadian to the Agency Clay is surprised the Indians already found out about the Comanche taking Lana. George Barber and Agent Miles meet the riders in front of the Agency and hurry to where they dismount.

"Have you heard anything Mister Kincaid?" The frail man is frantic.

"No Sir, but we're headed out after her as soon as we get supplies."

"I want to go with you."

Clay shakes his head. "No Sir, you're not used to riding long distances and we don't have the time to waste while you get ready."

"But she's my sister."

"Then do her a favor and let us handle this."

Nodding Barber turns back to the Agency. "Will they kill her?"

"We'll do our best to get her back."

"I know you will." Barber follows them into the Agency. "Whatever you need I'll pay for.

"Pressing hard to the west Slim pulls the gelding in as he spooks sideways from Rains dead horse. Looking down at the bloody spot where Rains was shot from his horse. He points at the tracks then off towards the river.

"Grey Moon has taken after them but they've sure got him outnumbered."

Clay nods. "You're figuring they're both dead by now, ain't you?"

"I figure, knowing them devils I hope the girl is dead." Slim lights a smoke. "Moon may be dead too but he'll take a few of them with him."

"You ride on in to the ranch in case you're needed. Tell the Guthries I'll try to catch up to Grey Moon."

"Thank you Mister Kincaid." Slim nods, "I'd trail with you but I've got to get back and see about Will and the Missus."

"You go on, I'll ride after them."

The warrior's trail is plain to follow where the tall grass laid over by their passing. Clay pulls the Winchester from its scabbard and jacks a shell into the chamber. He knows he is outnumbered but he does not have time or the inclination to go slow or use caution. Alternating between a short lope and a trot, he keeps the gelding traveling alongside the wide river. One shod horse was mixed in with the tracks. It must be Moon's horse and maybe soon, he will catch up to Grey Moon somewhere ahead following the trail.

Moon dismounts and studies the horse tracks that lead down to the river then straight into the muddy water. The Comanche did not try to find a shallow crossing but took to the water when they came to the banks. Without hesitating Moon kicks the gelding into the shallows and replaces the rifle in its sheath before hitting deep water. Slipping off to the side of the bay, Moon kicks strongly helping the horse swim across the river.

The river is deep but the current is not all strong as the bay horse swims powerfully towards the far bank. Splashing ashore Moon grabs the gelding's tail and let the horse pull him up the muddy bank before stopping him for a short rest. He heard stories all his life about the warlike Comanche and now he finally is going to get to see just how mighty they actually are. Around the livery back in Hayes City, he listened to the buffalo hunters, the soldiers, and the cattlemen who pushed their herds north. They all tell bloody stories of Quanah and his warriors. Now he is going to have to pit his courage and knowledge against theirs if he is to rescue Lana Barber.

Kicking the gelding, Moon rides through the tall grass and reeds following their trail. He knows the Comanche are well mounted, over the years he saw a few of the mustangs they rode and heard the stories of their hardiness and stamina on the trail. Apparently, the stories are true, the Comanche did not stop to breathe their animals as they climb up the deep sandy riverbank and ride away from the Canadian. Two hours later after pushing his horse hard, Moon climbs a small hill then dismounts and cautiously bellies up to the top for a look-see. His hunch is right; below him just out of rifle range a line of fifteen warriors follow the big warrior at the front in single file. Moon can see Lana riding double behind the Comanche.

Maybe his chances are getting better, tough as they are the little mustang carrying both the big warrior and Lana will tire. Mounting, he whips the bay across the rump with his rifle and lopes to where the warriors went out of his sight. He wants to fire on the Comanche in the worst way but even though it would narrow the odds, it will not help rescue Lana.

<h1 style="text-align:center">Chapter 15</h1>

<h2 style="text-align:center">The Missouri Jack</h2>

Clay finds where Moon and the warriors crossed the Canadian. Removing his boots, he ties them around his saddle horn and starts forward as a shrill whistle comes from downstream. Turning he sees three warriors coming straight at him at a hard run. Sighting the Winchester over the saddle, he takes careful aim then lowers the gun as the lead rider raises his arm and pulls his horse down into a slow trot.

"My friend Kincaid; Strong Bull and warriors have come to help you." The young Cheyenne reaches out and grabs Clay by the arm.

"It is good to see Strong Bull. How do you come to be here my friend?"

"My father, Charging Bull, sends me to help you find the yellow haired woman."

"Does Agent Miles know you are here?"

"Some of my people will tell him." Strong Bull looks down at the fresh tracks leading into the muddy water. "They tell agent everything. Come we go."

"Wait." Clay holds out his hand and stops the warrior. "I will give this good Winchester rifle if one of these men will ride fast to the Kiowa Villages on the upper Arkansas and ask Thunder Hawk for his help."

"Why do you want them to come here, they are Comanche same as these warriors?"

"I know." Clay acknowledges. "Thunder Hawk is my father's friend and I don't think he knows anything of this."

"It is two days ride to the Kiowa Village." Strong Bull shakes his head. "What if Thunder Hawk already left and is across the river in the Staked Plains?"

"Perhaps Thunder Hawk isn't." Clay persists. "If we can find him maybe he will come here and get the girl back before she is harmed."

"This warrior who has the woman is Snake Shield, very crazy and cruel, the worst of the Comanche." Strong Bull argues. "He will not listen to an old one like Thunder Hawk."

"It's a long shot alright but I'll give a rifle if one of them will try." Strong Bull shrugs and nods at the younger of the warriors. "She is your woman."

"Thank you my friend." Clay kicks his horse into the swirling water and starts across as the lone warrior races away to the northwest. "Tell me, how do you know this Comanche's name?"

"Many of my people have seen these warriors camped on our hunting grounds." Strong Bull laughs as his horse takes to the water. "This one has a shield painted with the snake on it."

Paddy and Moss sit above the Guthrie Ranch watching as the slender rider races his horse across the yard and makes a flying dismount before running across the porch. Paddy nods, something is amiss, he figures Galt set some of his plan in action.

"He sure is in an awful hurry."

"Yea, the Boss said he was gonna do something to stir up the hornet's nest." Paddy watches the house. "Reckon what it were?"

"Beat's me." Moss shrugs. "I reckon things are fixing to start hopping pretty soon now, that cowboy sure wasn't running that horse to death for nothing."

"Pine should be almost back to Galt by now." Paddy lies back on the grass. "We'll move down there right after dark."

Moss frowns. "I heard Galt tell him to stay and help us grab the mule."

"It don't take three men to steal a long eared donkey.

"Pulling his long skinning knife the scar faced Moss tests the blade. "You reckon they'll have him guarded?"

"Doubt it, why would they?"

Will sits listening to Slim as Alder pours him a cup of coffee. "When is the army sending the Doctor to see about Captain Rains?"

"He should be along anytime." Slim sips on his coffee and looks over where Rains lay. "The Colonel is sending two troops after the girl."

"They'll be too late to run them Comanche down." Will frowns, "What about Moon, did you happen to see him?"

"Sure didn't Boss but that Kincaid boy was at the fort, he rode back with me and picked up Grey Moon's track where it crossed the river."

"He alone?"

"Yep."

Rains turns his head weakly and looks across the room. "You see anything of Lana?"

"No Captain, I sure didn't."

Munday eases himself into an upright position and cusses. Alder looks up from where she is working over Rains wound and frowns. "That'll be enough of that language in my house young man."

"Shucks Ma, first excitement we've had around here and here I sit laid up with these broken ribs."

"Ain't you concerned about Moon or the girl?" Slim looks at the youngster and shakes his head.

"Sure I am Slim and I sure would like to be on the trail of them heathens." Munday frowns. "Just like the old days."

"Ugh huh." Slim turns his head not wanting Alder to see his frown.

"Missus, toss some grub together for Killian and the boys, Slim can take it out to the herd." Will nods over at Alder. "Slim you and the boys stay out with the herd tonight, might be them Comanche could hit us after dark."

"Yes sir, ya'll gonna be alright here alone?"

"Me, the Missus, and the boy can handle anything they throw at us." Will nods, "You boys stay alert out there and stay alive."

"Yes sir, I'm gone then."

Paddy watches from his place of concealment as the same slender rider that just rode into the ranch yard. He mounts and rides out due west towards the pasturelands. Slipping back, he kicks Moss awake and unhobbles the horses.

"Let's go, the place looks wide open."

The big Missouri Jack stands hip shot in a corner of the smaller corral watching the two men that are slipping quietly towards him. Anyone watching would have discovered the two men as the tall jack has his long ears pointing straight at the figures slipping up on him in the shadowy dark.

"You think that monster is halter broke?" Moss whispers. "Man he's a big one."

"He's bound to be, they didn't bring him here in a wagon." Paddy uncoils his rope and eases the gate open. "You scared of a donkey?"

"I've been around them igits my whole life and I know they'll dang sure bite and kick." Moss is dubious as Paddy approaches the Jack.

"Just pull the gate open and keep watch while I halter the ugly thing." Paddy advances towards the animal in the dusky dark. "I can't believe you're scared of a dumb animal."

"Say what you want, you best watch yourself Paddy." Moss shakes his head. "I heard a feller back in Missouri had three of his fingers bit clean off by a Jack just like this one."

Approaching the Jack as if it was a horse, Paddy lays his hand on the animal's hip and starts working his way up his back disregarding the ears that suddenly lay back pinned against the long head. From where he is guarding the gate, Moss hears the sickening thud of something hard-hitting against something soft then the ripping of cloth as Paddy races across the corral with the Jack in pursuit.

Slamming the gate shut as Paddy flies through it, Moss has to bite his finger to keep from laughing aloud. It is almost dark but he can still see the hefty Paddy running for his life then throwing himself bodily under the already open gate. Meanwhile, the Jack already stopped his pursuit and appears to be asleep in the middle of the corral.

Watching the Jack for a few seconds to make sure he I not coming over the gate Moss leans over and feels of his prone partner. "Dang Paddy, you dead or what?"

"I'm alive, I reckon." The words are shaky but at least the outlaw can still talk. "Did you see that sucker biting at me Moss?"

"I seen him and I warned you." Moss has to fight back his laughter. "Why that Jack done kicked you almost into next month and then he took a bite out of your hind side!"

"I'll kill him, danged if he's gonna kick and bite on me." Paddy gasps and then climbs slowly to his feet. "Man, how'd I get all the way over here?"

"Well, old Hoss you ran part of the way and that thing kicked you the rest, that's how." Moss shakes his head hiding a smile as he looks at Paddy's pants. "That ain't all either; the way he's looking over here he's planning on doing it again."

Paddy touches himself tenderly and cusses. "That thing is some kind of cannibal, that's what he is. Man my tail hurts."

"You gonna be able to ride Paddy?"

"I'll have to; we sure can't wait around here."

"What we gonna do now?" Moss still has a hard grip on the gate as he hides behind it. "That thing is just waiting on one of us to come back in that corral."

"I'm gonna get a rope on that Jackass, that's what." Paddy gets to his feet and shakes out a loop. "If we don't get him like Galt said; he'll be kicking us a lot harder than that long eared bag of bones."

Moss steps behind the gate and watches wide-eyed waiting for the wreck as the lariat settles around the Jack's neck. Pulling the loop tight, Paddy slowly works his way down the rope. Moss has to admit Paddy has guts or he is crazy. To his amazement, once the Jack feels the lariat tighten around his neck he leads docilely.

"Get the horses and let's ride." Paddy smiles proudly then touching his bottom tenderly, he looks up into the eyes of the culprit. "You're gonna get it Mister, soon as we cross the river, you're dead."

Grey Moon's long legged dun gelding pricks his ears, as he smells the Comanche horses ahead of him. Pulling him in, he studies the warriors that are crossing a large clear piece of flat land. He is curious, the raiders do not appear to be in a hurry and they ride as if they are out on a hunt looking for game. It is almost dark, he follows all-day and never gets out of a walk except for the first few miles. It does not make sense to him, why would Comanche Raiders be this far from their hunting grounds and why would they take only one captive? It is almost as if they want the army to follow or catch up with them.

Moon keeps a careful watch around him. They are Kwahadi Comanche, a warlike people adept at warfare and hard to surprise, yet he was following close to them all-day, surely they know he is here. He saw Lana Barber several times, as she was switched to different horses so not just one single horse would carry double. Besides being tired and dirty, she does not seem to be harmed in any way.

Circling a water hole, the warriors make camp and turn their ponies loose to graze. One lone warrior sits his horse watching the herd and riding in a large circle about the camp keeping watch for anyone coming towards them. Moon backtracks from the camp and unsaddles the dun hobbling him on the lush grass that grows belly deep on a horse. In a crouching run, he slips quietly back to a small knoll where he can study the camp and small fire while keeping an eye on the mounted warrior who guards the horses. From his vantage point, he watches as the Comanche warriors laze about the camp while the girl gathers small sticks and places them near the fire.

Lying hidden in the tall grass Moon keeps his dark eyes shifting back and forth between the sentry and the camp. The warrior set to watch the horses is young, he will have no problem killing this one but how could he rescue the girl who was being held in the middle of the camp and watched so close. He knows the Comanche, if he kills the sentry he will have to get the girl away to safety before the warrior's body is discovered or there is no doubt she will be killed in retaliation. Moon shakes his head, the girl is less than three hundred yards away but she might as well be a hundred miles.

Clay and the Cheyenne ride their horses hard catching up to the slow moving Comanche raiding party late in the afternoon. Moving ahead quietly they set their horses in a gully looking over to where Moon's dun gelding stands grazing. Pointing to a small knoll further out on the grassland, Strong Bull nods. "He is there, he watches the Comanche."

Clay looks past the horse but what he could see of the knoll seems empty of life. "How do you know he is there?"

"It is a good place to watch from." Strong Bull shrugs. "He would not leave his horse if he was not watching both the horse and the enemy."

"What will we do?"

Strong Bull dismounts. "We will wait here and let our horses graze. The breed will find us when he returns."

"Why do you call him a breed? He is half Cheyenne."

"Because he is a breed not a full-blood."

"And the Comanche?"

Strong Bull shrugs, "They are great warriors."

"But you are here to fight them?"

"They have come to our lands uninvited; my father says they will cause many problems for us with the whites. Besides it is a great honor to fight with warriors such as these."

"So they are your enemy?"

"For now, yes." Strong Bull nods, "Tomorrow maybe we fight with them against the pony soldier."

Moon watches his dun gelding as he circles stealthily back to where he left the horse. Several times the dun stopped grazing and lifted his head looking off behind him at a small grove of trees. Something or someone waits there, watching from the grove of trees.

"He comes." Strong Bull shifts his bow.

"You see him?" Clay looks out across the grassy flats trying to find the figure of Moon.

"No, but he is near." Strong Bull nods towards the dun. "His horse knows this and watches as he approaches."

"I am here, Cheyenne." Moon rises from the grass and walks to where the three lay hiding in the trees. "Do not shoot."

"Grey Moon, it is good to see you." Clay rises from the ground greeting the newcomer. "Have you seen the girl?"

"She is held captive just over that knoll." Moon nods at the small hill. "The Comanche watch her close."

"Has she been harmed?"

"No, she seems okay."

"What can we do to free her?"

Grey Moon looks over at Strong Bull and shakes his head. "If we attack we can kill them all but before they die they could kill her first."

"He is right." The Cheyenne agrees. "If we go in we must kill all of them before they know we are there."

"It is too risky." Clay shakes his head. "We cannot risk getting Lana killed."

Strong Bull looks at the white. "Death is better than being a woman captive of the Comanche."

"What do you wish to do?" Moon questions, "If we wait very long they may kill her."

Clay knows he is right, he heard horror tales of the Comanche all his life. "I sent a rider to Thunder Hawk for help; we will just follow these warriors and watch."

"You think a Comanche will come here and help free a white woman from their brothers?"

"I don't know but my father is their friend." Clay shrugs. "We have no choice, we will follow and watch close if we get a chance to free her we will, if not we will wait."

"You bring anything to eat?" Moon rubs his stomach. "I'm starved."

"In the bags."

"I will go back and watch the Comanche, you stay here." Moon pulls out biscuits and cooked bacon from the bags then walks away.

Pine dismounts and hands the reins of his tired gelding to one of the new men Galt took on before walking to where several men loaf around a small fire. Searching out each face as he passes to see if he knows any of them, Pine nods at the outlaw leader then finds a soft piece of ground to collapse on.

"They get the Jack?" Galt growls from where he is sitting.

"They got him." Pine lied; he did not wait to see if they got the Jack.

"Good, now if Guthrie goes after him it will leave his herd unguarded."

"What about the army?"

Galt smiles, "They got their hands full right now, seems some heathen Comanche shot Captain Rains and took a white woman named Lana Barber captive."

"And Kincaid?"

"No problem, someone took a shot at him, now he's laid up at the fort with a broken leg. What's better, I heard from Charlie Tom his kid is chasing after the Comanche band that took the girl."

"That leaves the horse herd almost unprotected. Why don't we just take them and clear out." Pine looks across at Galt. "Leave them hardheaded mules behind."

"No, I've had a man ride out to Kincaids; he's only got three men left out there to protect his herd." Galt shakes his head. "And that fool Guthrie is fixing to chase that Jack all the way across the Nations, we're gonna take both herds."

Pine shakes his head. "You're calling the shots Ewen but that's a lot of horse flesh to get rid of up north."

"I've got a perfect place to hide them while we sell them off."

"Okay, sounds good if we can pull it off."

"We've got twelve men left here, you take six and get the Kincaid horses and I'll take the rest and pick up the Guthrie herd." Galt rolls a quirley and lights up. "Leave no survivors behind. You understand me Pine?"

"I hear you, Boss." The lanky outlaw looks through the smoke at his leader. "Where are we gonna meet up?"

"North of the Canadian." Galt feels of his side. "When I get clear with the mules I'll send a man back to bring you in."

"If we pull it off, we'll have almost a thousand head of animals to push." Pine calculates what the horses will bring up in Missouri. "That's a lot of riding, how's your side?"

"It'll hold together, counting all that money makes it feel better already." Galt shrugs. "Get some rest; we're pulling out at daylight."

"Don't count your chickens before they hatch." Pine thinks it but says nothing. Ewen Galt is a hardheaded man, when his mind is made up nothing changes it.

Frank lies back on the army cot and stares up at the ceiling as something nags at him. So much has happened since the Guthries and his own herds arrived at the Darlington Agency. Him being shot, Captain Rains and Lana Barber attacked, and the Cavalry pulling away from the fort to chase after the Comanche. He knows the Comanche; he fought them for years before Quanah took a liking to him after the fight at his small ranch. Something about this does not seem right; he knows the Comanche mind, they would not just take the girl and nothing else. This far from their own country across the Red River, they would have killed a woman quickly and raided the Guthrie Ranch if they came this far into the Nations solely to steal and raid. No, there is something more to this; they did not take any horses, no plunder or captives, nothing.

Suddenly, he understands what is bothering him; it is too simple. Hollering for Emily, Frank sits painfully up on the side of the army cot. Hearing the door open he turns where she stands looking at him. "Have the team brought around and tell Bandy to hurry."

"What's wrong husband?" Emily tries to push him back on the cot. "You can't get out of bed yet."

"Just get the team wife; I'll explain it to you on the way to the ranch."

Emily nods. "Okay but are you able to travel?"

"Hurry wife." Frank orders gruffly. "I've got to travel, now please do as I say."

Dedrow pushes the bays as hard as he dares. Alternating between a fast trot and a lope, he looks into the bottom of the wagon where Frank lay on a corn shuck mattress, his face a mask of pain.

"Sorry boss, I can't miss all the rocks and holes."

"Just push'em hard Bandy, hard, I'll live through it."

"Yes sir, I'm pushing."

"What are you thinking husband?" Emily cradles his head in her lap.

"Just keep that rifle ready and keep a sharp lookout."

"You think the Comanche are fixing to raid into our herd, don't you."

"Something like that, I don't know who is coming but I've got me a feeling it won't be long." Frank looks up at the sky. "I can smell something wife and it sure ain't Comanche."

Dedrow pulls the blowing team into the ranch yard and helps the wounded man into the house. Emily follows with the extra shells and supplies they quickly gathered up at the Agency. Placing Frank in a straight-back chair where he can observe the yard and barn the foreman leads the team into the barn.

"Em, tell Bandy to come in soon as he unharnesses the team." Frank looks out the window. "And hurry."

"You still think someone is coming?"

"More than ever."

Dedrow pushes open the door and lays two loaded Winchesters on the long table. Looking around the room at the barred shutters and doors, he nods.

"You think we've got trouble Boss?"

"Ride out to the herd and have the boys push them in closer to the ranch." Frank tries to ease his leg. "Real close, put the old bell mare and a few others in the corral maybe that will hold the other horses from straying far."

"Yes sir." Dedrow heads for the door. "I'm gone."

"Turn down the lamps wife and get comfortable." He smiles over at her. "We may be in for a long night."

"Just like the old day's husband." Emily smiles, "And we're still alive."

"Just like the good old day's wife." He winks at her.

Chapter 16

The Herds

Guthrie straps his pistol on and starts for the door. "I'll feed the stock then we'll fort up, if anyone is gonna hit us it'll be at sun-up or a little before."

"I'll cover you from the porch Pa." Munday moves slowly following Will from the door and looks up at the darkening sky. "Watch yourself, tonight's gonna be what they always call a Comanche Moon down in Texas."

Will stops and looks back at the youngster curiously. "Now who told you that nonsense?"

"Slim."

"Figures." Will smiles, "Let me tell you boy, when a Comanche decides to raid he don't need a moon, just a target."

"And that's us maybe?"

"Yep, that's us."

Munday smiles, "Well I'm ready; we'll give them, what for, if they make that mistake."

Will was gone only a few minutes then he races back to the house and steps up on the porch where the boy is waiting in the shadows. "The Jack's gone."

"Comanche?"

"White men." Will swears and holds out a piece of cloth. "They left their boot prints in the corral and this, Comanche don't wear denim."

"There's blood on it."

Will chuckles, "Yep, I reckon that old Jack got a piece of one of them." Munday shakes his head bewildered. "Now why would anyone want that Jack except us?"

"I don't know boy, maybe they're figuring on pulling us away from the ranch on a wild-goose chase." Will follows Munday back into the kitchen.

"You going after the Jack?"

"No, I can't leave you and your Mother alone tonight." Will takes the coffee Alder offered. "Get some rest; I'll take the first watch."

Frank watches from the window as Dedrow and the other hands push the large herd of horses in close to the corrals and buildings then loads the bell mare and several others in the corral. Dedrow rides his horse close to the open window where Frank sits watching and stops.

"How you doing?"

"I'm alright Bandy, just can't move about real good."

"You figure we got trouble coming?"

"I don't know, just an old man's hunch I reckon."

Dedrow nods. "That's good enough for me. Where do you want us?"

"In the barn, maybe we can get them in a cross fire." Frank looks at his gathered riders. "Boys, I don't know who or what's coming. If it's Comanche, they'll probably raid us about daylight. I think it's whites that shot me and they could come anytime now but then again maybe not for a couple of days."

Emily carries biscuits and meat wrapped in cotton sacks out to the men then retreats into the house. "You want one of us to come in the house with you?"

"We're alright in here; you boys keep alert and be ready for whatever."

"We'll be ready Frank." Dedrow turns towards the barn.

Pine sits his horse and studies the dark Kincaid Ranch buildings. He purposely waits to close in on the ranch until after the full moon rises, lighting up the land so his men can see. The place is completely dark and silent as he studies the horses that graze around the near pastures. Pine does not like it. The horses are not out on the pasture as they should be and the ranch buildings are far too quiet. Hesitating several minutes he is undecided, the layout just does not look good but he has no choice. Galt is expecting him to bring the horses to the Canadian and he knows the man's temper if he does not follow his orders. Looking over at his men he shrugs and then finally motions them forward still feeling something is not right.

"We've caught them napping, boys." Pine whispers hoping he is right. "Kincaid is back at the fort and the hands will be in the bunkhouse. Remember no survivors."

Frank hears the low call of a whippoorwill come from the barn. Dedrow spotted something and sent his warning across the flat yard. Whispering to Emily, he cocks the hammer on his rifle and eases it out the open window.

"What is it husband?"

"I don't know yet." Frank touches her arm. "Bandy is in the loft and has a better view of the horses but I figure we got company."

"I'll take the other window." Emily takes two rifles and huddles beside the second window.

"You stay down now. You hear?"

Frank watches as six riders suddenly materialize in the yard right in front of the bunkhouse. Two men dismount; racing across the porch, they open the door and fire several shots into the empty bunks. Frank has his answer, sighting his rifle he takes careful aim on one of the men firing and pulls the trigger. The heavy slug flung the shooter forwards into the bunkhouse as several rifles open up from the barn emptying saddles as the Kincaid hands pour withering fire into the mounted riders. Two riders whirl their horses hard trying to escape but they drop from their saddles before they clear the ranch yard. Frank looks over where Emily is still firing into the down men.

"I think they're all down wife."

Emily lowers her smoking rifle. "I aim to make sure them back shooters don't get another chance at you husband."

"If I didn't know better, I'd think you were a cold hearted woman."

"You mess with my man and I can get cold hearted, real quick." Emily walks over to where Frank was reloading his rifle and hugs him.

Lanterns show across the yard as Dedrow and the others close in on the dead men cautiously. Leaning over and prodding the bodies to see if any lived they collect the weapons and start dragging the corpses onto the bunkhouse porch.

"They all dead?" Frank asks as Dedrow comes over to the house.

"Yep, to the last man." Dedrow rolls himself a quirley and strikes a match. "One said something funny before he cashed in his chips."

"What was that?"

"I dunno, something about counting your chickens." Dedrow shrugs. "That's all, don't know what he meant."

"Load them up. In the morning take them to the agency to that Marshal Vetter." Frank sets his rifle down. "Tell him what happened."

"I'd just dump them in a hole somewhere." Dedrow blows smoke. "They deserve nothing."

"That would be okay." Frank shakes his head. "Except I want folks to know what happens when they ride against the Running K Brand."

"I figure they'll know now alright." Dedrow looks over at Emily as she lights a lamp. "That was some pretty good shooting Miss Em."

The blue eyes flash. "Like ducks in a barrel Bandy but they reaped what they sowed I believe."

"Yes Ma'am." He agrees and smiles. "The way they came at us, they meant to kill us all."

Will heard a crescendo of shots coming from the north pasture just after the moon showed itself. Stepping out onto the dark porch, he listens as the far-off echoing of the shooting rises and then suddenly stops. Several minutes later Killian and Little Bit Dawkins ride into the yard and dismount on the run from their horses. Will holds the door as the two men duck inside the house.

"What happened out there?"

"They came up out of that deep gully north of here and surprised us." Killian peers out through a window. "They came up shooting, we didn't have a chance. Killed Andy and Slim right off."

"Slims dead?" Alder gasps aloud. "And poor Andy, no."

"He's dead Ma'am." Little Bit speaks up. "Like I said, we didn't know what hit us."

Will drops his head and cusses. "I sent him out there, I told Slim to warn you."

"It wasn't his fault or yours, he warned us." Killian shakes his head. "It was mine if anybody's, it was after dark and I figured we were okay for the night."

Will was about to answer when several shots rang out from the corrals sending lead through the thin walls of the house. Crouching beside the windows Will and Killian can see the rifle flashes of the shooters.

"There's only two out there Boss." The foreman ducks back down as the rifles fire again. "There were several more firing at us out by the herd."

"They're just trying to pin us down in here while the rest run off the herd." Will stands up. "Let's go."

"Where?"

"Out the back, you take the left side and I'll take the right." Will starts for the back door. "Munday, you and Little Bit stay with your Mother."

Alder takes him by the arm. "Wait until daylight so you can see."

Kissing her lightly he pulls loose. "No man kills my men, shoots up my house, and lives to brag about it."

"Then come back safe."

Galt has the mixed herd of mules and horses heading north and east in a hard run. After sending two men to keep the ones at the ranch under cover, he has four men counting Charlie Tom left to drive the herd. A few head will be lost in the run but he wants to cross the river and meet up with Pine and the Kincaid horses as soon as he could. The two long night rides he has undergone the last two days has his side hurting again but there is no time to rest until they clear the territory.

Galt knows Snake Shield took the woman and Paddy took the Jack so Guthrie and the Cavalry should be too busy to pursue them until they have a good lead. Reining his horse over to where Charlie Tom rides the left flank of the herd he looks over at the Indian.

"Did the men come in yet?"

"Me no see them come here."

Galt looks back over his shoulder. "They'll be along soon enough."

Will slips wide around the left side of the barn watching as the rifles spit fire and lead at the house. Gritting his teeth, he eases quietly up behind the first shooter and waits for the man to fire.

"You cock that rifle again pilgrim and you're a dead man." The rancher thumbs the hammer back on his Winchester. "Drop it and stand up with your hands high."

The man hesitates then finally pitches the rifle out in front of him. "Don't shoot mister."

"Now that's a good one after you've been shooting up my house." Will growls as several shots go off by the corrals. "We'll wait a few minutes friend but you better not move an eyelash."

"I ain't moving."

"I've got him Boss, come on in." Killian yells out from where the shooting came from.

Killian stands over another man as Will herds his man up to the corrals. Kicking the wounded man to his feet Killian shoves him roughly towards the other rustler. The man's left sleeve is bloodstained by a bullet that barely grazed him.

"He hurt bad?" Will can barely make out the hurt man in the dark.

Killian cusses the man then raises his rifle. "He'll live long enough to hang. I should have shot him dead and may still do it."

"We'll lock them in the storeroom, in the morning I'll send Little Bit for Marshal Vetter." Will prods the two men towards the barn.

"What about my arm?" The wounded man whines.

Only the whack of Killian's rifle sounds as he clubs the captive. "You should have thought of that when you killed Slim and Andy."

Little Bit arrives at Fort Reno almost at the same time Bandy Dedrow is hauling the dead bodies in from the Kincaid Ranch. Dismounting beside the wagon the rider looks over into the wagon where the bodies were stacked like cordwood.

"We've got two more for you Marshal out at Guthrie's ranch."

"What's going on here?" Vetter is curious that both ranches were attacked the same night. "I recognize these men as some of Ewen Galt's gang. I reckon he's behind this somewhere, probably aimed to run off some of your horses."

"Some of them." Little Bit scratches his head. "Shucks Marshal, he took every head we had and killed two men in the process."

"That's what it looks like, he's raiding both herds." Dedrow shakes his head. "He really didn't think he could get away with something like that?"

"Galt has run wild around the Nations since the end of the war." Vetter nods. "I wouldn't put it past him to try that very thing."

"Well Marshal he got away with some of it; him and his men killed two of our men and got away with all our stock." Little Bit steps back from the wagon. "They even took the big Missouri Jack that the boss was so proud of."

"You don't reckon this has something to do with the girl getting taken?"

"It could have been his way of getting the army out of the way."

"I'm heading back." Little Bit turns to his horse. "Will you be coming to get the prisoners Marshal?"

"Soon as I take care of these bodies and get saddled up."

"What should I tell Mister Guthrie about our herd?"

"I don't know, the army has all its men in the field after the Comanche so they can't help." Vetter shakes his head. "I sure don't have any men to go up against Galt and his crowd of killers; I reckon the herd will have to wait until the army gets back."

"Empty my wagon Marshal." Dedrow looks over to where Little Bit mounts. "Tell Mister Guthrie as soon as I can ride back to the ranch and get men we'll meet him north of the river and help him run down this bunch of horse thieves and killers."

"You coming Marshal?"

"I'll ride with you." Vetter nods, "Let me get these men under and I'll ride out."

"You better hurry, 'cause Will Guthrie ain't waiting." Little Bit spurs his gelding and rides away.

An hour before the breaking of the new dawn Moon slips back where he left Clay and Strong Bull. Quickly saddling his horse, he motions towards the northwest and rides off with them following. Passing the camp the Comanche just vacated an hour earlier, he dismounts and with Strong Bull's help, they examine the ground. The small heap of ashes from the night's fire still put off heat as they move about checking every footprint.

Moon shakes his head. "These warriors don't act like they're scared of anyone following them. Lighting a fire and keeping it burning through the night like that. They're not afraid or trying to hurry at all."

"Maybe they don't know we're here." Clay watches as the breed moves stealthily about the vacant camp like a hound smelling out a track. "The girl, is she okay?"

"They know we follow and the girl has not been harmed." Moon stands up and looks off towards the west. "Let's ride."

"How do you know she has not been harmed in any way?" Clay saw no sign of Lana at the camp, not a small footprint, nothing. "Tell me Moon, what should we do?"

"If the woman was attacked here in this place, the signs of a struggle would be on the ground. There is nothing."

"Then what would you do?" Clay repeats the question.

Pulling his horse to a stop Moon looks over at his two companions. "I think if your friend Thunder Hawk doesn't show soon, we should attack these warriors before they kill her."

"You think they'd just kill her?"

"Indians act on whims; the Comanche are wilder and crueler than most tribes." Moon looks over at Strong Bull. "They may keep her alive for bait but they could kill her quickly if anything happens."

"Moon speaks the truth, we should attack before they harm woman from Agency." Strong Bull nods. "And before horse soldiers come to this place."

"I forgot all about the cavalry, they'll attack if they catch up to the Comanche without regard for Lana's safety." Moon looks over at Clay then out across the flats. "Let's ride."

Moon takes the lead following the Comanche trail but keeps well back from the warriors. He knows the small Comanche Mustangs the warriors ride are like dogs, as they can smell a strange horse on the wind. They would warn their riders by the motion of their ears or nickering. He is taking no chances of being discovered and placing Lana in danger. He has a strange conviction the Comanche Snake Shield is just toying with them, using the girl to lure them further from the Fort before turning on them and attacking.

Clay kicks his gelding in behind Moon following next in line trying to figure out what to do. He has little experience fighting Indians. He listened to the tales of Indian fights from years past but personally, he was only in a skirmish with them once. He has no doubt Moon is right, if the cavalry shows up even at a distance the Comanche would kill Lana and flee. Kicking his gelding, he moves up alongside Moon.

"If Thunder Hawk hasn't arrived before dark we'll attack when they make camp."

Moon nods. "It will be just a gamble, we will slip close to the camp, maybe we can get her back alive but either way she could be killed."

"I know but if the cavalry rides in they'll kill her for sure." Clay shrugs. "Can they follow the Comanche, do they have a tracker?"

Moon nods at Strong Bull. "He's one but they've got others around the agency they can use."

"You think the soldiers are coming?"

Strong Bull grunts when he hears the question. "Soldier come, quick I think. Comanche take white woman but they shoot, maybe kill white soldier officer coat. They mad, I think."

Moon nods solemnly. "He's right about that, they'll be mad as a stirred up hornet's nest."

CHAPTER 17

THUNDER HAWK

Dedrow, Pecos, and two other Kincaid hands cross the North Canadian after riding hard through the night. Dedrow wore out the team returning to the ranch to tell Frank what happened. The rancher agrees with his foreman, they must catch the horse thieves and punish them so other rustlers in the Nations will know to give the ranches a wide berth and leave them alone.

"You and the Missus gonna be alright until we get back?" Dedrow leans from his fresh horse as he looks at them.

"We'll be fine, you boys be careful and come back in one piece." Frank assures him from his chair. "Lebo will be here if we need him."

Will and Munday stand up from their campfire and watch as four men swim the river. Munday who insisted on riding with the men despite Alder's objections slowly straightens to his full height giving his sore side time to stretch.

"Looks like Kincaid's men crossing the river boss." Killian recognizes Dedrow in the lead.

Will adds. "I see them, put on a fresh pot of coffee."

"Yes sir."

"How you doing son?"

"Sore and aching a little."

"You should have stayed back with your Ma instead of leaving Jace."

Will looks over at the youngster. "Can you pull that pistol?"

"Yes sir, I can pull it." The hand is just a blur as Munday pulls and cocks the weapon then grins. "You should have told me to stay home when we rode out."

"Would it have done any good?"

"No sir, I wouldn't miss this little showdown if I had ten broken ribs." He grins, "But you could have told me anyway."

Dedrow rides up to the fire and looks down at Will Guthrie. "We made it as fast as we could without using up our horses Mister Guthrie."

"You did fine, thank you for coming." Will holds out his hand as Dedrow dismounts. "Help yourself to some coffee and beans."

"Thank you Mister Guthrie." Dedrow nods at his men. "Ya'll heard the man, light and eat."

"You boys just call me Will."

"Yes Sir Will, my names Bandy Dedrow." Dedrow shakes hands. "I'm foreman for the Running K, the boss couldn't ride he's been shot."

"I heard he had, I hope he recovers. Galt is behind all of this, he's kicking up a real fuss around these parts lately."

"You find the trail?" Dedrow rolls himself a quirley.

"Right over there a hundred yards."

"How many riders?"

"Does it matter?" Munday studies the Running K men that lounge around. "Where's the young Mister Kincaid?"

Dedrow turns to where Munday sat. "Boy, out here everything matters."

"You heard Slim say he went after Moon and the girl." Will frowns over at his son, then back at Dedrow. "Just overlook my son Bandy, hopefully he'll mature one of these days. Anyway in answer to your question it looks like about five or six but he's bound to have more."

"He did have more." Dedrow looks hard at the fire. "We killed six of them when they attacked the Running K night before last. I don't know this Galt on sight but I don't think he was one of the dead. Marshal Vetter didn't identify any of the dead men as him."

"Galt isn't normally so eager to get his men killed." Will nods thoughtfully.

"He's never run into Frank Kincaid before either." Dedrow chuckles, "If I ain't mistaken this is his second run in with the Running K, once before when we killed Jack Fritch across the Red.

"I heard Fritch was dead, figured it might have been your bunch that got him." Will looks off towards the north. "Well, he was long overdue."

"He's paid up now."

"Well, let's get to it, Galt's got a lead on us."

"I still don't think he was with the ones that hit the Running K two days ago."

"Reckon not but I'll guarantee he planned this job out." Will tightens his cinch. "He just didn't figure on you bunch of Texas hellions."

"The good Marshal said he'll catch up directly."

Munday scowls. "What for, we don't need him. It'll leave more of them killers for the rest of us without him."

Dedrow only shakes his head and looks over at the youngster.

The mixed mule and horse herd of the Guthries cut a wide trail leaving prints a blind man could follow across the deep grasslands. Will leads the men in a hard lope eager to catch up to Galt before they cross into Kansas. The thieves push the herd hard to the north figuring safety is only a few miles ahead across the state line.

Waiting on help, Will lost valuable time but he has no choice. He must wait on the Running K hands at the river but that gives the horse thieves time to stretch their lead. Cussing, he slows his gelding down to a trot, he wants to catch up but the horses cannot keep up the pace he had set since early morning. As the sun stood high in the blue sky overhead, they begin to pass a few stragglers that had fallen out behind the herd too worn out to keep up.

"They're running my mules to death." Will fumes, his face turning beet red. "Ruining them!"

"We're getting close Will." Dedrow nudges his horse up next to Guthrie's horse. "We best be on watch."

Will pulls up and studies the post oak and blackjack trees that dot the bottomland along a small stream. "I agree, from here on in we need to be on our toes alright."

"I'll ride on ahead and take a look-see." Dedrow starts to kick his horse.

"No sir, I believe that'll be my job." Munday moves past both men. "After all, they are our mules."

Dedrow studies the slender frame of the youngster as he trots off down the grassy slope and splashes across the knee-deep creek. Watching from a distance as Munday rides up out of a gully and eases slowly to the top of another small hill the Guthrie riders see him suddenly rein his gelding back down the rise, then wave his hat over his head.

"He's spotted the herd." Will spurs his gelding and takes off down the slope.

"Let's go get'em boys." Dedrow waves his hat and races after Will. "Spur them broomtails."

Thunder Hawk and three older warriors ride easily alongside the young Cheyenne that was sent to find them. After hearing all the details the warrior could offer, the old Comanche figures Snake Shield will ride due west and try to rejoin Quanah across the Red River deep in the grassland of the Llano Estacado. The keen witted old warrior of the Comanche rode quickly from the Kiowa Village, heading due east to cut off the ones who took the white girl.

Some of the hostile Kiowa that did not give up the war trail still follow Quanah. The peace seeking Kiowa that came in swearing to no longer fight the whites, were allotted lands that lay to the west of the Cheyenne and Arapaho, a reward for them to stay at peace. Thunder Hawk still fights the whites, now he was sent east by Quanah to urge the younger warriors of the Kiowa to take up the war trail and join him across the Red. For months, Mackenzie followed Quanah and his Kwahadis relentlessly across the grasslands eager to fight. Several times the Comanche Chief outfoxed the white soldiers and sent them for cover but each time they come back stronger. Quanah knows he has to have more warriors, either that or he will be forced to surrender his people to the soldier chief at Fort Sill.

Thunder Hawk failed, none of the peaceful Kiowa, not even the younger hot bloods voted to join Quanah, rejecting his invitation to fight the white soldier. The old Comanche could only shake his head at their answer, it was over he knows the red race is doomed; they lost their will to fight the numerous white pony soldiers. With the appearance of the Cheyenne Fleet Hoof who brought word the son of Frank Kincaid is asking for his help the old warrior decides to ride back to the east. He knows Quanah needs all his warriors but five more will be of little use against so many white soldiers. Quanah pledged his word the Kincaids could live in peace, Thunder Hawk was bound to keep that word.

Thunder Hawk and Snake Shield are of the same tribe and village and both rode with Quanah but they were not on friendly terms. Both warriors fought the whites, killing, taking captives, and plundering the far-reaching farms and ranches. However, they are from different tribal clans, their dislike for one another grew deeper over the years as Thunder Hawk followed Quanah; Snake Shield followed Quanah too, but his loyalty wasn't like

Thunder Hawk, he wants to be Chief of the Comanche. Listening as the Cheyenne spoke the words of the white man Kincaid; Thunder Hawk mounts his men and heads back to the east to cut off his nemesis Snake Shield.

Thunder Hawk's party along with the Cheyenne sit their tired horses atop a tall canyon wall and watch the valley below them. Rays of sunlight glimmer on the clear water of a stream far below as the afternoon sun reached its zenith. Powdery, snow-white clouds float lazily just above their heads seemingly so close the warriors could reach up and touch them. Tall grass waves back and forth in the breeze as it whispers softly across the deep canyon floor. The old warrior knows this place. Several times over the years, before this land was split up and assigned to the tribes of the Comanche, he crossed this place riding away to the east to evade the white soldiers who pursued them.

"You think they will come this way Uncle?" Fleet Hoof signs over to Thunder Hawk. The Cheyenne language is different from the Comanche tongue but the hand signs are universal for the warlike tribes of the grasslands.

"They will come soon." Thunder Hawk moves his hands. "This is the trail we used before even my father's, fathers time."

Moon reins in abruptly as a bright flash comes from the high plateau ahead of them. Dropping to the ground, he points his dark finger skyward as the flash comes once again.

"Someone is up there, they want us to know."

"Maybe it is Thunder Hawk." Clay scanned the ridges.

For two days, Moon and Strong Bull follow the Comanche keeping a few miles back not wanting to ride into a trap. Clay changes his mind about attacking the warriors, as they make no threat to Lana. Moon creeps quietly forward each night as close as he dares and watches as she prepares meals for the Comanche. Other than being exhausted from the continuous traveling, she does not appear to be hurt. Clay decides to give Thunder Hawk more time to find them and try to persuade Snake Shield to release the girl or maybe collect some kind of ransom for her return. Now he knows he chose right, somewhere high on the canyon wall someone is signaling to them. Clay knows it has to be the old Comanche.

Thunder Hawk waits knee deep in water at the crossing of a small stream as Snake Shield rides down the steep bank into the water. The warriors from each band spread out facing one another as they enter the stream.

"What does the great Thunder Hawk do in this place?" Snake Shield places his brown arm around the waist of the frightened Lana. "I thought you joined our Chief Quanah on the Llano."

"I have come here looking for Snake Shield." Thunder Hawk looks over at the frightened girl. "And for this white woman!"

The warrior looks down at the girl and smiles, "As the whites who follow us do?"

Thunder Hawk is not surprised the wild warriors before him know that someone is following them. Trained on the back of a wild mustang, the warriors are as wily, maybe more so, as any predator. "Snake Shield knows Quanah has given the Kincaid's protection from all Comanche, yet you take one of their women captive."

"You lie; this is a woman of the pony soldier with two bars."

"I don't lie; Snake Shield has broken the word of Quanah by this act." Thunder Hawk's face is a mask showing no emotion. "This woman belongs to Clay Kincaid."

"He is one of the whites who follows us?"

"Perhaps he is following, I don't know."

"Why does he not attack and take the woman back?" Snake Shield raises his war club. "If he just follows, afraid to come close and fight for his woman, he is a coward."

"He knows to attack the Comanche under one such as you the woman would die." Thunder Hawk's old eyes look at the girl. "He follows and waits."

"This woman is now mine." Snake Shield jerks Lana by the hair raising her face. "Her hair is like the corn silk of the whites."

"Give her back to the whites, let us leave this place and join Quanah who needs our guns." Thunder Hawk looks at the girl. "Leave the white squaw here; if you harm this woman Quanah will banish you from the people."

"You!" Snake Shield points at Fleet Hoof. "Your people, the Cheyenne dogs, are with the white go bring them here to this place if they are not afraid. If you do not do this thing I will kill the woman now."

Thunder Hawk signs to Fleet Hoof then watches him ride away in a hard run. Not a horse moves as both parties sit and look across the creek at each other. The big hand of Snake Shield holds Lana by the hair in a viselike hold.

Strong Bull raises his arm as he recognizes the warrior riding toward them. Listening silently as Fleet Hoof speaks and gestures behind him Strong Bull nods and looks over at Clay and Moon.

"Fleet Hoof says the Comanche Thunder Hawk is ahead, he waits for us to come to him." Strong Bull nods to the west. "The Comanche Snake Shield says if you do not come the woman will die."

"We will follow you." Clay speaks up. "Let's ride but be ready for a trick."

Fleet Hoof turns his words to Strong Bull who quickly translates the young warrior's words. "There will be no tricks; I think this Comanche only wants to kill you to prove his bravery to the woman."

"Then let's see how brave this Snake Shield is." Clay kicks his gelding forward following the Cheyenne.

Fleet Hoof circles around the place where the Comanche wait leading the small party to a place they can get down the steep bank and approach the waiting warriors from downstream. Snake Shield turns his small war pony as they splash around a small bend revealing themselves as they approach where he sat. Grinning wildly, he tosses the girl from him and looks down as she falls backwards in the water and then tries to stand.

Pulling their horses in, Clay and the other's sit spread out facing the Comanche. Clay looks down at the soaking wet and terrified Lana and frowns. "We're here Lana, you're safe now."

"Is this your woman white man?" Snake Shield speaks in halting English then looks across the water to Clay for his answer.

"She is."

"Good, there she lies in the water." Snake Shield shakes his war club at Clay. "Take her from Snake Shield if you are man enough."

"He wants you to fight him for her." Moon hisses through clenched teeth then yells at the warrior. "I Grey Moon of the Cheyenne will fight the mighty Snake Shield of the Comanche."

"Hah, fight a breed." The warrior again looks at Clay. "Him only, she is his woman; if he wants the woman back he will fight me."

Thunder Hawk rides forward. "If this young warrior is harmed you will shame Quanah and our people."

"If the white does not fight me, I will kill the woman now." Snake Shield raises his war club and points it down at Lana. "Then he will carry the shame as the coward he is."

"Quanah will have your heart for this." Thunder Hawk does not dare move forward, one blow from the heavy war club would split Lana's head.

When the ground runs red with this white man's blood I will add yours to it old man." Snake Shield returns his crazed look at Clay. "Will you fight white man or will you run like a woman?"

"Get him off that little horse quick, anyway you can." Moon reaches out and takes Clay's pistol belt. "Then kill him."

"You make it sound easy." Clay stares across the water at the warrior and raises his hand.

Snake Shield looks down at the frightened girl and sneers, then suddenly turns and races his mustang upriver splashing and lunging through knee-deep water. Wheeling the little horse, he brandishes his war club taunting Clay. Turning his own horse Clay catches the war club Strong Bull tossed over to him then moves an equal distance downstream and turns facing the gesturing warrior. Moon starts forward to help Lana from the water but two of Snake Shield's men grab her by the arms and drag her from the creek.

"You die white man." Snake Shield yells futilely in Comanche not realizing Clay does not understand a word he just spoke. "Then she with the yellow hair will come to my lodge as my woman."

Raising their war clubs both men hit their horses, a clout on the rump then with a vicious scream they charge through the water racing towards each other. The running horses are midstream in water almost to their knees. Clay's yellow gelding is at least two hands taller than the Comanche's Mustang giving him the advantage of height and weight. Both men miss on their initial pass causing them to have to turn and charge again. Slashing and shoving into each other the men are knee to knee swinging wildly with intense force, each horse pushing against the other.

Spurring the palomino Clay pushes hard into the mustang forcing him to give ground. Finally, he knocks Snake Shield over sideways causing him to be momentarily submerged under the water and caught beneath the mustang. Sliding from his horse quickly Clay plunges through the creek water towards the kicking mustang trying to reach Snake Shield before he can get free and regain his feet. Reaching the Comanche as he rises blindly from the water, Clay swings at the exposed head. He misses as the warrior ducks back under the water and kicks himself backwards out of range of the war club.

Both fighters are wet and slippery making it hard for them to get a good grip on each other. Charging forward Clay feels the edge of the war club of Snake Shield as it narrowly deflects off his arm. Moving under the blow Clay ducks behind the shorter warrior and grabs him around the waist.

Physically lifting the man clear of the water then slamming him face first into the creek, Clay holds the struggling Snake Shield under the water until he quit moving.

Watching as the body floats a few feet downstream he turns on the other warriors who hold Lana in their grasp. "Tell them to release the woman or die."

Thunder Hawk speaks harshly as the warriors of Snake Shield threaten to harm the girl. "Let the white man and woman go in peace and leave this place with me. We will return to the camp of Quanah where all Comanche are needed."

"We will revenge Snake Shield." One of the warriors holding Lana's arm raises his own war axe.

The sound of the hissing arrow from Strong Bull, then the splashing of the warrior's body hitting the water is the only sound heard as Thunder Hawk raises his arm. "Stop Comanche's or many more will die here at this place."

"Snake Shield was a fool; he should not have listened to the white man with the promised rifles and whiskey." One of the Comanche warriors releases his grasp on Lana and retreats towards his horse.

"Galt." Moon speaks the name slowly. "It had to be him, what other white renegade would purposely sick the Comanche on his own people?

Clay wades through the water and pushes the other warrior aside picking up Lana and placing her on his Palomino. Handing the reins to Moon, he walks to where Thunder Hawk sits his horse.

"Thunder Hawk has been a true friend, if you ever need a place to go or a friend, the Kincaid Ranch is always open to you and your people."

"We go now to Quanah; we will fight more, kill and be killed." Thunder Hawk looks across at the remaining young warriors. "The Comanche are a great warrior people but now we are few. In the end, we will be defeated and have to surrender but we will surrender with pride not like whipped dogs. Quanah knows this, as I know it."

Clay shakes his head. "I know the Comanche are a great people and I am sorry that the cavalry comes into your lands my friend."

Thunder Hawk smiles and sticks out his hand. "It has always been so; our ancestors took this land many years ago from another people so now it is taken from us."

Clay takes the extended hand. "Good-bye Thunder Hawk, friend of my father."

"Your father should be proud; he has the bravest of sons." Thunder Hawk nods sadly. "As mine were when they lived."

Moon turns his gelding back to the east towards home as Clay mounts the dead Comanche's little horse. Neither party look back as both ride away in their own direction. Riding up beside Fleet Hoof, Clay hands him the Winchester as he promised. He shakes the Cheyenne's hand then kicks the little mustang into a trot until he catches up with Lana.

"Are you alright Miss Lana?" He smiles into her disheveled and tired face.

Nodding she tries to stifle a small cry then looks over at Clay. "I am now, thanks to all of you."

"Can you ride hard Ma'am; I'd like to get back to the ranch as quickly as I can." Moon looks over at her. "I fear Galt is up to more mischief back there."

"Yes Grey Moon, I can ride." Lana rubs her nose. "Did Captain Rains die a horrible death?"

Both men look curiously at the girl. "He's not dead Miss Lana, he was taken to the Guthrie Ranch last I seen him."

"He's not dead!"

Moon thought she was going to faint and fall from the Palomino when she heard the news. "No Miss Barber he's still alive."

Moon watches as Clay pulls his horse in and rejoins Strong Bull at the back of the procession. Shaking his head, he looks back at the rejected young man then kicks the gelding into a slow trot eager to cover the long miles back to the ranch.

Lana watches Clay's face change as well. "I hurt him didn't I Moon?"

"He's young and will live over it but he did fight Snake Shield for you."

"I really didn't mean." She hesitates. "I was just relieved the Captain was not killed."

"Well Ma'am, maybe you should tell him that, not me."

Chapter 18

Captain Rains

Moon reins up in front of the ranch house as Jace Tilden steps out onto the porch with Alder following close behind him. The Winchester in the man's hands lowers as the cowhand recognizes the mounted riders. Alder Guthrie rushes forward from the porch and hugs Moon as he dismounts then helps Lana from the palomino and into the house. Watching the women enter the house Moon looks over where Clay waits then motions him towards the house.

"I'll take the horses Moon." Jace reaches for the reins then looks over at the retreating back of the girl. "You mean to tell me ya'll got the girl back all by yourselves without the army's help?"

"We had help but they headed on home when we crossed the river." Moon looks about at the quiet ranch buildings. "Where is everybody?"

"They've gone after a bunch of horse thieves."

"What's been taken?"

"Haven't you noticed there ain't an animal on the place?"

"The herd's gone, stolen?"

"Yep, that's about the size of it, they even took that big old ugly jackass." Jace nods, "But that ain't the worst of it, Andy's dead and poor old Slim has been shot up pretty good."

Moon stares at Jace then back at the house. "Andy's dead?"

"Yep and Slim is shot up so bad I doubt he'll ever fully recover." The cowhand nods sadly. "The doctor from the fort came out and patched him up as best he could."

"Will's gone after the thieves?"

"Yep, the boss was fit to be tied, lit out of here in pursuit of the thieves with Munday and Killian. He's supposed to meet up with some of the Kincaid hands across the river north of here."

"How long have they been gone?"

Jace counts as he tries to remember. "Let's see, Killian and the boss brought Captain Rains in. Then Slim came back from the fort and Will sent him out to the herd. That night we had the fight here, I make it two days they been gone."

"Saddle me a fresh horse Jace."

"We've got five saddle horses left that were in the corral when the herd got taken." Jace shakes his head. "Can't figure why those skunks didn't turn them out when they stole the Jack."

"Saddle me one too; I'll be riding out with Moon." Clay speaks up. "Have you heard anything of my folks?"

"A squad of Cavalry rode in yesterday leading that long eared jackass Will was so proud of." Jace nods toward the corral where the Jack stood, his big head looking over the top pole. "They said six men raided your place the same night as our place was attacked, word is your Pa, Mother, and his hands killed all six. The Lieutenant said your people were all fine."

"Where did they pick up the Jack?"

"Somewhere across the river, he was wandering loose with a rope trailing from his neck." Jace shrugs. "They found two dead men stripped down to their long handles about a mile further on down the river."

"That's where old Snake Shield got the shod horses we found him with." Clay shakes his head. "Those men must have stolen the mule then ran smack into the Comanche when they crossed the river."

"I reckon, let's get something in us then we'll ride out." Moon looks off to the west. "Maybe we can get there in time to be of some help."

Stepping into the house Clay flushes deeply when he finds Lana sitting beside Rains who is lying on a daybed in the front room. Bandages cover his side and head. The Captain looks up as he walks over to where he lies.

"Good to see you alive, Captain."

"It's good to be alive, especially now that you and Moon brought Lana back to me."

Lana blushes slightly as Clay stares down into her face. "Well, you two have a lot to catch up on."

Rains smiles over at Lana then reaches for her hand. "Yes we do, I'm glad the post surgeon ordered me to stay here a few days until I recuperate. Now, with my lady back I'll get well in a hurry."

Moon comes from another room and asks Rains, "How are you Captain?"

"I'm fine now, thanks to you and Mister Kincaid." Rains holds Lana's hand as he looks up at the two men then back at the bedroom door. "How's your rider Slim?"

Moon looks over at the rigid face of Clay. "Slims hurt bad, he's pretty weak but he says he'll make it."

"Well, I hope so."

Alder hollers from the kitchen, "Come eat boys or I'll toss it to the hogs."

Moon grins, "That'd be a good trick, considering there ain't a hog on the ranch."

"Hog's might not be a bad idea at least we'd have plenty to eat." Alder calls back.

"We're coming." Moon notices Clay looking straight into Lana's blue eyes before following him from the room.

"Your horses are ready." Jace slams the door noisily. "You got plenty of water and I put some extra shells in your bags."

"Thanks." Moon mumbles between bites.

"I would ride with you boys but the Boss ordered me to stay at the ranch and guard Mrs. Guthrie and those folks."

"Grey Moon, I know you and Mister Kincaid are going after Will." Alder hands Jace several bundles of food. "Put these in their bags with the shells."

"Yes Ma'am."

"Figured on it Miss Alder, just as soon as we're finished eating."

She sits down at the table. "He's been gone almost three days. You reckon you'll get there in time?"

Moon hesitates then raises his fork. "We'll get there, that's what matters."

"Thank you."

Moon looks at her curiously. "I don't need thanks; he'd do the same for me."

Alder smiles, "Yes he would but you two be careful just the same. I want all of you to come back home in one piece."

"We'll be careful as we can."

Lana walks out on the porch and stands beside Alder as Moon and Clay mount their fresh horses. Walking over to where Clay sits his horse she laid her hand on his leg and looks up at him. "Thank you Clay Kincaid for risking your life to save mine."

Tipping his hat, he whirls his big gelding and with a wave, they were gone. Both women watch until the two men are out of their sight then turn back towards the house. Alder watched Lana's eyes as they never wavered or left Clay's straight back as he rode away.

"He's like a son to you isn't he Misses Guthrie?" Lana smiles over at the older woman. "Grey Moon I mean."

Alder nods. "Grey Moon is a son to me Lana; he's very special, same as Munday."

"He's a good man I know that. He didn't have to come after me but he did." Lana smiles at her.

"Speaking of good men young lady, you're going to have to make a choice one day." Alder looks across to where the men rode from their sight. "You've got two men very much in love with you."

"I guess one day I probably will." Lana nods and turns back for the house. "But not today."

Will with Killian, Dedrow, and the rest of the men rein in hard as they reach Munday. "We got'em Pa, man we've got them boys cold." Munday grimaces in pain as he turns in the saddle. "I count six riders, one each on the flanks of the herd, three bringing up the drag and one riding point."

"That's all?" Will is curious that Galt has so few men. "I reckon he's lost a lot of his riders."

"We going in?" Killian speaks up.

"We're going." Will nods, "Boy, why don't you stay here and rest those ribs."

"No sir, no disrespect but I ain't missing this showdown for anything." Munday grins broadly and pats the forty-four on his hip. "No Sir, not on your life."

Will shakes his head, "Okay son, they're your ribs."

"What's your plan Boss?"

"Plan, what plan?" Will pulls out his rifle. "I aim to ride over this hill in a dead run and shoot down every mother's son out there. They killed Andy and Slim and then stole my mules, now they're a fixing to pay for their wayward ways."

"They should be hung." Killian flips down his burned-out quirley and cusses.

"They will be, after we kill them." Will cusses, "You boys make sure your girths are pulled tight."

Killian looks over at the normally pleasant rancher and saw the change in his demeanor. Pure madness and hatred emit from the man's face. Pulling his pistol, he pushes the sixth shell into the cylinder. Nodding over at the rancher, he grins slightly and gathers his reins for a hard run.

"We're ready Will."

"You boys spread out; don't let one of them killers get away." Will checks his rifle then nods. "Not one, now let's go get them."

Galt whirls in his saddle as the sound of pounding hooves pour over the small knoll and horsemen charge towards them. The drumming of the horse's hooves and the sudden surge of the herd brought his attention back from his deep concentration. Watching as two of his men are shot from their saddles, Galt spurs his long legged roan hard and races away for the safety of a nearby ravine. He can hear the roll of rifle and pistol fire behind him as bullets buzz around him. Leaning low, he spurs the horse harder and disappears down in the ravine amid a smattering of trees and brush.

Firing rapidly, Munday charges into the herd headlong and shoots a rider from his saddle then pumps another shot into the prone man as he races by in pursuit of the man he recognizes as Galt. Several shots come from the ravine where Galt disappeared but Munday pushes on disregarding the danger before him. Reloading as the horse picks his way to the bottom of the deep gorge Munday studies the deep tracks Galt's horse left in the sandy bottom. Kicking his gelding, he follows the tracks unmindful of the danger of an ambush or the deadliness of the outlaw leader with a pistol.

"Come on out Mister Galt and let's settle this like men." Munday flings his challenge down onto the ravine. Only a deafening silence follows Munday's challenge. "Just you and me, what do you say?"

Two shots come from high above clipping a small limb above Munday's head. The outlaw found another animal trail out of the steep ravine. He shoots down in the direction of Munday's voice not wanting to show himself on the rim. With a loud laugh, Munday spurs his horse forward over the rim and rides out of the ravine.

Only the pounding of a running horse sounds out across the flats as Munday pulls his blowing gelding in. Gunfire behind him quiets and nothing can be heard. Patting the gelding, he eases down from the saddle and loosens the cinch so the horse can blow. Will with Killian and Dedrow close behind ride out of the ravine and pull up where he is waiting.

"You okay boy?"

"I'm okay." Munday looks off to the northwest. "Galt got away, his horse is fresh but mine is played out."

"We'll get him." Will looks across the ravine. "Before he gets far, we'll run him down."

"What about the others?"

"Four are dead, now I'm gonna hang them." Will cusses, "I think another rider got away with Galt."

"Seems like a waste of good rope to me." Killian speaks up. "They ain't gonna know the difference, they're dead."

"Nobody asked you." Will growls, "If you ain't got the stomach for it, ride for home. How many men were you after?"

"I only heard gunfire, never got close enough to see who I was after." Munday pulls his cinch tight. "I thought it was just Galt but there could have been two of them."

Killian sits his horse looking up at the four bodies swinging slowly back and forth on the bare limb of a huge oak. A quirley dangles out of his mouth as the rider pulls on it absently. He never saw Will Guthrie as mad and vengeful as he had been these past two days. Hanging men that are already dead is something he never seen before, for that matter ever heard of before.

"You gonna bury them Will?" Killian asks curiously.

"No I sure ain't and neither are any of you." Will growls, "Let this be a lesson for the next man that wants to kill my men or run off one of my animals."

"I figure this ought to dissuade the next man alright." Killian turns his horse and faces back to the east. "Sure dissuaded me alright, we starting home tonight?"

Will looks up at the bodies then shakes his head. "No, there's still two missing bodies that needs to decorate that tree. Galt and one other man got away and I aim to get both of them."

"Galt's mine Pa along with the other rider whoever it is, you take the herd home." Munday speaks up. "I'll put them up in that tree with the others."

"Galt's a killer boy, a very dangerous man." Will looks at his son, "I don't know who the other man is, maybe Pine Johnson and he's mean as sin too."

Munday smiles and adds, "So am I and those two are all mine. I'm going after them, alone."

"Boy, I can't let you ride out alone." Will shakes his head, "You're Ma would disown me if something should happen to you."

"I'm going alone Pa, I've never went against you on anything but this time I am."

Will looks over at Munday. "Alright son, they're yours. When are you going after them?"

"It's coming nightfall; I'll wait until morning then pull out."

"Alright let's make camp and get something to eat." Will looks towards a group of trees away from the hanging tree. "Downwind of these skunks!"

Munday shakes out a loop. "I've got to catch me something fresh to ride."

"I'll bring you in something." Dedrow undoes his own lariat. "You find you a soft spot and rest your ribs."

"Thanks Mister Dedrow, I can sure use some rest."

Riding through the herd of mules and horses looking for a good strong-limbed gelding for the Guthrie youngster Dedrow thought about Munday Guthrie. To him at first the younger Guthrie seems wild, a troublemaker but he has to hand it to the boy, he has guts. The way he thanked him back at camp shows the youngster has some respect for his elders. He could not be all that bad. In time providing he lives, he probably will make his mark on this land as his father did. His wild temper will cool and Dedrow figures he will make a good man one day.

Roping out a deep chested bay, he leads the gelding back to the picket line and ties him up. Unsaddling his own horse he walks back to the fire and drops his saddle to the ground then sits down on top of it.

"I brought him a blood bay with a pine tree brand on his left hip." Dedrow takes the coffee Will held out. "Hope he'll do."

"Old Baldy, he's as good as we got plenty of wind and surefooted." Killian nods, "You picked him a good one."

"Baldy? Dedrow looks over at the horse. "He ain't got a white mark on him."

Will laughs, "Nah, we named him after old Pete Sparks who raised him, Pete was as bald headed as a turtle."

Dedrow grins then rolls himself a quirley. "Sounds like a good name to me."

The squeak of saddle leather and the pounding of their horse's hooves beating against the hard ground is all that is heard as Grey Moon and Clay push their horses hard, following the wide trail of the mule herd to the north. Pointing with his finger Moon looks over at the trail ahead and nods.

Pulling in at the crossing of a small creek Moon let his horse drink lightly then splashes across and dismounts. "We'll walk awhile and let the horses rest some."

Clay looks down at the wide trail. "Looks like we're gaining."

"We are, the turned up ground is still damp." Moon agrees. "At the speed we're traveling we'll catch up tomorrow sometime."

Riding through the night following the trail by the light of a brilliant full moon, the two nod at each other tiredly as the sun starts to break over the furthest land swell in the east. With the beautiful sunrise, energy seeps back into their tired legs giving them a renewed burst of strength to keep following the trail.

Moon kneels and looks closely at the tracks. "We'll catch up today."

"I think we already have." Clay nods at the riders coming down the trail in their direction.

Moon smiles, "It's Will and Killian in the lead, I reckon they caught up to the horse thieves and the herd."

Will pulls his gelding in and stares across at the two newcomers. Shaking his head, he replies, "I figured you boys would be along."

Looking at the tired, wore out herd Moon replies, "Looks like you caught up with the horse thieves and got your animals back."

"We caught up with them last night."

Moon watches as other riders push the herd in and bunches them up. "Where's Munday?"

"We didn't get Galt, he took in after him and another rider we don't know."

"Who rode with him?"

"Nobody."

"You let him go alone?" Moon is in shock. "After a killer like Ewen Galt?"

"He insisted, wouldn't take no for an answer, he's a man now Moon, and he's got to cross the river alone sooner or later."

"Ewen Galt's a pretty big river to cross."

"I know but this time his pride was at stake." Will drops his head, "He's my son but to stop him this time no, he wants to prove himself and this might just grow him up."

Moon looks over at Killian. "Or it could kill him."

"The boy's my son, same as you are." Will looks over at Moon for understanding. "He's wild; maybe when this is finished he will settle down and make a man."

"The boss did right Moon, it was Munday's decision."

"Nobody asked you Killian."

"It was my decision Moon." Will looks over at the breed.

"It was a bad decision." Moon is disgusted. He cannot figure out either of the men for letting a boy go after two grown men alone.

"He rode out this morning at daybreak." Will did not bother to argue as he usually does. He is tired and he can see Moon is upset. He knows what Alder is going to say if anything happens to the boy. "What are you going to do?"

Moon looks over where Pete Jumper sat his horse. "Catch me a fresh horse Pete, a good one."

"Catch me one too, if you don't mind?" Clay dismounts and starts unsaddling his horse.

"Ugh huh." Jumper looks over at Will for a sign.

Will nods at the hand then dismounts. "You're going after Munday?"

"Yes sir, I aim to." Moon nods, "I just hope we won't be too late."

"You won't." Killian grins, "With a handgun that boy can take two Galt's."

"You should know you've put gun poison in his hands ever since we were kids." Moon glares at the foreman. "If anything happens to him I'll come looking for you."

Only a blur shows as Killian launches himself from his horse and lands on Moon's horse dragging him bodily to the ground. Will sits immobile and watches as his foreman punches at the prone man on the bottom. Shaking his head, he stops the rest of the hands from interfering as the two men wrestle around in the dirt. With brute strength Moon tosses the foreman over his head landing him under Dedrow's horse spooking the gelding into a bucking frenzy. The fight is over for the time being, the heavy gelding kicked Killian squarely in the solar plexus knocking the wind from the man.

"That's enough Moon." Will steps between the men as Killian crawls across the ground gasping, trying to catch his wind.

Jumper leads two geldings into the circle of men and hands Moon and Clay the lead ropes as he looks at the prone Killian then back over at Moon. He did not see the horse kick the foreman but he knows the power in Moon's punch and figures he hit the foreman.

Quickly saddling the horses, Moon looks over at the waiting men. "We'll catch up with him and see if he needs any help."

Will nods, "I appreciate that, he wouldn't have us help, he was determined and I doubt he'll appreciate your help any either."

"I know Sir, he can be hardheaded."

"If anything happens to the boy; Alder will never forgive me." Will wipes his face.

Dedrow helps Clay saddle his half-broke gelding. "You boys want me to ride with you?"

"No, help Mister Guthrie home with his herd, then you and the boys ride on home and check on the folks." Clay adjusts his curb chain on the young horse. "We'll get young Mister Guthrie home safe, if we can."

Dedrow nods, "You're the boss."

Stepping back as Clay steps into the saddle, Dedrow dodges sideways as the young green broke horse starts bucking across the camp knocking the coffeepot over that sat near the small campfire.

Moon watches and waits as Clay finally gets the young horse under control then looks down at Will. "We'll bring him back if we can."

Two hours down the back trail of the herd, Moon picks out the lone trail Munday left. Further along past a deep ravine, he finds the trail where two other sets of tracks joined his.

Pointing at the ground Moon nods then kicks his gelding into a slow trot. Close behind him Clay's young horse feeling frisky and still fresh makes a couple of crow hops before the sharp spurs sank into his sides knocking the buck out of him.

"You got one of Will's roans, I never seen one that wouldn't pitch every time you ride them." Moon looks at the young gelding. "But, they'll get you there and back."

Clay agrees. "He's a little salty alright but I'll bet he's loaded with bottom."

"They have heart alright." Moon nods. "Get a good hold and let's ride."

For four hours, Moon pushes hard holding to the trail like a hound on a coon's track. The ground turns from sand to grass then to solid rock in places along a ridgeback making the tracks hard to follow. Moon stays with the trail. He slows down at times then picks up his speed as the ground softens and the trail becomes clear again. Pulling up at a clear pond of water, Moon dismounts and drops to the ground on his stomach while his horse nuzzles the cool water. Clay studies the surrounding grassland then steps down out of his own saddle.

Rolling onto his side Moon looks across the water where Clay was drinking. "How come you came with me? Old Munday ain't been exactly sociable with you since you came to these parts."

"Respect." Clay rises to his knees wiping the dripping water from his chin. "For the Guthries and for you."

"Respect, well that respect can get you killed."

"It could at that but I don't think so this time." Clay pulls his gelding back from the water. "I plan to live to be an old man Mister Moon."

"Luck be with you." Moon mounts in one fluid motion. "Only time will tell."

"Don't you want to live a long life?"

"Don't know, ain't never thought much on it one way or the other." Moon looks over at Clay. "Course now, I ain't got a pretty blond haired girl to live for."

"And you think I do?"

"I do, if you play your cards right."

"What about that Captain Rains she's seems so fond of?"

"Just that Hoss, she seems but is she really?"

Dark is closing in as Moon crosses over the small river and wades out on the far bank. Shifting up and down the sandy banks, he picks up the trail that leads off to the north.

"Where is Galt headed?" Clay was never this far north and he does not know the territory.

"I'd say Hays City in a roundabout way but I don't believe he'll make it."

"That means we're getting close."

"It does, Munday's horse and ours are fresher." Moon studies the trail. "We've got him. He'll never make Hays."

"Who you figure is with him?"

"That I don't know but I'd bet it is Charlie Tom, a half-breed Comanche." Moon speaks slowly. "I've seen him around Hays and he's a bad one."

The deep night is upon the land, the darkness is intense as Munday sits beside a small fire deep inside a stand of plumb thickets. He knows the fire is too small to see at a distance but he forgot the smoke could carry on the wind. Huddling up to let his tired body take in the warmth of the blaze, Munday pulls on a quirley thoughtfully. Galt is close, his horses are worn out, and Munday can see how the toes of the two horses left drag tracks on the ground as they walk. Galt would not dare travel any further without rest, his horses need feed and water but mainly rest, if not he will be afoot.

Moon points with his chin, nods as he tests the wind, and smells the wood smoke from ahead. Easing to the ground, he hands his reins to Clay.

"Wait here until I give you the signal to come in."

"You reckon it's him?"

"Has to be, if it was Galt we'd of heard some shooting or found Munday's body."

Moving off stealthily in the faint light Moon disappears into the dark without a sound. Finding a dead log, Clay settles down to wait. From time to time, he catches a whiff of wood smoke on the still air. He cannot be sure it is smoke coming from a man-made fire; it could be just a small log or something still smoldering, the remnants of a grass fire.

Moon slips silently through the stand of trees sliding underneath the low thick limbs without making a sound. He is careful to stay upwind of the tethered horse so he would not snort and alert whoever is tending the fire. He crawls forward to within fifteen feet of the small fire.

Watching as Munday's head dips as he doses off, Moon tosses a small pebble hitting the sleeping man in the back. Rolling sideways the colt comes snaking out from under the heavy coat that was covering Munday.

"Hold your powder Hoss, it's just me." Moon ducks quickly to the ground in case in his drowsiness Munday fires a round in his direction.

"Moon, is that you?"

"None other, now I'm coming in don't cut loose on me." Moon pushes to his feet and shoves his way into the small clearing.

Munday holsters his pistol and piles a few small limbs on the fire. "How did you find me?"

"It's called tracking, brother."

"And you're Indian?"

Moon grins, relieved to find Munday alive. "You know, I believe I am."

"You alone?"

"Nope, Clay Kincaid is with me."

"What did you bring him with you for?"

"Weren't my idea, he wanted to come with me."

"Well, send him back."

"Nope, I've grown quite fond of his company."

"Then I'll kill him."

"Not till after we get Ewen Galt, then we'll discuss the matter." Moon shakes his head. "Now sit tight and I'll go bring him in."

Not a word is spoken by either man as the three sit around the warm fire. Both ignored each other's presence until Moon draws them into the conversation.

"You got any idea where Galt is camped?" Moon looks over at Munday. "He can't be far."

"He's not." Munday eyes the fire. "I had him and another rider spotted right before I pulled in here to make camp for the night."

"They close?"

"Yep, maybe two miles downriver from here."

"Why didn't you take them earlier?"

"It was almost dark; I sure didn't want to lose them in the dark and have to dig them out come daylight."

"They'll still be there come daylight then we'll move in." Clay chimes in.

"No, Galt is mine and mine alone." Munday shakes his head. "You two can have the other one whoever he is, divide him up anyway you want but leave Galt alone."

"Alright." Moon nods, "Ewen Galt's all yours."

Galt and Charlie Tom spend the night in a small draw that runs back from a large valley leaving their horses to graze on the lush bottom grass. The night passes quickly as the two men sleep throughout the night, too tired to even post a guard. With the new day and the coming of the sun, the half-breed rolls sleepily to his feet stumbling groggily and half-asleep to gather the geldings and get them saddled.

Moon and Clay watch from a stand of oaks as the outlaw walks from the canyon looking about for the missing animals. "Lose something Breed?"

Reaching for his pistol, as Moon's voice sounds Charlie Tom, it hardly clears his holster when the blast of Clay's forty-five sends lead into the man's chest. Another shot comes as the outlaw still tries to raise his weapon. Moon looks over at the smoking forty-five then lowers his own rifle letting it fall back towards the ground unused. He is in shock; he did not even fire his weapon when Clay pumped two rounds into the dead outlaw.

Moon knows Munday is fast with a handgun, he saw him draw and fire and now he saw Clay Kincaid in action. He shakes his head, in his few years he saw many fast guns in Hays City, Wichita and in the Nations but none have the speed and deadly accuracy of this youngster. The two holes in Charlie Tom's chest are less than two inches apart. Looking over at Clay, he takes a long hard look at the man for the first time. Clay Kincaid just killed a man that was intent on killing him, yet he appears as calm as a summer day.

Several pistol shots go off behind them drawing their attention away from the down man. Hurrying back towards where the outlaw camp lay they quicken their pace as three more shots ring out. Rushing into the draw with their pistols drawn Moon and Clay find Munday standing over Galt. Looking at the body Clay counts at least five bullet holes in the dead man. Galt's smoking pistol lay beside him on the ground.

Both men stand waiting as Munday stands over Galt for several seconds with his back to them before turning to Moon with his hand outstretched. "I got him Moon but he was faster than I thought."

Rushing forward Moon catches Munday in his arms as he collapses. Looking down at the bloody chest Moon closes his eyes and shakes his head. "No."

"It's okay brother." Blood comes from Munday's mouth as he whispers. "Tell them I love'em."

"I'll tell them." Moon squeezes his shoulders. "They know it already."

Munday looks over to where Clay stands. "We didn't get to settle our differences did we pilgrim?"

"They're settled Mister Guthrie."

Nodding weakly, Munday tries to smile. "I reckon they are now for sure."

"Brother." Moon calls the name as Munday's eyes roll back in his head, then his chest settled slowly. "Munday."

"He's gone Moon." Clay places his hand on the shaking shoulder. "I'm truly sorry."

Nodding his head, Moon wipes his eyes and laid Munday softly back on the sandy ground. "We'll take him home now."

"And these other two?"

Moon looks over at Galt. "There's a tree waiting for them like Mister Guthrie wanted and now I want it too."

"You thought a lot of him didn't you?"

Moon nods, "He was wild, always in trouble of some kind. That was mostly Killian's doings but he was good at heart."

"He died dead game for sure and thinking of his folks." Clay looks down at the ground. "Pa says in the end that's all that matters. He was a son to be proud of."

"Thank you for that Clay." Moon closes Munday's eyes. "You're right; he was all rawhide and guts even when I was mad at him. I was proud of him. We weren't brothers by blood but just the same we were as close as brothers, maybe closer."

Chapter 19

Lana Barber

Moon and Clay set their horses and look down at the smoke coming from the ranch house below them. Moon can see two men standing near the corrals and another sitting on the front porch. Raising his hat to block the sun Moon watches as Will Guthrie steps from the porch and looks in their direction.

"I'd rather take a whipping than ride down there." Moon looks over at the horse carrying Munday's body. "I don't know if I can do it."

"I know but you've got to." Clay looks into the dark face then at the front porch. "That looks like the cowboy that rode from the fort with me sitting in that chair."

Nearing the corral Moon speaks in surprise. "It is Slim; Miss Alder said he'd never get out of that bed."

Will drops his face as he recognizes Moon leading a horse behind him with what had to be a body draped across it. He knows it could only be Munday. Stumbling towards the oncoming horses, he shakes his head slowly back and forth then looks back towards the porch where Alder appeared. Moon waits quietly as Will unwraps the ropes that hold Munday on the horse and lifts the body gently from the horse.

Looking up to where Moon waits, he studies the sad face then turns and slowly carries Munday down the hill. Alder walks towards them her shoulders straight and square as they approach her. Taking her son's cold hand, she walks beside Will on to the house without speaking.

"His mother has him laid out in the front room." Will looks off towards the pasture then back at Moon and Clay. "You boys hungry?"

"No sir, we are alright." Moon shakes his head.

"She'll expect you to eat, you know her."

"Yes sir."

"Would you tell me what happened out there, how he died?"

"He died a brave man Mister Guthrie." Clay could not look into the haggard face before him. "The bravest I've ever seen."

"He was a good son." Will wipes his face with his red bandanna and starts towards the corral. "A good son."

Killian and the rest of the Guthrie crew sat in the bunkhouse talking about Munday and the Galt gang. "I can't believe Ewen Galt killed that boy in a fair fight, no sir, he was too fast."

"The Kincaid boy said it and I see no reason he would lie." Slim moves painfully towards the stove for a cup of coffee. "No sir, no reason at all."

"I say he lied."

"Your mouth could get you in trouble Tom Killian." Pete Jumper sits back down at the scarred table. "Moon says Kincaid is cat quick with his pistol."

"Maybe I'll just find out myself."

Jace swallows his coffee then lights himself a smoke. "It's your funeral Hoss."

Killian is about to say more as the door opens slowly and Clay walks into the bunkhouse. "Evening boys, Misses Guthrie wants you all to the house, Munday's ready to be viewed."

"Moon says you're pretty fast with that popgun of yours."

Clay looks across the room at the foreman. "I believe there's been enough killing and heartache around here to last a lifetime Mister Killian."

"Sounds like you're scared to me." Killian sneers over at Jace.

"Whatever you say." Clay turns towards the door.

"Don't turn your back on me Kincaid!"

Clay turns slowly back to where the foreman stood straddle legged staring at him. "Alright Killian."

Killian draws and cocks his forty-four pointing it at Clay. "Are you that fast, you young whipper-snapper? Well, we're fixing to find out because the next time I draw, you better do something or I'll kill you."

"He ain't kidding boy, he'll kill you for sure." Jumper tosses his burned-out smoke at the stove. "Let it be Tom."

"Now!" Killian starts for his pistol then stops midway as he looks into the deadly bore of Clay's forty-five.

"Don't do it boy." Jumper looks across from the table. "He ain't worth it."

The cocking of the pistol sounded louder than a clap of thunder in the small bunkhouse. "Don't kill him Clay, not now the Missus couldn't stand another death right now."

Jumper looks to where Will Guthrie stands in the open doorway and slowly stands up. "Tom pushed it Will, he was fixing to kill the boy."

"I seen it Jumper, you boys go on to the house for supper and the viewing." Will raises his hand as Killian starts forward. "Not you, get your things and clear out and thank your lucky stars I don't wring your neck right now."

Killian is in shock. "Will, we've been together through so much."

"It's over, now get!"

Killian turns pale as he quickly gathers his gear and walks from the bunkhouse. "I'll need a horse."

"Take one but come sunup don't let me see your face anywhere on this range again."

Alder Guthrie sat at the end of the table and watches Clay's eyes stare at the daybed where Rains lain while Lana sat beside him. "She's gone back to the fort."

"I'm sorry Ma'am, what did you say?" Clay turns his attention back to her.

Smiling sadly, she looks into his eyes. "Lana's gone back to the agency with Captain Rains."

"Thank you Misses Guthrie; in your sadness it's not right that I trouble you further with my problems."

"If you want her Clay, go to her and tell her." Alder looks behind her at the open door where the men were gathering around Munday. "Go to her and don't just give up, at least tell her how you feel and let her decide."

Clay nods slowly then looks down the table at the lady. "You're quite a lady Ma'am, quite a lady."

"And you're quite a man Mister Clay Kincaid." She smiles. "A man any woman would be proud to walk through this life with."

"I'm sorry for your son; I wish I got to know him better."

"I think you two would have gotten along wonderfully." Alder sniffs slightly.

"He was a brave man." Clay nods. "The bravest."

Clay sits his horse and looks across the broad plain at the Darlington Agency. Somewhere either inside the Agency or across the river he knows she will be in one place or the other. Her beautiful yellow hair and bright blue eyes are hard to erase from his mind but it is more, her demeanor and composure stand out even more. His mind went back to what Alder Guthrie said at the table yesterday as he sat looking down at the palomino mare that stood calmly beside him. He smiles down at the mare; she and the yellow gelding he is riding are almost a matched pair. The only difference is the mare has more white on her.

Kicking the horse, he starts forward a few steps then reins the gelding in again. The delighted look on Captain Rains face as he lay on the bed wounded looking up at the girl, crosses his mind. Then Lana's face materializes in his mind as she sat on the bed. He cannot get her out of his thoughts. She seemed happy and content as she waited on Rains. He wants to ride on towards the Running K but he promised Moon that he would deliver the mare and mule to Captain Rains at Fort Reno.

He smiles; he knows what Moon's intentions were and why he asked him to deliver the horse to the Agency. He still remembers the half grin on Grey Moon's face as he and the Guthries watched him ride away from the ranch.

Touching the yeller horse, he points him back to the east towards the faraway Fort and Agency buildings leading the mule and mare. He is anxious to see her but he does not know what to say to her. Going over the words he wants to speak to Lana, he knows it will not be the same. When she comes close to him, his legs freeze up, his mind goes completely blank, and his tongue becomes tongue-tied. Clay cusses himself for being a coward around the girl. He wishes Dedrow was here to do his talking for him. The distance from the Guthrie Ranch is at least ten miles but the miles seem to melt away far too fast, as he nears the Agency. He still did not plan exactly what he would say to her.

Reining in at the Agency tie rail, he looks across the noisy yard where the children play as their mother's pass in and out of the store. His hands freeze, not wanting to budge as he sits the horse. Despite the recent raid and the shooting of Captain Rains, the Agency is peaceful and tranquil as if nothing happened.

"Mister Kincaid, you're back." John Miles steps out onto the porch and looks over surprised at finding Clay sitting in front of the store.

Looking down at the Agent, Clay nods slowly. "Yes sir, that I am."

"Did Mister Guthrie get his stolen stock back?"

"He did, every last one of them." Clay did not mention Munday being killed. Bad news travels fast enough, it will get here.

"Lana told me when she came in with Captain Rains that you rode out to help against the rustlers." Miles smiles. "It was very commendable of you young man."

"Yes sir, is Miss Barber here?"

"Why no, she's gone over to the Fort to check on Captain Rains." Miles notices the disappointment on his face. "She didn't have any way of knowing you were coming in today."

Clay nods slowly as he looks off across the river then down at the mare. "Grey Moon asked me to bring these animals to her and the Captain."

Miles looks about the agency and shakes his head. "We have only the one small corral here to hold animals and it's already overcrowded."

"I see and then what would you have me do with them Mister Miles?"

Miles looks at the mare and smiles. "Perhaps if it isn't too much trouble you could take them across the river to the Captain."

"It's not too much trouble Sir but I didn't want to ride into the fort." Clay did not want to see Lana. He did but he just does not know what to say to the girl.

"You'll have to face her sooner or later lad."

Clay looks down at the man. How does Miles know what is holding him back? "I reckon you're right about that Sir. I'll take them to the fort."

"Good, good." The agent smiles mischievously. "Just be yourself Clay Kincaid when you speak with Lana."

"Yes sir."

"She's just a woman son, no different than any other."

Clay reaches down and cups his hand full of the warm river water to wash his face as his yellow gelding crosses the belly deep water. Replacing his Stetson his eyes search out the far bank then turn to the new fort in the distance. Soon he will be facing her, what will her reaction be to his words.

"Well young Mister Kincaid, I see you're back and all in one piece." Sergeant Ray walks from the stable doors and looks up at Clay. "The girl told us all about the Comanche and you fighting Snake Shield for her."

"She here?"

"Yes sir, she's over at the hospital with the Captain." Ray points with his chin. "You know the way she spoke, she was mighty proud of you."

"She say that in front of the Captain?"

Ray smiles. "Yes sir, she did, I don't think he was any too happy either."

"Sergeant, could you stable these animals for Captain Rains?" Clay leans over and hands Ray the lead ropes.

"I've got two empty stalls right here." Ray takes the leads. "You want your ropes?"

"No Sergeant, they go with the animals." Clay clucks to his gelding. "I'll just ride over to the hospital and say my goodbyes."

"Good luck to you Mister Kincaid." Ray smiles.

"And to you Sergeant."

Clay reins the yellow horse in and dismounts tying the gelding in front of the hospital. Looking up the five steps to the porch, he shakes his head then starts forward. Pushing open the door quietly he looks into the room to find Lana sitting beside Captain Rains with her back to him. His eyes cannot help but notice her small hand holding the Captain's hand. Reclosing the door softly he retreats across the wide porch and mounts his gelding.

Kicking the yellow horse into a slow lope, he rides the gelding back towards the Canadian without a backwards glance. Sergeant Ray watches as the proud straight back of the young man rides past without as much as a nod. He can see the hard look on Clay's face as he passes the stable. Chewing absently on a piece of straw he watches as the palomino horse slows at the river then splashes across the wide Canadian River.

Hurrying to the yellow mare's stall he quickly saddles the palomino and leads her over to the hospital. Opening the door he gets Lana's attention and motions her outside.

"Sergeant Ray." She blinks as she sees the reins of the palomino mare in his hands. "How did she get here?"

"The young Kincaid just brought her into the fort Ma'am."

Looking around the grounds quickly she turns her attention back to Ray. "Where is he Sergeant?"

"Gone Miss."

"Gone where?"

"He came over here and looked through the door for a second and then climbed on his horse and rode away."

Lana knows what Clay saw when he opened the door. "He did, did he?"

"Peered that way to me, Miss Lana."

"Thank you Sergeant Ray." Lana snatches the reins and quickly mounts the mare.

"He rode east Ma'am." Ray grins as he watches her race the mare away from the fort. "She's got you now Mister Clay Kincaid."

A mile from the river Clay hears the hard pounding of a running horse coming towards him. Turning in his saddle, he sees the flowing yellow hair of Lana as she rides the yellow mare in a hard run towards him. Reining the mare to a sliding stop beside him, she looks into his bashful face.

"You brought the mare to me Clay?"

"Yes Ma'am, Moon asked me to bring her to the Agency."

"And you left without saying a word to me?"

"You seemed very busy."

"No Clay Kincaid, I was doctoring an injured man." Lana glares at him frustrated. "I would never be too busy for you, never."

"But Captain Rains?"

"Captain Rains is a friend Mister Kincaid, only a friend."

"And Miss Barber, what am I?"

"You're very much more Clay." Lana smiles. "If you want to be?"

"I want to be Lana, a whole lot more."

Smiling she takes his hand as the yellow horses trot east along the Canadian River towards the new Running K Ranch in the Yukon Mountains of Oklahoma.

THE END

www.ingramcontent.com/pod-product-compliance
Lightning Source LLC
Chambersburg PA
CBHW070454120726
47910CB00003B/1042